Captain Lightfoot

CAPTAIN
Lightfoot
by W. R. Burnett

NEW YORK
Alfred · A · Knopf

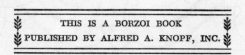

THIS IS A BORZOI BOOK
PUBLISHED BY ALFRED A. KNOPF, INC.

Author's Note

I ONCE HEARD an irritable critic define the *Serious Novel* as a novel with a dull and lugubrious subject treated in a dull and lugubrious manner. If that is true, then *Captain Lightfoot* is not a *Serious Novel*. It is an attempt, perhaps foolhardy, to reanimate certain limited aspects of life in the eighteenth century, and to compose a novel with the ultimate flavour of a folk-ballad. Captain Lightfoot himself is certainly a sort of folk-hero. (Although the actual dates of the action are 1817–18, the eighteenth century lingered on in Ireland long after its chronological demise, and in a sense still lingers.)

As I am no historian, the book is probably full of unconscious errors. I want to point out a deliberate one. Casanova's *Memoirs* are mentioned here and there in the narrative. Our time, as stated, is 1817–18. While it is true that the *Memoirs* were written before the close of the century—and even circulated, in part, among a select few—they were not officially published until 1826, in Leipzig. All the same, I like to think that as old Lord Clayton sat before the fire in Lightfoot's bedroom, waiting to touch the Captain for a hundred guineas, the old Lord was diverting himself with those magnificent *Memoirs*.

A word about *guineas*, which are mentioned often in the book. Money was sound in the British Isles in those days, and the gold guinea did not fluctuate in value, nor was it tampered with. It remained at twenty-one shillings for many years (in fact, until superseded by the sovereign), or, roughly, four pre-1933 American dollars.

AUTHOR'S NOTE

Guineas ceased to be minted in 1814, but were in use for many years after that date.

As to place names: Ballymore and Blackfountain are fictitious. All of the other place names, from Mooncoin on the Suir to the small Scottish port of Prestwick, can be found on any large-scale map of the British Isles.

W. R. B.

Contents

BOOK
I

Book I

IN DOHERTY'S SHADOW

It is time now, I think, to tell the true story of Michael Martin, better known to the people of Ireland generally—though not to his home town—as Captain Lightfoot. I have heard about him all my life, and he has become, after all these years, in a sense, a familiar of mine. Like myself, he was born in the Kilkenny market-town of Ballymore, and, as a matter of fact, he is a far-distant cousin of my own, his mother's name having been Conihy, my own name. There is no hurt to others in telling his story now; all who were connected with him and could be embarrassed or injured by the telling have long ago receded into the past along with the Old Ireland of our dreams: the Old Ireland of toll roads and coaching and red-coated dragoons and highwaymen on the Dublin Road and trouble in the back country and rebels shipping out from the West to the Americas and robustious but naïve politics and less Dublin whisky and more of the home-made kind and new songs being invented by the score by country people, songs better than Tom Moore's, and a gentlemanly English tyrant in Dublin Castle—the bad, good Old Ireland.

A somewhat prim contemporary wrote of Michael Martin in the following terms: "Lightfoot was a remarkably well-proportioned man, about five feet, ten inches in height; he had a very expressive face; his complexion fair, his hair raven-black, and his features indicating rather good nature than malignity. His frame was perfectly formed, and his bones and sinews put together in mighty power. . . . He weighed one hundred and eighty-five pounds, but he was so symmetrically formed that the most acute observer would have estimated him at thirty pounds less. . . . An uncommonly piercing blue eye gave a marked character of intelligence to the possessor, and seemed to crave the pity of the world that the mind which was reflected there had not been directed to better purposes."

Well, well; though it is a pretty good description of the brawny, blue-eyed, black-haired hero I've heard so much about, yet it is the work of an outsider, a history-book man, who could not refrain from a moral judgement, though he knew little or nothing of Michael Martin and his stresses, strains, and problems.

Michael Martin was born on a farm just outside Ballymore, Kilkenny, on August 25 in the year of our Lord 1795. There was great trouble in the world at the time, a revolution in France and a wave of rebellion against the old regime all over the turning globe. In America a new kind of government was wrestling with problems tough enough to sink an old, established empire. Ballymore, a backwater, paid little or no attention, and neither did the Martin family. They had their own problems, such as crops and pigs, and how best to age the home-made whisky.

Michael's mother, the former Brigid Conihy, died when Michael was but eleven, and this rather unruly young fellow was brought up by his father, his three older brothers, and an old patch of the name of Kathleen, who was eighty if a day at this time, smoked a clay pipe, worked all day long in the kitchen and was less tired at night than the men coming in from the fields. Kathleen was a distant cousin of the Martin clan. She had a will of iron, which she exercised by the means of weeping and wailing till the men cursed her for an old devil and let her have her way. When she died—at work in the kitchen, making a tasty stew for "Michael and the rest," as she always said—

Michael, eighteen now, lost his teacher and guide, and it is said he was never the same again. Bored with the monotony of farm work, he began to run wild with the young roughs of Ballymore and occasionally got into some slight trouble, such as tying the constable to a tree one night, stealing his chain of office (scrupulously returned), and breaking his official stave or pike. Michael and Tim Keenan saw gaol for this, to the great disgrace of the Martins, peaceful, religious men all—sandy-haired, freckled, nothing like black-haired, reckless Michael.

It is said by some that the old patch, Kathleen, did Michael a great disservice by educating him above his station. In Kilkenny at that time there was much illiteracy—in fact, Michael's own father could not read and write, and his brothers were but indifferent at both, caring for neither. Michael, unlike the others of his family, had a quick mind and a ready wit and took to learning as a horse to hay. At ten he could read anything he could lay his eyes on; at fifteen he wrote a hand an English notary might envy. "For why?" his father asked of Kathleen. "To write letters to the pigs in the pen? The black cattle in the fields? A summons to the oats, telling it to grow?" Kathleen would begin to shriek and wail, and the father would leave the house to be rid of her endless stream of melancholy invective.

Now I must tell you a little about the situation in Kilkenny as Michael, wild and unruly and hating the farm, became twenty-one and a man in his own right. To say there was trouble is to say nothing at all. In Ireland there is always trouble; if not, some is quickly arranged. And to say there was bad trouble is to exaggerate. The truth lies somewhere in between. The Union with England had pacified some of the country, especially around Dublin itself, where the English have always been strong and pre-eminent. But Kilkenny—in fact, a large part of Leinster—was a hotbed of resentment and rebellion. The market-town of Ballymore, our town, was partly owned and completely controlled by Lord Devereaux, an absentee. At best, an absentee was looked down on and resented, and when, to top it, he was a real Irishman himself, and no Sassenach, it made it so much the worse.

The Lord's factotum, one Angus Desmond, a Scotch-Irishman from Glasgow on the Clyde, was a taciturn, tight-fisted, rigidly honest teetotaller who thought in terms of contracts, documents, signatures, and the letter of the law. According to his lights, he was a good man, I suppose. But to the people of Ballymore he was an obstruction and a blight. His long silences irked them—who ever heard tell of a man who would not talk and pass the time of day? His tight-fistedness outraged them—what was money but a curse? His honesty—well, it is hard to talk against honesty—openly, that is; and yet a true man tempered honesty, at times, with a little sentiment. But his teetotallism . . . ! That was an appalling reversal of all the true processes of nature. Why, the man was abnormal, like a hunchback, or something of the kind. What—not drink good whisky? . . . Angus Desmond was just not the boy for the people of Ballymore.

Ireland, they say, is a land of secret societies. Due to the "oppression" of Lord Devereaux's man, Angus Desmond—so it was said—a new secret society sprang up in Kilkenny and spread like wildfire over a large part of Leinster until it became a noted and dangerous thing among the rulers of Ireland at Dublin Castle. The Lord-Lieutenant himself, Lord Castlewood, inveighed against it in a public speech and declared that it must and would be stamped out. It was known as the the S.F.Y.I.—Society of Free Young Irishmen—and its password was: "How many buttons on your coat?" and the reply was: "Five minus one." Owing to this password, a new name was gradually put upon the Society—a popularly devised name, later accepted by all—the "Five Minus One," and finally its symbol became 5 - 1, a sort of brand.

Now, like politics, secret societies make strange bedfellows. There are always the fanatics; then the sincere men of goodwill; then the maladjusted, who are really and basically against the world itself and not any one form of society, and are a drawback and a drag to everybody; and then there are the chowderheads, with no minds of their own, who merely go with a strong movement like leaves in the wind; and then, lastly, there are the wild boys who are always looking for trouble and a lark and an opportunity to flout the authorities out of high animal spirits and a sense of fun.

So . . . Michael Martin and his pal, Tim Keenan, joined the Society of Free Young Irishmen, and I leave you to guess for what reason.

The Society met in a ruined monastery dating back to the eleventh century. It was a good meeting-place because the country people of Kilkenny—the older folks, particularly—felt a cold terror of the "old grey ruin," as they called it, and gave it a wide berth. Its seat was awesome. Near by was the Great Bog, where a man could be sucked down out of sight in a matter of minutes, and at night devil-blue lights—the will-o'-the-wisp—could be seen travelling the bog just beyond the ruined monastery. Owls lived there and hooted dolefully till sunrise. If Old Horny was abroad at all, the country people said, his first stop would be "the old grey ruin on the darkling plain by the Great Bog."

A couple of tall, well-masked candles lit the meetings, which were held among the huge, fallen, moss-covered grey stones. Still-standing great walls loomed high above them in the darkness. The setting gave a great portentousness and mystery to the humdrum reading of minutes and the other dullnesses inseparable from such gatherings of men all the world over.

While the young bloods, like Michael Martin and Tim Keenan, picked their teeth in boredom or tried, under the cover of semi-darkness, to hug one of the many girls who had joined in with the men, the high officials of the order made speeches, and being Irishmen all and loving to hear the sound of their own voices, the speeches on the whole were not only long but irrelevant, wandering, and full of invective and vagueness.

One man spoke to the point: Regis Donnell—the leader, though only twenty-seven years of age. The people of Leinster had great faith in Regis—he was their man, a future political great, one for the Irish Pantheon. And he was no fanatic, but a man of goodwill, a moderate who believed in a peaceful penetration, a gradual acquiring of rights, a slow program of amelioration. As he said: "Ireland has been Ireland since the days of King Niall. Do you expect to change it in ten years?"

To which the fanatics in their hearts replied: "Yes," while Michael Martin, Tim Keenan, and some others pursued the laughing country girls among the ruins, and sometimes the speeches—even the speeches of Regis Donnell—were interrupted by loud feminine shrieks of protest.

"The owls have a new voice," Regis Donnell, who was not without wit though a dead serious man, cried one night when so interrupted. And from then on the girls of the S.F.Y.I. were known as "the Owls."

Michael Martin and Regis Donnell had little to say to each other, though they were friends. In the first place, they were miles apart in almost anything you could name. Regis was studious, Michael literate but wild and averse to grinding. Regis, though brave, did not like violence and would do his best to turn aside a quarrel; Michael was a very easy man to pick a fight with—his fists were always ready. Regis could not carry a tune; Michael could sing like a bird in a fine high tenor voice. Regis was wary of girls (except one, as we shall see); Michael loved them all, pursued them joyously and wittily and, it was said, with great success. Regis was a true patriot and felt a powerful responsibility towards the country and its people; Michael was proud of being an Irishman, but that was as far as it went; he could not think of the Irish as one people but only as individuals, some of whom he detested; and as for responsibility—well, let every man look after himself, and he would do the same. They agreed about one thing only: Catherine O'Herlihy.

This Catherine, though the daughter of an ordinary farmer, was the beauty of the place: Spanish-black hair, big black eyes, straight black brows, and a creamy Irish complexion. She was laughing, witty, and with a mind of her own. Her family was greatly flattered by the attentions to her of well-to-do Regis Donnell, and as for Mike Martin, they threatened to take a stick to him if he did not stay away with his blue eyes and his tenor singing voice, so well liked by Irish girls. But Catherine apparently could not see a straw of difference between them. She was serious and ladylike with Regis; romping and gay with Michael. When Regis importuned her to marry him, she told him that she was not ready yet for the "horse-collar of matrimony," being only nineteen; and when Michael, whose last thought was marriage, grew too bold, with her black eyes dancing in mirth she asked him: "What are your intentions, Mike?" And when he replied: "The worst, Cath, the worst," she slapped him hard and sent him on his way, but brought him back to the gate by laughing light-heartedly and then sent him away again, still unsatisfied.

To his cronies, Michael referred to Catherine as "the Dream." He was delighted with her because she was able to resist him. He respected her. "Why, by Gob," he said to Tim Keenan, "even when I sing to her the 'Bride of Mourne,' it's like nothing had happened. She resists the 'Bride of Mourne.' Incredible!"

And one day Tim said, shrugging: "It's in the cards. She'll marry the Donnell and be a big woman in Ireland."

"And good luck to her, then," said Michael sincerely. "She could marry a worse."

"Yes," said Tim. "*You*—and your stud of country girls."

And Michael suddenly got mad, and Tim, knowing him well, ran from him and hid. But half an hour later they were singing at the tavern over their whisky while a barful listened.

MICHAEL OFTEN HAD a barful listening. Too often. And that, in a sense, led to his first big trouble. It was the evening of a 5 – 1 meeting, and he and Tim Keenan were fortifying themselves at the Bonnie Prince Charlie, a large inn and tavern owned by Gilroy Donnell, the father of Regis. Michael was in very good voice that night and sang loudly and well many old country ballads beloved by those of Bally-more. He sang so well, in fact, that he was bought round after round until finally even Tim Keenan, partaking with him, began to complain. "Whist, Mike. We've got a skinful, and there's the meeting. The bloody 5 – 1."

But Michael sang on. And it happened that evening, as if destiny was a party to the business, that Angus Desmond was having his frugal supper in a back parlour of the inn, alone and with one candle. He was eating porridge and drinking buttermilk—enough to turn the stout stomach of Michael, who saw the lanky Scotch-Irishman through a partly open door. He also saw on the table beside Angus a small black bag, and he knew, as did everybody in the town, that the black bag meant money—Angus had been out collecting the rents. And in the middle of a song Michael turned to Tim and asked: "Didn't I hear that the blessed 5 – 1 needed money? That the dues of many, especially those of the 'Owls,' are uncollectable through poverty?"

Tim Keenan stared in surprise, but nodded. Neither he nor Michael had ever paid any dues at all.

"Well, then," said Michael, "fetch me mine host's brassbound pistol. You'll find it at the end of the bar."

"Michael! What now? Stop singing and drinking and go clear your head."

But let's not forget that Tim Keenan had been drinking right along with Michael, so he did not argue very much and in a moment stole the pistol, slipped it down inside his trousers, and after a short while and another song they drifted out. Once in the street, Michael explained what he was going to do. At first Tim laughed, thinking it a great lark; then suddenly he sobered and said: "Mike! It's highway robbery. A capital offence. They'll hang you at the next assizes as they hanged Patrick Flemming and Paddy O'Bryan in the bad old days."

But Michael was very well fortified against anything that smacked of sense and only laughed. "What—hang me for borrowing money from a usurer? Why, that would be contrary to King's Law."

But Tim Keenan was not that drunk. He begged, pleaded, and expostulated, but to no avail, and finally he said: "Hang if you like, Mike Martin! But not me. Why, Angus is Lord Devereaux's man, and the Lord is the most powerful noble in Kilkenny. No, thank you, Michael." And he departed.

Michael called "coward" after him and even "caitiff" and "Englishman," and at last "Orangeman," but none of these killing-matter insults had any effect on Tim Keenan, who was by now stone-sober with fright.

Tim did not know what to do. In Ballymore when anybody did not know what to do, he eventually ended up at Regis Donnell's house. Regis always knew what to do. Though only twenty-seven, he seemed to have the wisdom of a patriarch. But he had already left on his way to the 5 - 1 meeting at the monastery. Tim ran after him through the boggy land, panting, and in danger of falling in to kingdom-come.

Michael waited impatiently for Angus, whistling a back-country jig, and when at last he saw Lord Devereaux's steward coming, he pulled a white neckerchief up over his face, presented his big pistol at Angus's breast, and remembering the highwayman tales of his childhood—remembering Patrick Flemming and Paddy O'Bryan and also remembering the whispered exploits of the newest knight of the road, Captain Thunderbolt—he cried loudly in an awful voice: "Stand and deliver."

Angus gave a jump; then he laughed and said: "Michael Martin, you are drunk, so do not try to fool me with this highwayman masquerade, but stand aside." Then he laughed again. "Highwayman, where's your horse?"

Now Michael, as you know, had a very quick temper, and these gibes infuriated him. "What—can a Scot see through a handkerchief?" he cried. And then he hit Angus hard on the point of the jaw with his left fist, and Angus went down like a pole-axed steer, and Michael grabbed up the little black bag, flung the pistol back towards the inn, and made off fast to the monastery with enough money, as he was well aware, to set him up in business for life. But money, as money, was not and never would be Michael's cardinal concern. At the moment, all that he thought about was the faces of those of the 5 – 1 when they saw the bag of gold.

In this comedy of errors, as Michael was going towards the monastery by one route, Tim and Regis Donnell were hurrying back towards the Bonnie Prince Charlie by another.

Michael found a goodly crowd of young members of the 5 – 1 waiting, so he jumped up on the rostrum, poured the gold out on an old wooden farm-table, and made a speech and even sang a song about the wrongs of Ireland to tremendous laughter and applause. Even Catherine O'Herlihy did not seem to realize the seriousness of what had happened, and told the other girls in a delighted voice that "Mike Martin is the greatest buck in the county." What bravery! Robbing Lord Devereaux's steward. What impudence! The "Owls" all shrieked —but not in protest this one time, only with delight.

But it was a different thing altogether when Regis Donnell appeared, followed at a distance by Tim Keenan, who was shaking with apprehension.

Regis got up on the rostrum and tried to explain to the company that they had no reason to crow whatsoever, that a heinous crime had been committed by a drunken member of their beloved Society. But for once he was booed into silence, and Michael Martin stood laughing at him. "Regis," Michael cried, "we need money for a good cause —Ireland's cause. So we take it. You can talk till you're blue in the face and it won't get us a penny. There's gold. Two hundred pounds of it, and the Society is rich at last."

He was cheered. But little by little Regis Donnell made them understand what had happened. Armed robbery on the highway was a capital offence. Michael could be hanged for it, and oh, what a wide embarrassment that would be!

"Yes," said Michael, "then my face would be red indeed."

After the laughter had died down, Regis gathered up the gold pieces, put them back into the black bag, and said that he must at once return the money to Angus Desmond and plead with him that no report of the matter be made to the authorities; otherwise the dragoons would descend on Ballymore in full force, and they all knew what that meant.

"Well, in that case," said Michael, "I resign from the Society. You are all a bunch of fools making unnecessary and meaningless noises in the night. Talk, talk. And where will that get Ireland?"

"I will take up the matter of your expulsion from our Society at my leisure, Mike," said Regis.

"You will take nothing but the back of my hand, you Englishman," cried Michael, and to the horror of all, he tried to strike Regis Donnell, who merely stood looking at him sadly.

That gesture cooked Michael's goose. Nobody ever raised a hand to Regis. You just did not do it. Regis himself would not raise a hand to the dirtiest and meanest cur dog lying in the middle of the Ballymore highway. It was like a sacrilege to think of striking Regis.

"Out with him," cried a man in the crowd.

"Oh, it's you, Pat?" called Michael. "Have you paid your dues lately?"

But this time Michael did not raise a laugh. The meeting broke up in confusion. Michael, sober now, tried to take Catherine aside and talk to her, but she would not listen, brushed him out of her way, and went with Regis into town to see Lord Devereaux's steward, who was lying at home with a great blue lump on his jaw and a badly damaged ego.

Tim Keenan hid in the bushes from Michael, but a dozen or so of the wild ones rallied to Michael and, hoisting him up on their shoulders, carried him home to his father's farm and made such a ho-lo-boloo in the dooryard that Michael's father came out with a cudgel and chased them away.

"What have you been at, Mike?" demanded the father.

"Nothing, sir. A bit of a sing, a party."

"At least you've been at somebody's whisky, and how you stink of it!"

Michael jumped into bed, laughing at the memory of Angus falling in the roadway with a look of surprise on his narrow, canting Scotch face.

BUT THE NEXT NIGHT the joke turned wry. After supper Michael was surprised to see Regis Donnell and Tim Keenan approaching the house along the road. He went out at once. Regis offered him a wallet, and both he and Tim began to talk at the same time.

"Wait! Wait!" cried Michael. "Does it take two of you to expel me from the Society? And what is this wallet?"

"Listen to me, Mike," cried Regis impatiently. "Take this wallet and go at once. Get out. Angus Desmond has changed his mind in spite of us returning the money. He has gone to the authorities. The bills will be out on you for robbery, and the dragoons will be here before morning. It's a hanging matter till it cools off, Mike, so don't delay. Get out at once—now."

Michael was astonished. "The dragoons? Why, the skinflint has got his money back, and lost nothing by the deal but a crack on the jaw."

"The crack on the jaw did it, Mike," Regis insisted. "You've hurt his dignity sorely. Remember—he's Lord Devereaux's factotum. You do not crack such men on the jaw with impunity."

Michael was bewildered. "But, Regis, for the love of God, where does a man go to run away?"

"There are three pounds in the purse, enough to see you through to Dublin, a great city, where a man can hide himself from the dragoons, melt into the crowd. Take the country roads parallel to the Great Dublin Road, or, better still, the woods and fields, but keep a sight always on the road so you will not get lost."

"And good luck to you, Michael," said Tim Keenan, weeping a little. " 'Twas all that Bonnie Prince Charlie whisky did it."

"A slob is what you are, Tim," said Michael, "but my friend, and thanks for the wishes. And as for you, Regis—I will not take your wallet, and be damned to you and your parliament of talking, do-nothing Irishmen. I will do something. Mark me."

"Something rash and foolish," cried Regis. "Take the money. It is not mine, but the money of the Society. Take it, Michael.".

It was reported that Michael used such language in speaking of the Society that it could not be printed or even repeated in mixed company, and to such a length that Regis finally paled with anger, flung the wallet into a hedge, and left, followed by Tim Keenan, who was afraid to stay and afraid to leave and compromised by walking backward all the way to the road.

When Michael's anger cooled, he plucked the wallet out of the hedge, put it into his shirt with a shrug, stuffed a fresh pair of socks and a change of underwear into his pockets, and without saying good-bye to his father or his brothers—out of dislike for explanations and useless family expostulations and wrangling—he set off across the dark fields towards a country lane and the whitewashed stone house of John O'Herlihy.

Though only a little after eight of the clock, it was already dark at Catherine's. There wasn't even a glimmer of light showing anyplace. Buffer, the big mongrel dog, did not bark at Michael's approach, but hurried over to him and licked his hand.

"Hello, Buffer," said Michael, "and in a short minute—good-bye. Would like to take you with me, dog. You could watch while I sleep."

Catherine slept in a little curtained-off alcove at the back of the house; slept with her window shut and barred, as was the custom in those long-gone days. Buffer watched curiously as Michael picked up a few pebbles and tossed them at the window. After a long interval, Catherine, in a heavy, voluminous white nightgown, appeared at the window and looked out. When she saw Michael's face at the glass, she started back, and it was some moments before he could get her to open the window so he could talk with her. At last she motioned for him to stand away, and then she opened the window. Little by little, she let him approach, but when he had explained what had happened and had told her that he was leaving Kilkenny for Dublin and the great world beyond, she began to cry and kissed him passionately and wept a little. And Michael said: "And so you love me, then."

"I don't know, Mick; truly I don't know," cried Catherine, all upset and weeping. "Sometimes I think so, sometimes not. You are a drunkard, Mick, and a ruffian; and I'm sure you will come to no good end. Father says so, too; and all the others of the family."

"To hell with the likes of the O'Herlihys. A Martin is just as good any day."

And then they quarrelled, and finally Catherine slammed the window shut in a rage, waking the whole house, and Buffer barked in glee, and John O'Herlihy appeared with a blunderbuss, and there was much yelling and carrying on before Catherine could make them all understand that Mike was going away to Dublin suddenly and had come to say good-bye.

"He's going away?" cried O'Herlihy, the father, while the sons laughed with relief. "Why—fine, fine! And good luck to you, Mick. Make a great name and stay in Dublin. That's the place."

But Michael was delighted in spite of all because Catherine, pretty as a sunrise and fresh as the dew thereof, kissed him good-bye in front of all of them, standing there only in her nightgown and her bare feet, with old O'Herlihy glowering and fondling the blunderbuss.

Buffer saw him to the gate and licked his hand good-bye. A big moon was rising over the dark fields. Michael looked back and saw Buffer standing there watching him go, and he felt a great lump in his throat, and so he broke out whistling a lively tune called the "Tinker of Armagh," and Buffer barked and other dogs answered him from far away and near—and this was how Michael Martin, aged about twenty-two, set out for the great cosmopolitan city of Dublin, in the year of our Lord 1817.

As you know, Michael was a green hand. He had never before been farther from Ballymore than the ten miles to Blackfountain, where they raced the home-grown Irish thoroughbreds in the middle of the summer. Time after time he got lost and wandered in circles in a wood, trying to catch a glimpse of the Dublin Road without showing himself, till finally he lost his temper and said: "Be damned to this," crossed a wood and a field and a farm, and came out at last on the Great Dublin Road itself, which stretched off ahead of him, flat, straight, endless but promising, towards the faraway capital city on the Liffey.

As long as he could remember, Michael had heard talk and stories of Dublin: its high houses from the top of which a man could fall to his death, its crowded streets full of foreigners from all quarters of the globe, its great harbour full of masts and spars, its glittering taverns, ale-houses, coffee-houses, and theatres—its handsome, easy-going women. Excitement began to grow in him as he walked along the King's Highway like any free, unmenaced citizen, whistling the "Tinker of Armagh," paying little attention to things about him.

Later he heard a thunder of hoofs, and a big fine equipage passed on its way to Dublin: the varnish of the coach flashing in the sun, six fine, high-stepping cobs of horses with a postilion in livery riding one of the leaders—the fast-turning wheels winking and throwing off light . . . a vision, truly a vision, Michael told himself: a vision of luxury and ease; a vision of the Great World. He had caught a glimpse of a man in a pale-blue coat and a shiny hat cocked over one eye sleeping in the depths of the coach. Lucky fellow! A great noble, no doubt, on his way to his mansion in Dublin. Merrion Square, perhaps.

The coach disappeared ahead, raising a pillar of white dust, and then Michael saw a crossroads and a big parson in black coat and white tabbed collar riding in a cart pulled by a fat pony and turning from the side-road into the main highway . . . and he was thinking what a big, impressive-looking man the parson was when, from behind a tall hedge at the side of the road, a lone red-coated dragoon on horseback eased out with a sabre in his hand and in a rough, authoritative voice told Michael to halt in his tracks or he'd split him from head to heel.

"And for what?" cried Michael.

"Because," said the dragoon, "you are a wanted man with bills out on you, and a ten-pound reward. Eh, Martin?"

Well, Michael was caught. If he ran, the dragoon would ride him down and slash him with the sabre. If he did not run, he was fair taken and would appear at the assizes and maybe hang or at least be shipped to Botany Bay in the far Antipodes.

With hardly a thought in his mind, his body acting almost of itself, Michael left his feet in a tremendous diving leap, took the dragoon full in the belly with his head, and they both sailed through the air from the saddle and fell to the ground on the other side with Michael on top, the tall hedges screening them from the roadway. The sabre went through the air in a long arc and fell ten feet away with a loud clatter of heavy metal. Michael hit the dragoon several belts on the jaw, and the dragoon lay as still in the dust as Angus Desmond had lain at Ballymore from the one punch only.

Michael glanced down at the dragoon, knew that he'd be there for a long time to come, then he eyed the dragoon's fine horse. It would get him into Dublin in style; then he walked over to pick up the sabre. Now he had a weapon and was not a naked, helpless man at the mercy of any one at all armed. But he heard a footfall and looked up. The big parson he'd seen in the pony cart at the crossroads was looking at him round a hedge. The parson had remarkably bold, black, unparsonlike eyes.

"Leave the horse and the weapon, man," said the parson. " 'Twould only make it worse for you if caught."

"And who the devil are you?" cried Michael. "And what business is it of yours—a Protestant?"

"My son," said the parson, "you are a likely lad, and it aches me to see you in trouble. Come with me. I'm on my way to Dublin—by a slow route, it is true, as I have to make many stops, owing to my profession, but I'll see you safe there at last. I warrant it."

"And why should you see me safe, a wanted man?"

"Why, because I'm a Christian, my son; and I like neither the English dragoons nor the Lords of Dublin Castle."

Michael stared at him suspiciously, but horses went past on the highway, unsettling him somewhat, and finally he took off his hat and scratched his head, and said: "Well, I'd as well trust you as another, parson; but—look now—I am no man to tamper with. I must get to Dublin uncaught. That's all."

"I warrant it," said the big parson.

Michael got into the cart with the parson, who clucked to the strong, fat pony and they were off down the side-road, which wound among fields of oats, showing in the distance the straight chimney-smoke of small farm-houses.

"As you see," said the parson, "the cart is full of pamphlets and holy tracts, and if we are flushed—as pheasants in a covert, that is— hide yourself among the tracts and leave the rest to me."

Michael said nothing. Thrust among the tracts was a huge bell-muzzled blunderbuss. After a moment Michael asked: "And the weapon, parson?"

"It's loaded with nails. It is to protect myself from the petty male-factors of the back roads."

Near sundown and many miles away from the Dublin Road they were flushed indeed, by half a dozen dragoons, and Michael hid himself among the tracts with his right hand on the blunderbuss. But the dragoons were respectful with the parson and listened with interest to the following:

"You are far off your course, gentlemen. I saw the man you want at the Dublin Road. He was making his way across the fields to the hills. You are miles off your course."

And the dragoons thanked the parson, saluting, and galloped off down the country lane towards the Dublin Road.

"By Gob," cried Michael, emerging from among the tracts, "you gave me a true word, parson."

"Ay," said the parson shortly, and clucked to the fat pony.

THE SUN SANK beyond the rolling farm land, and it grew dark at last. The parson pulled up at the gate of a little farm, and the whole family ran out to see what it was—back-country people who seldom saw a strange face: an old man, a middle-aged woman, two tall young sons, a handsome daughter with pale-blue eyes and red hair, and a flock of jiggling, yelling children.

The old man lit a wood torch and held it up, and in the flickering light Michael eyed the red-haired girl and smiled his best Ballymore smile for her and showed his strong white teeth, and the girl covered her head with a shawl, hid in it, giggled. Meanwhile, the parson asked the way to the nearest inn, and while the old man told him, in a long, confused manner, Michael got down and talked with the girl.

"And what's your name, little one?" he asked.

"Moira Shay. And yours?"

"Is Mike good enough?"

"It would be Mike," said the girl, giggling. "Are you long for here?"

"No. But I might be back."

"Then we'll unleash the dogs when we see you coming," said the girl, giggling again.

Michael turned at the chink of money and saw the parson offering some coins to the old man, who refused, hesitated, then took them reluctantly.

"It's only because of the need," he explained, embarrassed.

"Ah, yes," said the parson. "Ireland is in great need. While the aristocrats sup and gamble, the true Irish starve."

Michael was deeply moved. Turning, he hit the parson on the back, a blow strong enough to fell a steer, but the big parson did not even wince. "By Gob," cried Michael, "you're a true man, parson. I love you." Then he turned, laughing. "And I love you, too, Moira, with your pretty red hair."

The girl giggled. "All the same," she said, "when I see you coming back, I'll unleash the dogs, and they are big ones and fierce."

There was great good humour all around, and as the parson and Michael drove off, the jiggling, yelling children ran along beside the cart for quite a way until they were called back by the old man.

"A lovely girl," mused Michael, as they drove off into the dark.

"There are lovely red-haired girls all over Ireland," said the parson. "Why stop for one?"

"You say that? A parson?" cried Michael.

The parson made no comment, but merely laughed loudly.

THEY WERE well suited at the mossy old country inn, which had stood on this ground since the time the Normans came. The parson took a big room with two beds and called for a bottle of country whisky and a tableful of food.

Michael ate like a wolf-hound and drank as if there was no more whisky to be had at all—but the parson, in most unparsonlike greediness, kept him company to the full.

And when they were through and the remains had been carried away, the parson sat back with a sigh and smoked a white clay pipe with a long stem and put his feet up. Michael studied him narrowly. There was something about this parson . . . well, what a parson! Bigger than himself, wider, heavier, with a strong, smooth, bold face and a formidable dark eye. An ill man to cross, it was obvious, even to Michael, who seldom gave such a thing a thought. If a man must be crossed, cross him and be damned to him! Yes, yes, this parson . . . and he sat staring at him. And finally he had a wild thought and gave a start.

"How many buttons on your coat?" he asked abruptly.

"Why, five minus one, naturally," said the parson, laughing.

"Be Gob!" yelled Michael, and then he jumped up and did a furious jig to his own mouth music, and presently the big parson jumped from his chair, breaking his pipe, and joined in the jig, his clerical coat-tails flying . . . but then all at once he gave a loud bellow of pain and sat down abruptly. Michael stopped, astonished.

"Damn you, you wild back-country gossoon!" cried the parson. "You've made me forget myself, when I shouldn't."

And now he stripped down his coarse stocking and showed a bad wound far around in the calf of his left leg, and Michael stared as before. The parson whipped out a large pocket-knife, held it to the candle flame for a moment, then handed it to Michael.

"There's a pistol ball in that leg," said the parson. "Dig it out. It's behind me. I can't reach it."

Too full of pride to refuse, but sweating badly from distaste and apprehension, Michael knelt, and after a long nerve-racking search, finally found the pistol ball and dug it out. The parson gave a muffled bellow or two and sweat as badly as Michael, but when the ordeal was over, he clapped Michael on the back, praised him highly for a brave, steady fellow, and called for more whisky.

"You puzzle me, parson," said Michael, recovering after a long drink.

"Ay! But the puzzle will soon be over. Look, lad. I need one like you in my business."

"What business? Five minus one?"

"Why, yes. If you put it that way. You are a bold fellow, Michael —though you need guidance, and I will be your mentor if you say the word, and I'll make you rich. 'S Faith, how many young gentlemen of the road have struck for two hundreds pounds on the first try?"

Michael was dumbfounded. "Gentlemen of the road?"

The parson took from an inside pocket a bill or wanted-poster. It was for the apprehension of one Michael Martin, and the reward was ten pounds; said Martin had robbed Lord Devereaux's high steward of two hundred golden pounds on the open street by force of arms.

"Where did you get that?" Michael demanded.

"I am interested in such things," said the parson, and then he drew another bill from inside his coat and handed it to Michael.

It was a King's poster—no local thing: very important. It was for the capture, dead or alive, of John Doherty, the notorious murderer and highwayman, known as Captain Thunderbolt. Michael read the description in awed silence, and when he glanced up at the parson at last, his mouth was wide open and there was a chill along his spine and he wanted to rise and run back to Ballymore—for he was, he knew, just a country boy, after all, and not one to be associating with this celebrated knight of the road, whose depredations and cruelty were known all over Ireland from the West to the East.

"Now the puzzle's over," said John Doherty. "No more puzzle. And now you understand?"

"Yes," stammered Michael.

"Well, now, you have no choice, my boy. You know me. I've trusted you. Did you note the reward? Five hundred pounds—an unheard-of rich sum for the body of a man, you'll say—and yet this carcass is worth it and more, much more. In Dublin I am a rich man. I must get back, that's the only problem—and I have a leg wounded which may fester, God forbid!—and you must see me back."

"I'll do what I can, sir," said Michael, "and you saving my life, and giving to the poor like a kindly man, and a joiner of the 5 – 1 like all proper bucks—though you're a little old for the Young Irishmen."

Doherty roared back at him. "Old is it, you country simpleton! Is forty old? I'm a better man than you, game leg and all—and I'll prove it if you say the word, right now."

"Well," said Michael, "it is my principle to back up from no man —nor the devil neither—and I'm ready."

Doherty roared with laughter, slapped Michael on the shoulder, and pushed him back into his chair. "Well said, Michael. Well said. And we'll take it up later, if you insist. Right at the moment we've got business. You see, there was a little difficulty in Dublin, so I took ship for Waterford on the Suir. I was pursued, you understand, but I slipped away. Now the trouble is over, and all I need to do is get back. I heard they were watching the ships at the small ports, so I came back by land, but I've had my troubles, lad, many troubles—including a ball in the leg from a gentleman from whom I borrowed a small sum of money. My purse is getting very slim. . . ."

"I have three pounds," said Michael.

Doherty roared. "Oh, the simplicity of the fellow! Three pounds, is it? A tip for one pretty doxy, nothing more."

"Three pounds?" cried Michael, horrified. "Why, more like tuppence, I'd say."

"Listen, lad. We'll soon be in Dublin and flying high. But we may have to borrow a little money from some rich gentleman. You see, if you are taken without money, there is the devil to pay. But if you are taken *with* money, why, there are those who will smooth your way. You see? Well, well, you'll learn. Take no chances with poverty. But once in Dublin, my sister, Lady Anne More—"

"A Lady?" cried Michael, astonished.

"Why, yes," said Doherty. "A Lady with a fine mansion of her own and good connexions in the town. Fine beds for us, Michael, with expensive linen sheets, servants, food for the gods, French brandy of the best. What do you say to that?"

"Why, it sounds like a dream," said Michael.

"And so," said Doherty, dipping his fingers in the whisky, "since you will help me and be my second, you must have a true professional name—and I will christen you as follows—" and here Doherty flicked some whisky into Michael's face. "I christen you—what shall it be?— yes: Captain Lightfoot."

And Doherty laughed and clapped Michael on the back, and Michael sat there, pleased in a way, but worried and bewildered. Was this the thing? The right thing?

"And now," said Doherty, "to bed. Sleep makes us all Pashas."

Michael was much taken with the remark. "What saying is that?" he inquired.

"I heard it from a Turkish fellow in London."

Michael stared at Doherty in awe. Here was a man who had known a Turk and had been to London. "And what might a Pasha be?"

"A Pasha is a great noble," Doherty explained. "It is as if to say,

sleep, like death, makes all men equal. The Turkish fellow was quite a strong man, but they hanged him at Westminster. Very sad."

A short time later Michael went thoughtfully to bed.

IT WAS broad morning now, the sun was almost halfway up the sky, and the larks were singing in the fields. Doherty and Michael, with the pony cart and the fat pony near by, were loitering among the high hedges of the Dublin Road, waiting, as Doherty said, for "prey." Michael kept glancing at Doherty, who was a new man, and a fine figure of a man, in gentleman's dress, with half-boots, and a shiny hat with a cock feather in it, and a slim gentleman's-sword at his side.

Doherty was explaining about disguises. "You must learn the art, my boy. Most people are born gulls and take a man for his dress and look no farther. A man in a black coat and a tabbed collar is a parson —no more, no less. Presto! I'm a gentleman, and your average fellow would not recognize the parson in me. We live in a world of phantasmagoria, lad; a world of false forms, and false faces. Each man wears a mask against his fellows. Ah, well. Enough philosophy for the morning."

Michael stared, speechless, at such talk. A great man clearly, Doherty.

Peasants' carts passed along the road; then a jaunting-car, which turned off the main highway and followed a track through the fields; and then a drover going to market with a score of fine black cattle; and then nothing for a long time—until finally a pillar of dust appeared down the roadway, fast-moving dust, and Doherty perked up and said: "Remember, now. Grab the lead horses by the bridle and watch the driver or the postilion, as the case may be."

Michael found himself shaking, and this infuriated him so that he gritted his teeth and cursed to himself. Now the vehicle came into sight, a smart calash pulled by two powerful black cobs, with a driver in gold and grey livery: no postilion. It was such a rich-seeming equipage that Michael was overawed, but Doherty stepped out at once with the wicked-looking blunderbuss, and the calash came to an abrupt stop. Michael jumped to the horses at once, grabbed the bridles, then looked at the liveried driver, who had a tough Irish phiz and began to grin at Michael and winked one eye slowly. Michael stared and then whispered, loud enough for the driver to hear:

"How many buttons on your coat, man?"

"Five minus one," answered the driver and winked again.

Beyond them the following conversation ensued as Doherty "borrowed" some money and other objects from a bored-looking English Lord in a uniform:

"What—a highwayman! You look like a gentleman, my man."

"And gentleman I am," said Doherty. "You may see now that ill luck may sometimes befall a courtier who follows nothing but inconstancy, admires nothing but beauty, and honours nothing but fortune."

"Well spoken," said the English Lord. "It's a pity I will see you hanged at Dublin Castle, sir; a great pity. And now I mind not my hundred guineas and pistoles, and my gold snuff-box, and my two diamond rings—but I would appreciate it greatly, my man, were you to return my gold watch. It has a sentimental value beyond price."

"To me, my Lord," said Doherty, "while I respect sentiment, your watch has a great *monetary* value, and that at the moment is the important thing, though later I may have leisure for sentiment."

"I see," said the English Lord. "Yes, yes; a terrible pity that a man of such great parts as yourself should be hanged, but never forget the saw:

> Little villains must submit to Fate
> That great ones may enjoy the World in State."

Doherty bowed at this and gave the Lord back his watch. "I see that you, my Lord, are no hypocrite and understand the true workings of the world. Good day to you, sir."

Michael stood aside, the driver cracked his whip, and the calash drove off.

"Now," said Doherty, "we are almost ready for the rest of our journey—we have at least three hundred pounds worth of what is vulgarly called booty. We sell the fat pony and cart, buy us two fine horses—the best only. A fine horse is one which leaps a high hedge, a wide ditch, and a five-bar gate. They are not to be stolen. Keep watch while I get back into my parson rig, then we'll be off through the back country again."

IT WAS night. The lights of Dublin winked ahead of them through the thin, blowing mist, and Michael's heart was beating like a hammer on an anvil.

Doherty gestured expansively. "Dublin. Our town. Now we leave the highway and ride by the river. It's safer, and I know every foot of it."

Little by little, Dublin came towards them as they walked their horses along the embankment. It seemed so vast to Michael that he felt a sort of panic and longed for a moment to be back in little old Ballymore, where he knew every face, every stone in the roadway, every tree, and every dog.

"We rest the night at Nine Steps in the stews. It's an unsavoury neighbourhood, but we are well taken care of there. Big Tom is friend to us all, and we are protected from constables and narks alike. Mahony, the blind harpist, who sings like a lark, keeps watch on the front pavement—he is not so blind after all, you see—and when danger approaches, which is seldom, Mahony plays and sings the "Highwayman's Song," softly if the danger is not great, loudly if great, and he bellows if it's the Lord-Lieutenant's men. Mahony has not bellowed for many a year, as the Lord-Lieutenant's men have had too many broken heads in that neighbourhood and are now wary. 'Tis a great thing to sleep peacefully among friends."

"That it is," said Michael, staring about him at the big warehouses, the quays, the thronged gin shops and the lights—the forests of streetlamps, casting golden-yellow zigzags into the black water.

"And tomorrow we'll have in Mr. Stitch, and he will alter some of my clothes for you, Mike. I have a superfluity of same stored at Nine Steps—all gentleman's clothes, and then we'll go on, the night, to my sister's, Lady Anne More's, and dance to the sound of violins and hautboys, and meet a lovely woman or two, and perhaps risk a guinea at the tables."

"Gaming, you mean?"

"Of course. There is as much gaming in Dublin as in London. Each night there's a faro bank at Lady Anne More's, and the quality come there to gamble. We see fine people there, Mike."

"Quality, you say?"

"And why not? I'm of the quality, myself—though fallen on evil days. Here, Mike—before I forget—are fifty guineas for your own use. I'll keep the snuff-box and the diamond rings, as they are beyond your competence to handle."

"Fifty guineas, God above!" cried Michael, almost falling off his horse.

"Nothing, I assure you. Nothing," said Doherty, laughing.

"Could I send a good half of it back to Ballymore for the Society?" cried Michael. "How would I do that?"

"'S Faith!" said Doherty. "Don't be impatient to part with your money. Later, lad, later. Perhaps we'll both go to Ballymore one of these days. Dublin may get hot again. Who knows?"

Michael rode towards the slatternly big tavern called Nine Steps, shaking his head with wonder. It was all like a dream. Jack in the Beanstalk, for sure.

THEY HAD a fine big room on the fourth floor at Nine Steps—or so it seemed to Michael—and there was a fine wide prospect from the window out over the narrow streets of the stews, with, beyond, dimly seen through the mist, the masts and spars on the river and the riding-lights swaying gently with the tide.

"A fine room indeed," said Michael as Doherty blew out the candle and got into his bed across the way from Michael.

Doherty laughed in derision. "A stable! A pig-sty! Wait till to-morrow night, lad. Then you will see a room, many rooms; and then you may crow if you like."

Doherty fell at once to sleep, but Michael, used to the country quiet of the Ballymore farm, turned and tossed as the bleakly unfamiliar sounds of Dublin at night drifted in through the open windows:

shouting, singing, a harp playing a jig and accompanied by wild drunken shouts; the ringing of a bell and the voice of the night crier, calling the hour; the rumble of carts and the cracking of whips and cursing; the whizzing roll of a calash and the iron ring of shod horses on the street; the heavy footfalls of the Watch and the sound of pike-butts against a door: the cry of "All's well," later, from a rich, coarse, beery bass voice; and then the mad playing of the harp again, and more jigging, and the shrieks of a doxy being pinched, or worse; and then the clatter of dragoons, and strange high alien cries from the river quays, and a heavy ship's bell tolling, and more carts and whipping and cursing, and then a great clatter as a big night-coach drove by with outriders and the blowing of a horn at the corners . . . and on and on until finally Michael gave a shout of rage and leaped out of bed and ran to the window.

Doherty woke at once and sat up. "What is it, lad? Trouble?"

"Trouble enough," cried Michael. "Don't any man sleep at all in this hellish town?"

"It's early yet. At Lady Anne's they've scarce put the counters on the faro bank table, and the last act of the play is not yet over at the King's Theatre."

"Musha," groaned Michael, deeply impressed. "At home a man is waking up from his first long sleep and looking at the window to see if morning's greying yet."

Doherty gave a grunt of derision, turned his back on the room, and pulled the covers up over his head, but Michael stayed at the window and stood looking out at the brawl and moil of night Dublin with something that was almost fear—and yet was not quite fear, but maybe the awe of the exile far from home.

And presently an old cracked tenor voice rose on the night, accompanied by a harp, and the voice was singing the "Bride of Mourne," and Michael put his head down on the sill and listened, and pretty soon a tear or two stole down his cheeks. The "Bride of Mourne"! The old back-country story of the poor sick hopeful betrothed girl who did not quite live to see the hour of her wedding, though she heard the summoning bells—all set to music of such gentle sweetness that it melted the heart.

"Damn old Mahony," cried Doherty suddenly in the darkness; "he will sing those damned old back-country, moss-grown, gruesome songs, enough to make a man's hair stand on end, sad as a debtor's tale who wishes not to pay."

"He sings very fine for an old man," said Michael, who should know. "Very fine indeed."

"And talks even better," cried Doherty, sitting up with a curse. "Talked his way from the gallows with the help of a priest. Benefit of clergy. Reads and writes as well as I do myself, and I'm a school-educated man."

"From the gallows?"

"Ay! In his time Tyburn still stood in London—Mahony's on for eighty. They banished him to Jamaica's Isle, but he was back in a year, across all that water, three thousand miles of it, I hear. Yes, Mahony's quite a man, though he's like a reformed drunkard—the worst sort of bigot. He will warn you to lead a life of holy toil and then you will not end a half-blind harpist in the streets of Dublin. Don't listen. That old one is handed many shillings a day, guineas even. He's rich, I'm told. And for what? Even if they bury it with him all in gold, the worms won't eat it."

"He was a highwayman, then?" asked Michael.

"Ay. And a pirate, too, so he says, though he is a great one for talk and vain to build himself up in past evil so as to contrast with present virtue—though he keeps the watch for Nine Steps and hates a constable as a thief hates a nark. Go to bed, Martin. Sleep. To-morrow the sun will shine on our doings, and once you are in gentle-man's clothes—mark me—you will feel and act like a gentleman. The way of the world."

The song ended below, then Mahony broke out with another jig and there was the scuffling of dancers. In a moment Doherty began to snore. Michael went back to bed and lay with his hands under his head, looking up at the faint patterns of reflected light on the ceiling. Here he was in Dublin! He couldn't believe it; he just couldn't believe it . . . and then suddenly all sounds seemed to cease, and the world went black. . . .

Somebody had him by the shoulder, shaking him. He woke with a start to broad day, violent clamour of voices, wheels, and hoofbeats in the street below, and Doherty in a fine frilled shirt bending over him, grinning. "It's ten of the clock, man. Are you going to sleep all morning?"

Michael was astonished. He had never slept later than six in his whole life before. And then immediately he got another shock. A plump Negro girl brought in a huge tray of food, and flashed her big ivory teeth at him, and then scuttled out with a happy squeal as Doherty made a certain gesture in her direction.

"Why, Gob!" cried Michael, flabbergasted. "She's all black—black as an ebony cane."

"You haven't seen a Negress before?" cried Doherty, laughing. "Why, they're thick as flies in London. Oh, a real back-country boy."

"And be damned to you, Doherty," cried Michael, jumping out of bed, incensed, already growing familiar with Doherty and losing some of his awe. "I'll learn. I'll learn. Give me time."

They ate at the window, looking out now and then at the masts showing above the house-tops and at the green-bronze twinkling of the water of the bay in the distance.

Michael looked down into the street in wonder. "Why, the old man's back with his harp already. When does he sleep?"

"Only a few hours," said Doherty, "maybe less. He lives in the basement, not ten feet from where he takes his stand."

"They're giving him money in his hat—and it's only ten of the clock in the morning."

"All day it's like that. 'Tis an honest form of thievery. Leave it to Mahony to think of one, with his twisted mind."

THE TAILOR came at one o'clock. He was a little dancing fellow with a dark Italianate face. From time to time, as he was being tried and suited, Michael addressed him politely as "Mr. Stitch," and got a black look, and heard a strange coughing sound from Doherty; until at last the tailor tore off his measure and threw it across the room, and Doherty collapsed against the wall, doubled over with laughing, and the little tailor cried: "My name, sir, an it please you, is Signor Perini. I would be obliged, sir, if you would call me by that name and not by the common and facetious designation of my trade."

Michael lifted the little man from the floor by the front of his coat and shook him as a terrier shakes a rat.

"Don't raise your voice to me, man," cried Michael, very much embarrassed and feeling like a bog-trotter of the far West country and furious because of it. "I'm a stranger in Dublin. Give me a chance. The fellow Doherty referred to you as Mr. Stitch. How was I to know it wasn't your true name?"

Doherty intervened and laughingly apologized to little Mr. Perini, whose face was almost black with rage and humiliation.

"He treats an artist in this ruffianly manner?" he cried. "What sort of man is this—this friend of yours, Captain Doherty?"

"A fine fellow," said Doherty, still overcome by laughter, "but odd, very odd."

"Odd indeed," muttered Mr. Perini, and from that moment on did his work in absolute and injured silence.

Michael kept glowering—to top it all, the man was a foreigner, with strange foreign ways, and should he be reproving a true Irishman?— but Michael's expression changed to one of abashed and astonished wonder when he saw himself in the cheval-glass in the dress of a gentleman with a slim sword at his side, varnished half-boots, a shiny hat with a feather, a dark-blue coat with red facings, and a canary-yellow waistcoat with deep pockets and gold braid.

"If those at the Bonnie Prince Charlie could only see me now!" he cried, preening himself like a young girl getting ready for her first ball.

"There is fine blood in this man," said Doherty judiciously. "He is none of your peat-gathering bumpkins from the woods. Is there a manor-house close to your farm, lad?"

Michael did not take Doherty's meaning at first, but when he did, there was hell to pay, and Mr. Perini fled down the stairs away from this "young rustic barbarian," and Doherty, almost helpless with laughter, had a hard time holding Michael off long enough to explain that it was only a manner of speaking, a mere witticism, a facetious comment among gentlemen.

"Don't be so ready to fight," said Doherty when Michael had calmed down a bit. "As partners in a nervous business, we'll be at it soon enough. But let it come by natural means. I'll accommodate you, boy. But not over nothing. You must get used to quips in Dublin. If not, you'll be fighting duels behind the University, one after another—or, if you are not a good shot, there will be only one. You are a gentleman now. Gentlemen do not use their fists. They use pistols, swords, or sabres. Have you ever handled a sword or a sabre?"

"I have not. Nor a pistol, except in fun."

"Well, then, don't jump for a throat at a quip. There is no sense in living as long as Mahony, of course; but there is even less sense in dying with fuzz on your cheeks."

And Doherty spent the rest of the day till candle-time showing Michael how to draw a sword, how to thrust and parry, how to advance and withdraw. Doherty was astonished at the Ballymore boy's aptitude and determination. "You'll do, lad. You'll do," he kept saying. And then later he went patiently into all the mechanics of handling and loading, unloading and reloading a pistol, till Michael was almost ready to drop with weariness. "You'll do, pistol or otherwise," said Doherty, "and now we'll have a light repast, and then a hackney coach to Lady Anne's, and some gaming and a supper at midnight, and then perhaps a coranto or two with the fillies, eh?"

"A what?"

"A dance. A dance. What—don't you know the coranto?"

"No," said Michael, bristling. "A foreign dance, I'm sure."

But Doherty showed him, humming an air, and when the Negro girl, Bessa, came in with the tray, she almost fainted at the sight of these two big broad-shouldered brawny Irishmen daintily dancing the coranto together.

It was nearly ten o'clock when they set out in a coach for an evening of pleasure at Lady Anne's—and to stay there the night, and for many nights to come, Doherty insisted, rubbing his big hands in delight. As for Michael, he was half asleep in his corner of the coach. What—start out at ten for a party, like a chicken thief, while all respectable folk slept? It seemed abnormal.

But he woke with a bang when he saw Lady Anne's mansion and the liveried callers and doormen and the blazing lights and the equipages along the street, and heard the sound of violins and hautboys and the chink of gold coins and the subdued, thrilling laughter of real gentlewomen.

And then inside, the elegant furniture of English design, and the chandeliers with a thousand candles, it seemed, and the smooth polished floor reflecting the lights with a golden shimmering, and the silver, and the well-dressed, polite, bowing men, and the lovely ladies whose décolletage embarrassed him so that he didn't know where to look—what a plethora of pink nakedness!—and the heavy scent of flowers and perfume, and the winking of great jewels under the candle-light—and then, there suddenly, was Lady Anne More smiling at him —a statuesque blonde woman with her hair piled high, and wide, oddly shaped green eyes of such a brilliance as to dazzle him. Michael felt faint, bowing before her as Doherty had taught him. What a place for Farmer Seumas Martin's youngest boy, Mick!

"Your servant, ma'am," said Michael, trying not to get entangled with his sword. Doherty had warned him repeatedly about sword-en-tanglement. One of the greatest ruffians of England, William Cox, had been taken, due to tripping over an unfamiliar sword he'd only put on that morning.

"Why, the man's handsome, Jack," said Lady Anne, turning to Doherty. "Captain Martin, is it? Welcome, Captain. Welcome."

And then she had to turn away to greet a slim old buck of sixty who had been announced by a bawling footman as: "His Excellency, Lord Clayton."

And Michael stared at the Lord as if at a tiger, and Doherty, noting the stare, hurried him off to show him the house.

Michael never said a word as Doherty led him through the huge, elegantly furnished mansion, room by room. Now and then he gave a sharp exclamation of surprise and awe, but the words wouldn't come. He was stunned—and wandered through the many candle-lit rooms like a sorely troubled man walking in his sleep.

But his silence was not missed or even much noted. Doherty talked fifteen to the dozen, explaining how this piece was from Italy and of Renaissance design, how that big sumptuous gilt mirror was from Venice and had hung originally in a boudoir of the Doge's palace— and Michael did not even ask: "And what might a Doge be?"—how this table had been built by the cabinet-maker to the King in London, and how that great wall tapestry was from a Norman castle of the old Irish days. . . .

But finally Michael was moved to speak. "Gob, your Lady Anne must be richer than the greatest usurer in Ireland."

Doherty winked his left eye slowly and pursed his lips. "Lady Anne, is it? You're looking at Doherty's Castle, lad."

Michael was staggered. "But Lady Anne—what of her?"

Doherty roared, then sobered. "Why, she lives here, minds the place for me. Look, Michael. You are in for a long education at my hands, so you may as well begin now. What costs a noble five hundred guineas may cost me a matter of shillings, or nothing at all. Now take that hundred-guinea mirror. A present from a friend. Or, let's say he was in a tight squeeze and was happy to give it to me for a favour."

"A favour?"

"Ay! He was menaced by parasites—a very indiscreet Lord indeed. The parasites were moving in on him, owing to a folly he had committed with a young lass, a very young lass, but old in evil. I had often remarked that mirror when gaming with my Lord. Well, I spoke a sharp word to the parasites, and the mirror was mine. The tapestry? A receiver of stolen goods could not turn it. I traded him a saddle for it. A good saddle can always be turned. And so on—I'll not bore you with the rest. But there is a point, a moral, you might say. There are no stable values in this world, lad. It's all a matter of intelligence and desire. Or cunning and lust, if you like. There are men—and women, particularly women—who would sell their souls for my tapestry of the Norman Conquest. I acquired it for a second-hand saddle." Doherty looked at the dumbfounded Michael narrowly, and sighed. "I see I am going too fast for you, lad. Well, never mind. There's plenty of time. Shall we go back downstairs?"

They went down to the dancing-room, where an elegant rout was disporting itself, and Doherty danced a coranto with Lady Anne More to the delight of everyone. A pretty sight, this brawny dark-haired man and this tall, statue-like golden-haired woman, dancing in the blaze of candles to the expert music of French musicians.

Michael stood back against a wall, watching. Beyond, through huge wide-open doors, he could see the gaming at the faro bank tables, and could hear the calling of the dealers. A moment later a small, handsome, black-haired girl accosted him and asked him if he were for the dancing, the gaming, or the reception rooms upstairs. Her dress was so low in front, showing a soft, deep cleft, that Michael kept his eyes on the gilt moulding around the ceiling and said in a shaky voice: "Why, I'm for looking on at the moment, dear one."

The girl laughed. "What a nice Irish voice you have, and how nicely you say 'dear one' as if you meant it."

And at that Michael's instincts overcame his shyness, and he grinned and said: "There's no great difficulty in a man calling you 'dear one.' It should be easy as breathing." And then he lowered his eyes from the moulding and looked at her, and he felt his blood rising. A lady this, and yet careless of her charms, very careless. What if her dress should fall off altogether, and from the look of it, it might!

The girl's smile stiffened, and Michael turned. Doherty was bearing down on them.

"What have you been saying to him, Aga?" Doherty demanded.

"Why, nothing at all," the girl replied, showing what Michael took to be deep agitation, maybe even fright.

Doherty said brusquely: "This is Captain Martin, my second, a young lad who will go far. Captain, this is Agatha McDonald, a Scottish girl."

Aga seemed overcome, and a flush showed on her neck and bosom. She curtsied to Michael, who stood staring at her in amazement; then he bowed abruptly, hitting the wall with the end of his sword scabbard.

"The sword, the sword!" said Doherty, grimacing.

"Ay!" cried Michael, flushing with embarrassment.

Aga curtsied again, then made off quickly towards the gaming-room.

"If you want a girl, let me know," said Doherty. "A lady of quality, eh, lad?"

"I pick my own girls," Michael replied stiffly, still angry about Doherty calling him on his ineptitude with the sword.

Doherty stared at him hard for a moment, then finally he shrugged. "Well, well; you've a lot to learn, and you can't be expected to learn it all in one night. Be guided by me; that's all I ask."

Michael felt very uncomfortable, like a man taking part in a masquerade against his will. "When do we leave?" he demanded.

"Leave!" shouted Doherty. "We don't leave at all. This is our home."

And while Michael was digesting this, a small mincing young man in gold braid that must have cost him a hundred guineas came timidly up to Doherty and said: "Your pardon, sir. 'S Faith, I have had a run of bad luck, and—"

"To what amount?" Doherty demanded shortly, and Michael was a little shocked at Doherty's curtness with this elegant young man, obviously one of the quality.

"Two hundred guineas, Captain. And, 'S Blood! I'm strapped, for the moment."

Doherty's face softened. "Two hundred guineas, you say? Ah, well, then, play on. You have credit, sir, up to two hundred more. I'll tell your table-man so."

"Thank you, Captain," said the mincing young man. "A thousand thanks. I've always said that you were a sporting man of the old school."

He left, and Doherty laughed coarsely. "Should I not trust him for two hundred more when he's already dropped two hundred? His father will pay, in any case. You've heard of the Earl of Aire?"

"Of course," said Michael.

"That short simulacrum of a man is his fifth son. Each son is shorter than the last as the Earl's powers wane, and the final one will be a midget, I have no doubt."

Michael was shocked at Doherty's levity over the fifth son of the powerful and awesome Earl of Aire. Not only was he shocked, he was completely bewildered. He simply could not understand what this business was all about. Doherty, a highwayman, with his house full of the finest quality. It made no kind of sense at all to Michael.

Later Michael stood alone, watching the dancing. It was getting very late, and Michael was sleepy and began to wonder when these people made off to their homes and went to bed. But more kept coming.

And then at last there was a great commotion at the door, bells rang, and there was loud bawling and shouting from the footmen, and side doors seemed to burst open of themselves, and women screamed, and in a moment the stairway was full of struggling humanity—and Michael stood frozen as threescore of High Constable's men, led by a tall fellow in a red officer's coat, converged on the gaming-room in a flying wedge.

And now suddenly it was all like a nightmare to Michael, who stood staring. He saw from the corner of his eye Doherty escaping by a back window, helped by Lady Anne More and Aga, the Scotch girl. He saw the Earl of Aire's fifth son slap the tall red-coated officer in the face with a glove. He heard Lady Anne More's indignant, peacock-like cries, and finally he came to attention as a constable's man cried: "See the quality safely to their carriages, Malone—take three men. I'll look after the trulls and pimps—a nice haul!"

And then Michael saw three brawny policemen roughly handling a harried flock of women, who were screaming and lashing out with their feet, and Michael's blood rose to the boiling-point. He forgot that he was a "gentleman," he forgot his sword—and leaping in at once, he battered the three policemen about the hall in good old Ballymore Fair style, and ignored their amazed cries of: "Sir! Sir! What are you about?"

Till finally half a dozen of them bore him to the floor and tried to reason with him, but, having no success, they bound his arms behind his back with straps and arrested him, as they said, for his own sake.

"Wild drunk, this fellow," said one of the constable's men. "An hour or two in the jug will cool the temper of the young gentleman."

A MINOR MAGISTRATE sat behind a high desk, smiling at Michael, as an officer of the constabulary explained what had happened.

"Ah, yes," said the magistrate. "And may I ask your name, sir?"

"I give no name," said Michael sullenly.

"Quite right. I understand," said the magistrate. "But, sir, while I do not choose to take note of your having been apprehended in a house of ill-repute—that's your affair—I must, you understand, take note of your violence towards officers of the law."

"They were manhandling the ladies."

The magistrate was astounded. "Manhandling the . . . ! Nothing of the kind, sir. They were only doing their sworn duty in regard to these trulls and trollops, who spread the pox about the town in spite of their nice ways and their costly habiliments. You are in error, sir— but I must say it does you credit."

"I saw them," cried Michael.

An officer whispered to the magistrate. "He was drunk as a Lord —begging your pardon, sir—drunk as a lord. A most violent young man, and strong as the Bull of Bashan."

"You saw with befuddled eyes," the magistrate went on. "Now, I feel sure that a young man of your quality does not want to be remanded to a cell, but I have no choice unless . . ."

"Unless . . . ?" asked Michael.

"Of course," said the magistrate, "I could fine you, but the fine, according to the new code, would be very heavy indeed, and then if you couldn't pay it, you'd be thrown into the prison for debtors, and there the way of release is hard. I have no choice in this matter, I'm sorry to say. But actually it is very simple. A person of quality must vouch for you. Then I sign a release, and that is the end of the matter entirely."

Michael was silent, not knowing what to say or do. As far as he could see, he had been abandoned by Doherty and was once more on his own, a bungling, bewildered country boy from Ballymore, homeless and friendless now, and adrift on the sea of Dublin. Should he pay the fine? Would fifty guineas be enough?

But at that moment there was a slight commotion in the anteroom, then a huge bailiff entered and bawled: "Lord Clayton, Your Honour —to see you on the matter in hand."

The constable's man straightened up and stood at attention, and the magistrate put on a strained, obsequious smile.

Lord Clayton, the little shrivelled buck Michael had seen at Lady Anne's, entered stiffly, attended by a huge flunkey in livery.

"Your Excellency," murmured the magistrate.

"Why have you arrested this fine young man?" shouted Lord Clayton.

"I was about to release him, Your Excellency," said the magistrate, fawning, while the constable's man turned white.

"Well, then, consider him released, damn it." Lord Clayton turned to the flunkey. "See the Captain to the coach, Myles. I'll attend to the details."

Blindly bewildered, Michael went out, followed by the towering flunkey.

Now Lord Clayton drew out a huge purse, but the magistrate cried:

"It's only a matter of a signature, Your Excellency. Nothing more, an't please you."

Lord Clayton put back his head and laughed. "What—an honest magistrate? Dublin, Dublin, what is happening to you!"

The magistrate smiled feebly and offered a book for Lord Clayton to sign. When it was done, Lord Clayton handed the magistrate his snuff-box, a beautiful thing of gold and enamel, and then he tipped the constable's man, who flushed heavily and bowed low. The magistrate took a pinch of snuff and made a move to return the snuff-box, but Lord Clayton wheeled abruptly and went out.

"Forgetful as a Lord," said the magistrate, pocketing the expensive snuff-box, and the constable's man grinned broadly.

Michael was astonished to find Doherty waiting for him in Lord Clayton's coach. Doherty was rocking with laughter as Michael was obsequiously helped in by the flunkey.

Doherty said: "The last I saw of the lad, he had constable's men strewn all over the carpet. 'S Blood, Martin, what a brawling Irishman you are!"

"What happened?" asked Michael, and Doherty almost fell on the floor of the coach laughing. After a moment Michael said: "Will you stop nickering long enough to tell a person why Lord Clayton bailed me out?"

"Why, he's a close friend of mine," said Doherty. "Why else? I am able to do many favours for the old boy, who loves women and gaming and hasn't a pistole to his name—nothing but a grand title, the lustre of which he's tarnished badly."

Michael sat shaking his head in bewilderment, and finally Doherty said: "Well, lad, it's back to Nine Steps for us until Lady Anne can find a new mansion and move the furniture. The old place has been burnt, badly burnt."

"God above!" cried Michael. "Did they set fire to the house, too?"

And now Doherty actually fell to the floor laughing, and Lord

Clayton, returning, was amazed to see the great Captain Doherty rising from the bottom of the coach to greet him.

Michael froze in the presence of Lord Clayton, and neither the Lord nor Doherty could get another word from him.

LORD CLAYTON'S COACH dropped them at Nine Steps, and the old Lord raised his hat politely as he drove away, and Michael returned the salute and bowed low. Doherty mocked him by outdoing his bow and sweeping the ground with his hat. But Michael was too tired to care.

It was so late now that even poor old Mahony had disappeared into his basement for a cat-nap, but Big Tom, ex-pugilist and proprietor of Nine Steps, was still up and sitting in the hallway with his chair tipped back, smoking a short clay pipe.

"You are back soon, Captain," said Big Tom, grinning and showing a gap or two in his teeth. "Bessa will not be expecting you. I hope your room is tidy."

"If not, it's no great matter," said Doherty, yawning. "All I ask at the moment is that the bed hold still."

Big Tom roared and dropped his pipe and broke it in his merriment. "Oh, damn the pipe!" he cried; then: "As Thatch's parrot used to say: 'Out with the lubber. He's brittle as an Irishman's pipe.' Too true."

"Thatch?" said Doherty. "You couldn't have known Thatch, Tom."

"No," said Tom. "But my grandfather did."

"He's speaking of Blackbeard," Doherty explained, but Michael yawned in his face. "Well, to bed. The lad's more tired than myself."

Tom called good-night, then rose to find another pipe. As they went up the stairs, Michael said: "With you, Doherty, a man lives many nights in one."

Doherty liked the remark and kept repeating it over and over. "Yes," he said finally, while they were undressing by candlelight. "And though I'm only forty by common chronology, I'm a hundred and forty in the true annals of time. There was a Frenchman who used to say: 'A man who lives more lives than one, must die more deaths than one.' I don't quite take him there. One death and it's over, and God be thanked that it's so. I've seen many men die, and with some of them it is a very hard thing. Once is enough."

Now they both fell into bed, and that was the end of them for many hours.

DOHERTY WOKE very early for him, but Michael was already at the window. It was raining gently and mistily, a real Dublin summer rain, and the old city was a silvery grey in colour, the chimney pots shining like billycock hats.

After breakfast and a brief, laughing tussle with Bessa, Doherty felt philosophically inclined. "There was this Roman writer," he began, "a fellow of the name of Petronius. He said a true word: 'It is not wise to place much reliance upon any scheme, because Fortune has a method of her own.'"

"You could call it Providence," said Michael.

"Be damned to Providence," cried Doherty. "I call it Fortune. Oh, yes—and she has a method of her own! Let us take last night. For weeks I'd been longing for the Mansion, and the ease and luxury of it, ready to settle down for who knows how long a time. What was to prevent it? Why, Fortune, sir. She prevented it. She laughed at my little scheme of contentment, and presto! it was gone. Now let's be fair. The Mansion is a heavy burden and a constant source of drain and anxiety, and yet when I was on the road running from the dragoons, I thought of it as Paradise." Doherty hesitated, then said: "Lad, there is only one Paradise. Paradise lost."

But Michael did not know what he was talking about, so Doherty broke off, sighed, and rose. He glanced out the window at the rainy day, then he observed: "If it was always night, I think I'd be a happier man. What does one do with the daytime? It's only good for a single thing, sleep. I think I'll sleep till the lights are lit again."

But there was a knock at the door, and opening it, Michael found Big Tom on the threshold.

"Captain," said Tom, addressing himself to Doherty, "there's an unsavoury fellow to see you whose name I pronounce only if absolutely necessary."

"Pronounce it."

"Clagett, the nark."

Doherty's face darkened and his lips set grimly. "To see *me*, you say?"

Tom nodded. "He says he wants nothing, only to help you, like a friend."

"A likely story. Clagett helps Clagett. But send him in, Tom."

A strange-looking little man with something vaguely nautical about him came in after a moment, cringing and fawning before he was halfway through the door. He was poorly dressed, but there were several fine cameos on his thick fingers, and when he whipped off his hat you saw that he had a tarred pigtail like an old-fashioned pirate, and that he was wearing a gold ring in his right ear.

"Captain Doherty, your servant," he said, bowing. "Young gentleman, your servant—whoever you may be."

"A friend," said Doherty shortly, staring at Clagett as a girl stares at a fat toad, and waving Michael to silence. "I am told you want to help me like a friend. Well, many friends of yours have swung, and many more have been shipped to Botany Bay to live among the savage blacks and the jumping kangaroos. Is this how you want to serve me, a friend?"

Clagett glanced significantly at Michael, but said nothing.

"You may talk in front of the lad," said Doherty, "or keep silent and get out, whichever pleases you most."

Clagett cringed and smiled at the same time, showing large, yellowish, badly discoloured teeth. "A *close* friend, then, the young man. Ah, yes. Captain, you know well I've never done you a disservice."

"And for good reason. I'd see your throat was cut for it if it cost me a thousand guineas."

"Exactly. And yet a man of your acquaintance has just done you a disservice of the greatest magnitude, and you are doing nothing about it at all. In fact, I can't see that you're even angry or at any kind of loss, as if nothing had happened."

"This is news to me," said Doherty airily.

"Ah, yes," said Clagett, tapping the side of his nose in an odd gesture; "then you don't really know. I suspected as much."

"And the fellow's name?"

Clagett hesitated, then spoke quickly. "The one they call Sir George Bracey."

"That rogue! But what has he done to me?"

Clagett laughed unpleasantly, but cringed away from Doherty, who glared. "It seems, sir," said Clagett, "that Sir George has turned nark —a gold-braided nark, for certain—and has sent the High Constable's men down on you at the Mansion."

"What!" cried Doherty, his face dark with rage, his body seeming to swell enough to burst his clothes.

"As a friend," said Clagett, "I tell you this. I want nothing for it. Nothing."

"You lie," said Doherty. "Perhaps you lie all around. But I might believe you if I knew what you wanted out of it. Not that I doubt Sir George is the worst rogue in the British Isles."

"Well," said Clagett, "Sir George has set up a gaming-place of his own on money borrowed from a usurer. His business has been a little slack, while Lady Anne has prospered beyond anything yet seen. So Sir George played nark for the High Constable. With you elimi-nated—"

Doherty broke in. "I begin to see you may have the right of it, Clagett. And where is Sir George holding forth?"

With surprising alacrity Clagett whipped out a piece of paper and handed it to Doherty, who glanced at it briefly. "Ah, quite a nice address. Very nice. And now, Clagett—what do you want out of this?"

Clagett was silent for a moment, lost in thought, as if calculating what he should say. "Captain, I'm a man of business, of many busi-nesses. Sir George was bankrupt—sold up, you know—and hadn't a farthing to his name. He was for ending it like a Roman. But I found the usurer for him, I found the gaming-house, I found him expert card-men—and to date I have not even been invited to sup, let alone been paid my rightful commission, or dividend. So," Clagett went on with an evil grin, "I want nothing of you, nothing. Only your good-will, Captain."

"My goodwill you will never have, Clagett," said Doherty. "But my thanks—yes."

Clagett nodded. "You see, being a man of integrity myself, Sir

George's prosperity at the moment irks me sorely. Good day to you, Captain; and to your close young friend."

Clagett looked Michael over carefully, then withdrew.

"Sir George, is it!" cried Doherty, raging about the room. "Set the constables on me, will he? Chase me from my Paradise? Better for Sir George had he ended it like a Roman, as he'd wanted to."

Michael was, as usual, bewildered. "This man is a Lord—and yet he runs a gaming-place and is a rogue?"

"I never saw his patent," cried Doherty. "They tell me he's quality. But he's a rat, for all that. Michael, we've got business tonight—the two of us."

"And what business is that?"

"Why, to collect poor Clagett's dividends," cried Doherty; then he began to laugh loudly and strut about the room.

THAT AFTERNOON while Doherty was getting dressed to go out, he noticed that Michael was sitting on his bed, still half dressed, lost in thought. Finally Doherty turned and asked: "Is something bothering you, lad? Your face is as puckered as a parson's on Saturday night thinking out a Sunday sermon."

Michael sighed. "I don't grasp it at all."

"And what's that?" Doherty demanded. "Maybe I can explain. I'm a great explainer." He laughed loudly as he began to hitch on his sword.

"Well, Doherty, I may be green—I *am* green, Lord knows—but how is it that you're so well known, with posters out and a huge reward, and yet you move about in Dublin as you please and call yourself Doherty in the open? Why, when I was in my sixteenth year, I remember seeing a poster out for John Doherty, Captain Thunderbolt. It was on a tree in Ballymore."

Doherty threw back his head and laughed. "Lad," he said, "you understand neither the law nor the perversions of the law. Now, look. In the first place, there are many men in Scotland and Ireland of the name of Doherty; and then, what's to prevent any rogue at all from calling himself John Doherty or even Captain Thunderbolt? A man must be caught on the spot, you understand? While I avoid being taken in town like the plague; if taken, they must charge me at once and they must produce witnesses to prove that I am veritably Captain Doherty, or Captain Thunderbolt. Otherwise I am merely Captain John Doherty, of the same name, a well-known man in sporting Dublin, with fine connexions, mark you, such as Lord Clayton, Aire's fifth son, and others I could name. Do you begin to comprehend the confusions attendant upon catching one John Doherty and convicting him of a capital offence? Why, lad, even faced by a witness who is willing to swear that I relieved him of his guineas and perhaps his watch, there are ways . . . but we will not go into all that. Let's say this: for a matter of ten years I have been badly wanted—or, at least, said Captain Thunderbolt has been wanted—and here I am strapping on my sword ready to go out on a matter of business like the most respectable merchant in Dublin. Don't think so hard, and stop wrinkling your brow. Again, remember. You must be taken on the spot— or red-handed, as they say. So rest easy about Captain Doherty, Captain Martin-Lightfoot."

Michael still did not see, but he sighed and dismissed that part of the subject and took up another. "Now about the business of the blessed 5 – 1."

Ready to go out, Doherty turned and grunted irritably. "The blessed 5 – 1, is it? What would you have me do, go to meetings and listen to the braying of every disaffected jackass from Cobh itself to Dublin? For why? No—I do better, much better. I divide my money with the poor. When my purse is full, it's open to any poor devil in the land. Do you likewise, and you will be of more service to the Irish than the screamingest fanatical politician in the whole Movement. Now, goodbye. I'll be back for the evening meal. You stay close. At Nine Steps you're safe. I have business." He went out with a swirl of his coat, slamming the door.

MICHAEL FINISHED DRESSING at last, but, restless and lonely, not knowing what to do with himself, he paced the room for a while, looked

out into the street at the hubbub of traffic, and stared off at the masts
and spars showing above the house-tops; then, bored with everything,
of a sudden he went out and down the stairs to the lower part of the
inn, where ruffianly men were arguing at the bar and where there
was a great clamour and shouting in all the rooms as the dice rolled
and the cards were slapped down, and the sweating waiters hurried
through the narrow hallways, balancing huge trays of drink and food.

Men on their way in, seeing Michael and taking him for a gentleman
by reason of his fine clothes, glowered at him, but made way, and
some of them even touched their forelocks respectfully and bowed and
murmured something like: "Your Worship. . . ."

Michael emerged at last on the front steps and stood looking up and
down the street at the concourse of people and gigs and carts and men
on horseback and laughing sailors from the quays with sea-bags over
their shoulders and black-suited business men from the warehouses
and slatternly women walking heedlessly in the mud of the street.
"By Gob, it's like ants," Michael told himself. "It's a marvel they all
know where they are going in this ho-lo-boloo."

Where should he walk to? What could he do in this jammed, alien
place? It was a marvel, too, that all the hundreds of faces were different and that he had never seen a one of them before. Bells tolled at
the quays; a coach roared past full of travellers, the postilion whipping
his horses at the cross-street; countrymen in battered old carts bumped
by on the way to the huge market beyond; a green-coated constable's
man on a white horse turned in from the cross-street and ambled his
way through the press, getting furious glances, and Michael eyed him
boldly as he passed, a big fellow with red hair. And then as he hesitated,
somebody plucked him by the sleeve, and turning, he saw a wizened
old man reaching up from the basement steps to accost him. The old
man's eyes were so pale they were almost white. His nose and chin
nearly met. His complexion was as dark as a Latin's, and his surprisingly thick hair was darkish tinged with grey. Was this Mahony?

"Sir," said the old man, "don't go out. Stay."

"How's that?" asked Michael.

"I saw your guardian, the great ruffler Captain Doherty, pass out
some while back. You are new to Dublin. Stay at Nine Steps. You are
safe here."

"Are you Mahony, the harpist?"

"Ay! Come below along with me. We'll have a chat."

Michael hesitated. Here was company, and, truth to tell, that was all he wanted. And yet he felt a certain irritation at Doherty and Mahony both. Did they think he was a child to be told to stay? Still, why offend the old one? He could go on later.

Turning from the street, he followed old Mahony down into his basement room. It was nicely fixed for such a place, with engravings of sailing-ships on the walls, a stove in the middle, a solid old table with chairs about it, and the harp in one corner, its gold figure-head glimmering darkly in the filtered daylight. They sat down, and Mahony handed him a long clay pipe and started to light a taper at the stove, but Michael said:

"Thank you, Mahony, but I haven't as yet acquired the habit."

Mahony took the pipe from him and lit it for himself and puffed contentedly. "And don't, then," he said. " 'Tis a filthy habit, to be sure. You see a man sitting here before you who over a long life acquired and rejected many filthy habits and has now but one left—tobacco; unless you include good ale, which I do not." There was a pause, and old Mahony puffed on his pipe. "Did not Doherty tell you to stay in, lad?"

"He did. But I'm past twenty-one, and Doherty is not my father."

Mahony cackled drearily, then he sobered. "Is it possible at all for you to go back to your native village?"

Michael stared, then he understood and replied: "At the moment, no."

"Ah, well," said Mahony, with a sigh, "that's the way it all starts. Take me. Of respectable folks, I was apprenticed to a tailor when I was twelve. But no tailoring for me. I was too wild. I hung about the quays, listening to the sailors talk of places far away, and when I was but fifteen I shipped out as a cabin-boy. It was a rough voyage— kill or cure, you know. But it neither killed me, though I almost died of home-sickness and the brutal punishment of a crazy mate, nor did it cure me—not of the wanderlust, that is. At sixteen I was a rough young fellow and reckless. I'd left the Church and was a thorough-going heathen." Mahony sighed and relit his pipe. "My father tried to reason with me to no avail. 'Keep on,' he told me, 'and you'll end at Execution Dock.' Which I nearly did. I shipped out with a villainous crew. I did not know it, but it was a piratical bunch, and we took a ship off Barbados and sent the whole crew to the bottom. Two days later we were taken by one of His Majesty's frigates. 'Twas only my youth saved me. I was small for my age and claimed to be thirteen, otherwise I would have been stretched at Execution Dock as were the rest of those who survived the battle with the frigate. Ay! But did that teach me a lesson? It did not, even though a kindly priest said to me—as I intended saying to you: 'Go home, lad. That is the best place, after all.'"

Michael listened with interest. The old man had a very taking way of telling of his life.

"And then," Mahony went on, "it was one ship after another, some good, some bad; a full pocket at the end of the return voyage and an empty one a few days later—what with liquor and women and all the rest—and then back to sea with the ruffians. They left me for dead in Jamaica one voyage, but I fooled them and came round, and on the return, a passenger this time, I met a plausible rogue of the name of Captain Cunningham, who'd been condemned to death in the Colonies but had managed to slip away to Jamaica, one way or another. Well, he was a 'knight of the road,' as they called them then, and back in England I rode with him till one night we were set upon by sheriff's men, and Cunningham was killed dead at the first shot, and I was taken in a net as natives in the brush take a wild beast. You see, the sheriff's men wanted somebody to hang as an example to others. It was a barbarous time, nearly sixty years back, and it was the custom then to hang the caught highwayman at the nearest big town and then remove his body to the place of his greatest crime and hang it there in chains for all to see and as a deterrent to others. Good God! It was an awful thought to me—Mahony hanging in chains at a crossroads for the bumpkins to laugh at and the crows to pick. A priest saved me. Benefit of clergy, though very unusual in a capital case. But I was only twenty and looked far, far younger."

"The priest saved you from hanging?"

"Ay! Yet he couldn't save me from the branding, though he was able to mitigate its severity. See? I am branded on both hands with a T—'Thief.' And on the forehead, here, see?—under this fringe. 'Thief' again—T. I carried these marks into the King's Navy, and was laughed at and derided for them, though I fought well and was half blinded when a deck-gun exploded in a sea battle."

Michael struggled to keep himself from shuddering at the ugly scars, the seared cicatrix, of the branding, and his heart turned over in his chest, and he felt cold sweat on his forehead.

"With hot irons, was it?"

"White-hot," said Mahony, "and my flesh sizzled like pork in a pan."

"God above!" cried Michael, wanting to rise and leave.

"Men who are at war with society must look forward to final suffering," said Mahony. "There is no other conclusion, lad; believe me. Only the priest saved my neck. We appeared before an old magistrate. *'Legitne vel non?'* asks the magistrate. And then I had to read from a Bible, the Fifty-first Psalm, to prove myself literate, and to bear out the priest that I had or would study for the clergy; and so, being literate, I read the verse out, though I was shaking like a dog, and then the priest said: *'Legit ut clericus.'* It is always the Fifty-first Psalm, called the neckverse because it has saved many from hanging—and a thousand rogues who could not read a line of print had the verse by heart, hoping it would save them at last." Mahony puffed on his pipe, meditatively. "Yes, I escaped hanging, though not branding, and here you see me a lonely old man, without kin or friends, playing a harp in the streets for a living, and tied down for ever to the stews of Dublin and the life of an outcast. Lad, if ever you can go back to your native village in safety, go back."

Michael sat lost in thought, staring at the floor, shaken, perturbed, wondering. He'd lost all desire to roam the streets of Dublin, whose clamour of traffic and humanity came in through Mahony's open door but faintly muffled.

"Yes," said Mahony, nodding, "if you ever can, go home. Stay there. Lead a quiet, respectable life. Marry a fine village girl. Raise a family. It is the best life."

And Michael sat thinking sadly of Catherine O'Herlihy, and little by little, lines from the "Bride of Mourne" began to run through his head, and he kept back his tears with difficulty.

He was so silent and looked so thoughtful that night when he and Doherty were preparing to go out and pay Sir George Bracey a call, that Doherty finally demanded: "What the devil is it with you, lad? You look like a man going to his own funeral."

"And might I not be?" asked Michael.

Doherty roared with laughter. "Oh, good God, lad," he said, "this is nothing, nothing at all, a mere formality. 'S Faith, what has happened to the brawling boy from Ballymore who had six big constable's men down at one time?" Now something struck Doherty, and he turned and looked hard at Michael. "Have you been talking to that auld prattler James Mahony while I was away?"

"We exchanged a word or two, yes."

"Damn the auld croaking crow of a spoil-sport and frockless priest! One day I'll break that Irish harp over his head for him. Lad, don't listen to the man. He's a laughing-stock for his preaching to the young. He's lived his life and now would live yours. Listen, I've got news for you. After we pay our respects to that great gentleman Sir George, we'll sup with Lady Anne and the little black-haired Aga. They've found a nice nest for themselves, pending removal to the new mansion we've got our eyes on. What do you say? A roast chicken and a bottle or two of claret with the women, and a nice fire, and to hell with Dublin and its rain and mist for the night."

Michael perked up at once, his face flushed pink, and the natural optimism of his nature took charge once more. "Why, fine, Doherty. A remarkably pretty girl, Aga. The idea suits me as hardly anything in Dublin has suited me up to now. Will it be long before we see her?"

"Not long," cried Doherty, clapping him on the back.

They went out laughing.

THE FINE THOROUGHBRED HORSES they had bought on the way into Dublin from the south were ready saddled for them at the stables back of Nine Steps, and they rode northward through a large alley, crossed many streets and avenues, bewildering to Michael, and finally came out onto a broad thoroughfare lined with tall old trees where hackney coaches, calashes, gigs, and vehicles of all kinds were bowling towards town and away from town, passing and repassing beneath the mellow, flickering lamplight falling from tall standards.

Michael shook his head in bewilderment. "Some going, some coming, and they all seem to know which. Where in the name of God do all these people come from? Horses enough for ten regiments. Conveyances enough to move all the people of Kilkenny to a new county. It makes a man dizzy."

Doherty laughed. "Gigmanity, lad, gigmanity—the animal on wheels. 'Tis a new world, eh? I like it. On the move—that's the way it should be. Time enough to sit in a chair and poke a fire when you're an old man like Mahony, that mealy-mouthed, hypocritical old ruffler and pirate!" Doherty laughed again. "Excitement in the air. Women about. Fine horses. Plenty of gold guineas. Something stirring. That's the life, lad. We'll be a long time dead, and then who will care? A pox on the virtuous life, the flannel nightcap, to bed at nine with the stale wife of your bosom, church on Sunday, business during the week—and heaven for reward. A pox on't!"

Michael began to catch the excitement, and when a pretty girl waved a lace handkerchief from an open carriage at the two handsome gentlemen of quality riding so jauntily on their mettlesome thoroughbreds, Michael laughed aloud and kneed his horse up beside her and swept his hat from his head, and the girl showed delightful dimples and tossed her dark-red curls . . . but a stern old face leaned forward and stared hard at Michael, and steely eyes met his with a shock, and false teeth glared in a snarl, and behind Michael, Doherty cried:

"Leave off, lad—'tis Lord Crewe himself, who will not thank you for meddling with his toy."

Michael reined in so fast that his horse reared and almost threw him. "Lord Crewe, is it?" he shouted to Doherty, as the carriage rolled on. "What a lovely daughter the man has!"

"Ay!" cried Doherty, laughing. "Many a lovely daughter, but not his own. You have just seen the main adviser to the Lord-Lieutenant, which proves you to be a lucky fellow, because I myself have not seen him close these ten years."

They rode on.

"It was not his daughter, then?"

Doherty shrugged. "Do you think the daughter of Lord Crewe would be waving a handkerchief at a stranger on the streets of Dublin? Probably naught but some young Parisian doxy, free and easy in her ways. I am told the great Lord prefers the French—that is, for certain purposes; not diplomatically, needless to say. For he once said: 'The only good Frog is a dead Frog.'"

Little by little the vehicular traffic thinned, the thoroughfare narrowed, and after a while the houses were more widely spaced until it seemed that they were almost in the open country. Lights of big estates glimmered back in among the shrubbery, and at last Doherty turned off into a wide, winding, well-cared-for road with a black archway of trees, and they rode for a quarter of an hour, passing one small estate after another, until Michael began to wonder if there was any end to Dublin at all.

Doherty reined in at last and pointed with the butt of his whip. "A lovely spot for us," he said. "If there's trouble—which I don't anticipate—you understand, we escape northward into the open country. We have better horses than any of the dragoons or constabulary, and who is going to worry about the rest? Under cover of night, no one can overtake us. That's if there's trouble. If there is not, why, we amble back to town, and in half an hour's time we'll be supping with our ladies and drinking claret and toasting our toes before a cannel-coal fire in a pink and mirrored boudoir. Eh, lad?

"Down this lane, now," Doherty went on. "There's a wooden gate in the wall with neither lock nor key—it merely swings on its hinges."

They halted in pitch-darkness. A high wall loomed over them, and beyond the wall there were the big lighted windows of a large mansion.

"Sir George does well for himself," said Doherty, as they dismounted. "Now, lad; the most important part is yours."

"How can I believe that, Doherty?" asked Michael, nervous but resolute.

"Because I tell you so. You are to remain with the horses and guard my rear approaches. You must not run away, no matter what happens. Stand firm. You have sword and pistol. Defend yourself if necessary, but do not run away, and do not lose the horses. I'm speaking only of an extremity. Actually, it will go like clock-work and I'll be back in ten minutes. Stand by the gate and keep it open so you can see what is going on. Tally-ho, lad. I'm off."

Now Doherty adjusted a mask. "The best carnival mask I could find. It has black lace on it and slanted eyeholes. Why, they'd take me for a Venetian tart if it wasn't for the pants. Ha! Ha! Stand firm."

Michael stood in the darkness at the gate, watching Doherty go. He crossed a long formal garden, disappeared among the shrubbery, then reappeared again at a higher level, crossed a terrace, and went boldly in at a French window which was open on the night.

Michael heard a ho-lo-boloo inside, then silence, and he stood holding his breath in the darkness, feeling lost, alone, befuddled, inadequate, but completely resolved to do his duty and prove his mettle. Loud voices rose on the night. Somewhere a door was banged. There were feminine shrieks. Then, at last, Doherty burst out through the French window and made for the shrubbery, but in a moment a bareheaded man burst out after him with a huge upraised sabre in his right hand, and the man was crying: "Doherty, you filthy rogue! You swine! Doherty, I say!"

And at that moment Michael gave a loud gasp and almost abandoned the horses. Doherty had tripped over a root and fallen to the lawn, and the bare-headed man had slashed him with the sabre. On the ground Doherty seemed to turn swiftly. There was a red glare in the night, lighting up the bushes, and the shattering report of a pistol. The bare-headed man dropped his sabre, reeled backward across the terrace like a drunken man falling downstairs, then plunged headlong into the shrubbery. No one else appeared, although there was much shouting and screaming. Michael stood firm, but his heart was beating so heavily it was jarring his chest.

Doherty dragged his right leg across the formal garden and through the gate. "So much for Sir George," he said jeeringly as Michael helped him onto his horse, then mounted his own.

"Back to town," cried Doherty. "He slashed me bad in the back of my right leg. I'm bleeding like a stuck pig."

Behind them the shouts and screams died away as they tore off down a back road towards the faraway misty lights of Dublin.

"Good boy," cried Doherty. "You have won your spurs—you've drawn first blood, and it's blue. I peeled the rat-like Lord for a good four thousand guineas, and I let the moonlight into him, besides. 'Twas his own fault, the fool. What—pursue me with a naked sabre? Asked to be given his *quietus est*, the fellow did. Oh, God—I'm bleeding hard!"

They galloped in silence for a while, then Doherty reined in to a wrack and Michael followed suit. "No use killing the horses," said Doherty. "We're not pursued."

After another silence Doherty said: "If we don't staunch this soon, I'll be too weak to walk up the one flight to Lady Anne's nest. We must stop."

They turned off the road into a clump of bushes, dismounted, and Doherty lit a wax match to look at his leg. "God above!" he cried. "This calls for a tourniquet at once. Fortune, thou bitch! Doherty tripping over a root when he was away clean! It has never happened before."

Gritting his teeth to keep back retching, Michael helped Doherty with his leg, and at last the flow of blood was staunched and a handkerchief bandage tied in place. "It's bad, bad," cried Doherty. "Ah, well. Perhaps I need to be bled. Once a sawbones told me so. 'Doherty,' he said, 'your blood's too thick, and in your forties you'll fall down in the street one day with a stroke.' Well, by God, I've took the cure at last with a will."

All at once a blunderbuss spoke thunderously out of the darkness and Doherty was hit again, and for a moment there was a panic of men and horses as Michael and Doherty mounted and finally got away through the clump of bushes and into the meadow-like open country with the river glimmering in the distance like a silver platter in the moonlight.

"An ambush, by the gods!" cried Doherty. "And I'm tagged again —in the arm. A nail, I think. It's getting to be too much of a good thing, as the tart said on Saturday night."

They rode hard towards the gleaming river, pursued by a score of horsemen who seemed to materialize out of the darkness.

"Dragoons!" cried Doherty. "And where in God's name have they come from?" Then he laughed loudly. "All on broken-winded cobs procured for them by some thieving government horse-factor. Let's show 'em what kind of horses we ride, lad."

And Doherty belted his horse with the whip, and Michael followed suit, and they were off with the wind screaming round them, and they took a high hedge with never a bobble, then a ditch, then a wooden bridge over the river, and then another series of hedges and three wide ditches, and then they were in a flat, grassy country where the going was marvellous, and little by little they lost the dragoons and were soon riding alone in the moonlight, and finally Doherty turned, laughed jeeringly, and shouted at the vanished redcoats: "Lobsters, how do you like the colour of me arse?"

And Michael roared with laughter, but mostly out of excitement.

TOWARDS DAWN Doherty's pallor became so noticeable that it began to bother Michael greatly, though he could not bring himself to speak till long after the sun had cleared the hedge-rows and was finally sending long, rayed beams down through the tall trees lining the road. "Doherty," he asked at last, "are you all right, man?"

"I've been bled to the bone," said Doherty with a wan smile, "and the nail from the blunderbuss is giving me fits in my arm. I need food and brandy and a new bandage. There's a market-town up ahead."

They reached the big, sprawling market-town about noon. "We do not rest here," said Doherty. "We get supplies and move on to a country road I know where there's excellent cover."

Leaving his sword with Doherty as an encumbrance, and hiding his pistol, Michael went boldly into the inn on the highway while Doherty remained with the horses. The inn was full of loud-mouthed drovers who looked askance at the handsome young man in gentleman's clothes, but mine host was most polite and made up a package of food for the travellers with dispatch, and was greatly pleased and grinned and touched his forelock when Michael bought his most expensive bottle of brandy.

"Is it far you are going?" asked mine host, as Michael paid the score. "I have excellent horses here if your cobs are tired of the road. I'll trade or sell, as the case may be, sir."

"We're well suited," said Michael; "but thank you and good day to you."

Michael and Doherty rode off at once, but many came to the door of the inn and stared after them as they disappeared up the broad highway, northward.

"I don't like the look of that," said Doherty. "We've been remarked, and a man in gentleman's clothes is as conspicuous away from the great cities as a bear in a poultry yard. We'll head for the back country immediately."

They turned off at the first by-road and walked their horses for nearly an hour before Doherty began to sway in his saddle. "I'm beat, lad," he cried finally. "It's a thing a man does not like to admit, but there comes a time . . ."

They had halted. Michael turned to glance at Doherty. He gave a start and jumped off his horse at once. Doherty's face was a livid green colour. Suddenly, with a husky groan, Doherty turned in his saddle and fainted. Michael tried to catch him, but Doherty was too heavy and a dead weight now, and they fell to the road together, with Doherty on top. After a brief struggle Michael managed to get out from under him, produce the brandy bottle, and force a little of the liquid into Doherty's mouth. In a moment Doherty's eyes opened; he blinked rapidly, took in the scene, and came back to reality with a start; then, to Michael's surprise, he laughed.

"By God," he cried, "'tis my first faint. What a pass Doherty has come to when a man has to force good brandy down his throat!"

Michael laughed loudly, relieved.

As Michael, leading the horses, helped Doherty to a grassy bank in the midst of a dense clump of bushes, Doherty said: "I've lived my life by hunches, and this has been the best hunch yet—teaming with Captain Lightfoot. 'Tis a miracle I did not try the chastening of Sir George alone, as I might have done."

Michael hoppled the horses, and they sat down by a little stream to eat. The water was as clear as glass, and they could see the sandy bottom and small silver fish flicking past, in and out of the shadows cast by the stream-side trees. A soft breeze blew about them.

"Now," said Doherty, when he'd eaten his food like a wolf-hound and drunk nearly half of the bottle of brandy, "there is a time for running and a time for thinking. This is the time to think. Did the ambush seem somewhat strange to you?"

"It did," said Michael.

"Ay! Passing strange. It may have been our dear friend Clagett, killing two birds with one stone, though one of the birds flew the coop."

"Clagett, is it? I did not like that little man. He had the look of a ferret about him."

Doherty laughed. "A libel on the useful ferret, lad. A tame ferret will catch hares for you and destroy rats. Yes, I think we may well say that Mr. Clagett arranged the little party at which we and Sir George were the honoured guests. Now if I was a fool, which I trust I'm not, I'd rush back to Dublin and cut Clagett's throat. He is counting on that, and they will be looking for me. And Mr. Clagett, he will have shipped out to Liverpool on one of his many mysterious voyages; the fellow is a pirate at heart—and was in fact, I hear—and can't keep off the sea. Lad, I have a brilliant plan. First, I wore a mask at Sir George's. Sir George thought he recognized me and called out my name. But is that evidence? It is not. Second, we have made famously good time because of these 'noble steeds'—God, how I love a good horse; I'll take him to a man, any day. I don't suppose, lad, that you've read *Gulliver's Travels*? I thought not. Well, the Dean was of like opinion with myself. Yes, we've made fine time, and we can make better if poor old Doherty—fainting like a maiden aunt!—holds together. I have friends at Lisburn in Antrim, good friends. It's a normal four-day ride from the market-town we just passed through. We'll make it in two, lad, and then I'll send letters back to Lord Clayton and Aire's fifth son, Clonmel, by the fast mail, telling them I'm on my way to Scotland for a little trip for my health and to see my poor old father—who hates me, by the way, as the devil hates holy water— and there is evidence, if you like! The letters will be dated Belfast, so how could I have been in Dublin the night Sir George met his well-merited and inevitable fate? You see, Doherty has a head on his shoulders and intends to keep it there. Lad, there is only one difficulty."

Michael sat looking at Doherty with deep admiration. Here was a man, indeed. But in a moment he came to himself and asked: "And what may that be?"

"Why, Doherty, lad. Doherty himself! Can he make it, empty of blood as a wrinkled wineskin is of wine?"

"I think he will make it," said Michael firmly.

"Ah, well said," cried Doherty, delighted. "And now for the little business of the nail. It must come out."

Michael felt himself wincing inwardly, but made no protest. Doherty whipped out his clasp-knife and cleansed it in the flames of several wax matches; then, baring his arm to the shoulder, he said: "Cut away, lad; cut away."

It was a long, slow, hard, gruelling process. Twice Doherty almost fainted and grabbed for the brandy bottle. But at last it was over, the nail out, and the arm bandaged, and Doherty, though pale as death, was drunk on the brandy and in high spirits. " 'Twas like an uneasy conscience gnawing at me, that blasted nail—and rusty at that! An uneasy conscience, says Doherty, as if he knew what that meant."

Michael took several long pulls at the brandy and sighed with relief that the business was over at last. "Doherty," he said, emboldened by the brandy, "the next nail that comes your way, dodge it, for the love of God! I'd rather have it in myself than taking it out of you."

Doherty roared with laughter, and Michael laughed with him.

BUT THEIR WHIRLWIND RIDE to Lisburn was no laughing matter. To Michael it seemed like a protracted nightmare as they galloped northward over back-country roads, endlessly; the stops were few and short, and there seemed to be neither day nor night, but only a blurred greyness—the very colour of fatigue. More than once he was on the point of begging off, of asking for a good breather, but Doherty, his face waxen-pale now, but his eyes hard and his heavy jaw set, kept urging his tired horse forward, cooing to him one minute, whipping him the next—and remembering Doherty's wounds, his loss of blood, his fainting, Michael, sound as an English guinea and twenty years younger, flushed with shame at his own desire to quit, and with tight lips, said nothing.

A portentous red dawn flamed over Lisburn one morning as Doherty reined in his staggering, lathered horse at the side of the road beside a tall hedge and in a weak voice said: "There it is, the roof of the mansion. Between those trees. See? We've made it, lad; and sooner than I hoped. Now we'll dismount, get our weight off the backs of these poor beasts, and walk them in."

Michael stared about him in wonder as they emerged from a wood and saw before them what had once been a great formal garden all run to weeds and ruin, and a huge square George I manor-house with broken windows and unpainted wood and a look of brutal neglect, and as he turned to Doherty to see what his reaction might be to all this desolation, Doherty cried: "God above! And what is this? Mc-Candless must have wrecked himself at last with the cards, the horses, and the red-haired women."

"It's abandoned," gasped Michael. All the way along the road he'd been thinking of this place as a haven of refuge, a place where a man could rest for days and eat his fill and soothe his raw, chafed thighs and breathe in peace without a struggling horse and a rush of wind and the danger of a mortal fall.

"It's abandoned to the elements, God knows," said Doherty, "but there's someone here. Look at the smoke."

Michael glanced up. Sure enough, a thin column of smoke was rising straight up in the still dawn from one of the rear chimneys of the big house, and as they hesitated, a tough-faced red-headed groom in a tartan waistcoat came round the corner of the house and stood staring at them. Doherty, wavering on his legs now, motioned for the fellow to come over.

The groom came grudgingly and touched his forelock with a surly air.

"I'm a great friend to Rob McCandless, my man," said Doherty, "and we've had a long ride and our mounts are spent, and we'd like to pass the night. What's happened to the place?"

"What's happened indeed, sor!" said the groom, but his attitude had changed abruptly. "So you are friends of the Master? It was a sad day when he left for London, as he's in the debtor's prison there, and his brother, Alfred, is now the Master, and you see what has come of it."

"Alfred? I don't know the man."

"Nor none of us do. He's a Frenchman-like kind of creature, an author, by'r Lady! Writes books, he does, and sits up the night and sleeps the day and won't spend a farthing on the auld place."

Doherty gave the groom a gold guinea, and the groom's eyes lighted up unbelievably, and he bowed respectfully now as he touched his forelock.

"Look, my man," said Doherty, "these beasts have been hard-ridden. Cool them out slow if it takes all day, and there will be another guinea for you."

"At your service, sor—and they'll be cooled out like Darby winners. An't it please you, sor, and no offence—you're a mite pale and weary-looking from your ride. I'll have Cathcart, the butler, make a place for you. The Master will not be up till sundown—and to bed at sunrise." The groom shook his head. "The likes we never any of us saw. In a dream, he is."

"And could I have stationery for a letter or two? And could we make the fast mail for Dublin?"

"We could that, sor. I'll ride to the Admiral myself as soon as it please you. The Admiral's where the coach stops outside Lisburn, if you don't know, sor."

He let them in by the front, and as they waited in the hall for the butler, they saw the groom leading the staggering horses off towards the stables beyond the mansion house.

Doherty, pale as paper, leaned against the wall to support himself. "Poor Rob," he muttered. "A great man for the horses. Has run a third thrice in the Darby. Could never quite win."

A sad-eyed, grey-haired old man in rusty livery came hurriedly into the hallway and bowed nervously. "Gentlemen. How himself will greet friends of Mr. Robert's I have no way of knowing. But you are welcome, gentlemen." He studied Doherty for a moment. "Why, aren't you Mr. Doherty of Glasgow? I remember you, sir. I might say, sir, I remember you from the good old days."

"LAD," said Doherty, "looks like we've done it, though I'm more dead than alive."

He was stretched out in his shirt on a huge canopied bed in the great old bedroom Cathcart had assigned to them. He and Michael had just picked away all that remained of a big cold roast pheasant and drunk some very poor claret, but tasty enough with the bird. The letters had been dispatched, and the groom had already returned with the word that he had made the coach for Dublin with them.

"Yes," said Doherty. "We've done it. What do you say to Scotland?"

"Fine. And how do we get there?" asked Michael, somewhat vague in his geography.

"Why, we charter ship at Belfast. 'Tis only a matter of thirteen miles from Torr Head to the Mull of Kintayre, though farther to port —say, Prestwick."

"A ship, is it? On the sea?" asked Michael.

Doherty laughed weakly. "Did you think we'd ride across? It's naught but the North Channel, a pond. Or like a pond at times, let's say. In this summer weather it should be a pond, though a storm whips up sudden-like. I've seen them in my many passages."

"And the horses?"

"They ride aboard. You walk them up a gangplank and there you are. Now I sleep. Lock the door."

Michael obeyed, but showed some surprise. Doherty glanced at him ironically.

"Countryman," he said, "we have more than four thousand guineas in our clothes—a fortune in any time and land. If Rob were here, I'd still lock the door. A friend is a friend, you say? True. But a friend is also a man, a human being—and being human, he can be led into temptation. Look, lad. You must learn, so that is why I'm talking. Remember this. Each man, smile though he may, puts his own interests first in this sorry world. There is no man—*no* man!—who thinks of himself second, nor woman neither, except your mother, lad. . . ." Doherty broke off abruptly and seemed lost in thought for a while, and then he murmured as if half asleep: ". . . except your mother. . . ."

THEY HAD dinner with Alfred McCandless in the great, high-ceiled dining-room of the manor. The parsimonious fire in the big grate was too meagre to warm it, and the evening had turned coolish. Michael felt himself shivering and struggled not to show it. The old place was very damp and had an overpowering dank, musty smell like a long-abandoned mediæval castle.

Alfred McCandless was a sick-looking little man with pointed, supercilious eyebrows. He was wrapped in several mangy old dressing-gowns, and he wore a nightcap at the table and shivered delicately from time to time.

"A touch of fever," he explained, nibbling at his food.

"Fever? I doubt it," said Doherty bluntly. "You're wanting enough fire to warm this beast of a place."

"Oh, it couldn't be that, Doherty," said Alfred. "No, no; it's the fever."

"Well, then," said Doherty, looking askance at the meagre, wineless meal set before him, "I have it, too; a tertian ague, as I'm shivering like a bone-fed dog."

Alfred ignored the pointed remarks, picked at his meal, and tried to engage Doherty in a conversation in French, but finally shrugged and gave it up. "Doherty," he said, "you speak French very poorly, and with the worst and coarsest Irish accent I've ever heard on the Continent or elsewhere."

"Should I speak, then, with an Italian accent?" cried Doherty, bristling. "I make no especial claims for speaking the Continental jargon. It pleased you to start the conversation so. Plain English is good enough for me."

"A dreadful language," said Alfred, shivering slightly, with distaste or cold, who could tell? "No nuances. No subtlety. No elegance. No charm. No . . . *je ne sais quoi*. Are you a reading man, Doherty? As a friend of my brother's, I suppose not."

"You suppose wrong, sir," cried Doherty. "I am as well-read as yourself, I warrant. Perhaps not in Frog literature. But otherwise."

"Spare me these vulgarisms, Doherty."

"I've had enough of the 'Doherty,' sir. '*Mister* Doherty,' if you please," said Doherty in a dangerously quiet voice. He looked ill. His face was greyish and drawn, but his black eyes snapped and sparkled with vitality.

"Quite so," said Alfred vaguely. "You are cold, you say? There is not enough fire? You don't seem to care for your dinner? Well, well.

Since you are paying guests, order what you like, *Mister* Doherty."

"Why, yes," snapped Doherty, "we'll pay. We are willing and able. We are vulgarly rich, if you like. We'll be glad to pay, and be damned to you, sir."

Alfred McCandless rose slowly from his chair and stood peering weakly at Doherty. "And would it interest you to know, *Mister* Doherty, that I've sent for the dragoons—and that they should be here shortly? I don't like the look of you, my man, nor your swagger—and I'll say this: I know a gentleman of fortune when I see one. I knew my brother well, the extravagant, ruinous rogue!"

Doherty's chair went over with a crash. But Alfred had raised a huge pistol from below the level of the tablecloth, and it was aimed at Doherty's belly. Doherty stared opened-mouth, amazed, it was obvious, that a poor creature like this should show even a moment of resolution. But Michael wasted no time whatsoever in thought. He knocked over the candelabra at once and leaped across the table, catching Alfred full in the chest. The master's chair fell backward and Alfred with it. Michael, on top of him, hit him a few light taps on the chin. Alfred lay very still and white in the flickering firelight.

"Well done, lad," said Doherty. "I'm weak and shaky on my feet, and my head's not working as it should."

"We've got to get out, Doherty," cried Michael, nettled at Doherty's hesitations.

"Ay! Ay! And I was looking forward to a good night's rest. This business will be the death of me yet."

Michael laughed loudly, but for once Doherty did not join in.

WRAGG, the red-headed groom, and a little Negro jockey saddled the horses with great haste, and Doherty gave them each a gold guinea.

"Now, boys," he said, "I take it that you do not greatly love your master."

The Negro would say nothing and seemed worried, but Wragg spoke up at once. "That is to put it too mildly, sor. Starving us, paying us nothing. What—is the man mad?"

"Good. The dragoons will be here. Insist that I struck you, Wragg; then they will believe you when you tell them we set off south on the Dublin Road."

"Very good, sor," said Wragg. "I'll do it. And good-bye and good luck to yourself and the young gentleman."

Michael and Doherty gestured good-bye as they rode off towards the northwest, away from the Dublin Road.

IT WAS after ten o'clock now, and ahead of them they could see the widely spread-out lights of Belfast. It was raining, and a nasty-seeming wind was blowing treetop-high across the open country, and the great branches were tossing wildly and making a fearful racket overhead. They were walking their horses along a country lane. The horses, with such a short rest, were now as badly spent as the men, and it was becoming a question if they'd make it.

Of a sudden, Doherty gave a loud, despairing groan and fell from his saddle onto a wet, grassy bank. Michael, appalled, got down at once and knelt beside him.

He hardly recognized Doherty's voice. "Don't leave me here, Michael. I know you're sound in wind and limb and I've got four thousand guineas in my pocket and am no match for you now . . . with the weakness and all. God above, how can a man be this drained and live . . . ?"

"Doherty! Doherty!"

"See me through, lad, for the love of God. I have a wish to go home to Glasgow and look at the old place once again . . . but now I'm a poor hulk, the simulacrum of a man . . . so go on, lad—take the money. Leave me behind. It's the way of the world. I'd do it myself. Should you hang at Dublin Castle for Doherty?"

"Talk sense, Doherty," cried Michael. "But tell me what to do. I'm as lost as a song-bird in the snow. How do we get to Glasgow?"

He started back suddenly. Doherty had raised up and was holding a pistol on him. "Oh, no you don't, now, you young rogue! I'll blow you to kingdom-come. Doherty's not through yet—though he's close, lad, close. . . ." The pistol fell from his hand, and he lay back.

Michael jumped up, shaking badly, and fumbled in the saddle-bag for the brandy, but as he found it, he heard a great clatter of hoofbeats along the country road, and he just managed to get Doherty and the horses back into the bushes when a cavalcade went past thundering at a wrack towards the lights of Belfast. But it was a party of young men, apparently, and they'd been drinking, and some of them were singing and some of them talking loudly and cursing good-naturedly. "Odds on," a voice was borne back on the breeze. "Odds on—and beaten ten good lengths. Something amiss there, my boys, something amiss in . . ."

As soon as Doherty had had a good pull at the brandy, he sat up and looked about him dazedly. "For the love of God, when did it start raining?" he cried. "Michael, it's raining, and I never knew it. I'm wet to the skin." He was silent a moment, then he said in his natural voice: "God—another faint, eh? Even the ladies will begin to disavow me."

A little later Michael helped him back onto his horse.

"It's not long now," said Doherty, "and then the quays of Belfast Lough, a boat, and home. Ah, yes—home to Glasgow with all its rows of little mean houses just alike. A barren place, lad. A barren place indeed for an Irishman, but home."

At first the lights of Belfast seemed to recede, and Michael grew worried, but at last they topped a rise and there before them lay the great northern city, its thousands of lights blurred by the driving rain which slanted across in front of them like an avalanche of slender silver spears.

"Doherty, are you all right?" cried Michael.

"As could be expected for a hollow man," Doherty replied, with a weak laugh.

They skirted the town and came out at last on the quays, where the boats were rocking wildly at anchor and the hawsers were sawing and creaking and the timbers of ruinous old hulks were groaning; and overhead the riding-lights tossed and swung as in a hurricane. Doherty reached down and stopped a man in oilskins.

"I'm turned around in all this rain and blow, man," he said. "Where's Cavendish's from here?"

The man looked up in surprise. "Why, right in front of your face, sir; and I'm the old man's foreman."

"We would charter a ship for Prestwick."

"The two of you? Two horses? Ay. We've got the very thing. She can clear at dawn, if the weather settles. The Channel's rough as sand-paper, I hear."

"Not at dawn," cried Doherty; "*now!*"

And Michael started slightly and looked off into the darkness across the black water that was heaving a hundred reflected lights on its bosom.

The man in oilskins looked up strangely at Doherty. "Now?"

"Ay. We've plenty of money, and old Cavendish is a friend of mine and has put me down safe at Prestwick, many's the time."

"Not in weather like this, I'll warrant. But come in out of the rain, gentlemen, and yonder is a shed for your horses."

They dismounted. Doherty went into a quay-house with the man in oilskins, and Michael took the horses into the shed and unsaddled them and bedded them down and gave them water. They were staggering with weariness, and Doherty's mount lay down at once and fell asleep. Michael's slept standing.

As Michael made his way towards the blurred lights of the quay-house, he felt like a man on the moon, a pioneer of the interstellar spaces. God, how far away the pleasant fields of Ballymore seemed in the driving rain of this far-northern port with Scotland just across the black, tossing waters! Thirteen miles from Torr Head to the Mull of Kintayre, Doherty had said. But miles on land were one thing, and on water another. In all his life Michael had never been in a boat of any kind.

WHEN MICHAEL ENTERED the quay-house, he found Doherty sitting beside an iron stove with a coarse-featured, white-haired old Scotsman who was smoking a short clay pipe upside down. He'd just come in from the weather and hadn't thought to turn his pipe over yet. Doherty looked bad, Michael thought; very bad indeed. His wide, rugged countenance seemed warped and sunken, and his colour was the worst it had been yet, a bluish white.

"The man's mad," old Cavendish was saying. "But for that kind of money . . . providing, of course, I can get the hands to put to sea in this weather. The *Ballantrae* out of Stranraer just came in, and she'd took quite a buffeting. The Channel's rolling mast-high, the skipper told me, and the *Ballantrae's* a much better ship than I can let you have, Mr. Doherty."

"My father's ill, I'm telling you," Doherty insisted, "and I always promised him I'd be in at the death; he wouldn't die easy otherwise."

"You look a mite under the weather yourself, Mr. Doherty," said old Cavendish, "if you don't mind my saying so, sir."

"'Tis a touch of the fever," said Doherty, trying to give a natural laugh but failing woefully. "Nothing, Cavendish. Nothing at all."

Cavendish turned and looked up at Michael. "And you, young man —are you game to risk it in this wind?"

"Ay! What is thirteen miles? That's not far, surely."

"Thirteen miles!" cried Cavendish. "It's more like a hundred; eighty, for sure, if you don't get blown off your course. You're thinking of the distance from land's end to land's end as the crow flies. That means nothing, lad. You're bound from Belfast to Prestwick, an entirely different matter."

Michael stared in surprise, appalled by the thought of crossing one hundred miles of stormy sea in the darkness. Doherty glanced up, and Michael read appeal in his dimming eyes.

"Old Cavendish was always a great one for making difficulties. It ups the price. He'll find obstacles on a still, moonlight night," said Doherty, making a very heavy attempt at lightness. "Lad, there is not twenty miles of open Channel water; all the rest is land-locked. Am I not right, Cavendish?"

"More or less," said the old man, "but she rolls mast-high tonight, land-locked or not. Even the Lough, a reasonably still place, is pitching, as you can see by glancing out the window." There was a brief silence. Finally Cavendish spat on the stove, making it sizzle; then he rose and put on his oilskins. "All right, Mr. Doherty. Very well. We'll see what we can do."

He went out. Doherty turned quickly. "Got the brandy, lad?"

Michael nodded and handed Doherty the bottle. He took a quick pull, then gave it back. "We'd better get another before we sail," he said. "Perhaps two. I'll need them. Now look, Michael. See me through. That's all I say. See me through. And you'll never regret it. I promise you. Lad, I've got a momentous desire to go home. Let's not examine into the why of it. I just have. If I was a sensible man—which God knows I've never been—I'd look out a friend of mine in Belfast and lay up till I was fit, but . . ."

"Perhaps that's best," Michael put in quickly. He felt like a man tied to the tail of a meteor and wanting to drag his feet to slow down the dizzying forward motion. He'd felt like that ever since his arrival in Dublin. With Doherty there was much excitement, and excitement was good; but no rest, no pausing at all—and that could become as wearisome, Michael decided, as sitting at home twiddling your thumbs.

"Oh, it's best. No doubt of it," said Doherty. "It's sensible. It's reasonable. But as I said, I have this momentous desire driving me, and let's not inquire into it."

After a long while Cavendish came back and nodded. "Very well, Mr. Doherty. I had more takers than I bargained for. 'Tis the talk of gold guineas does it."

Michael's heart sank, but he said nothing as he saw the pleased smile on Doherty's drawn, pale face.

THE RAIN was driving almost horizontally as they took the horses aboard, and a whistling wind was blowing in from the east across Belfast Lough. There was a heavy tarpaulin shelter forward for the horses and a mighty stanchion with iron rings to tie them to. Taking horses from Belfast to Scotland was done every day of the week. Exhausted, the horses were scarcely any trouble at all and made themselves at home at once in the straw put down for them. A little Portugee with gold rings in his ears moved forward with the nose-bags and strapped them on.

"Feed them," he said, grinning. "Keeps them busy, you comprehend?"

Michael stood on the heaving deck, watching the horses eat. They munched quietly, their eyes half closed as if they were safe and sound in their home stables and not on the swaying deck of a meagre ship that had little business sailing out into the North Channel on a night like this.

Doherty had gone below. When the ship put out in the Lough, Michael left the Portugee with the horses and went down a battered little companionway to the cabin. The ship was already creaking and groaning as if in mortal agony, and the roll and pitch startled Michael to such an extent that he expected the ship to turn turtle at any moment. At the bottom of the stairs the big Irish mate grinned at him. "The Lough an't half so bad as I thought it'd be, sir," he said. "It's right smooth, considering."

Michael stared at him in amazement. "Smooth, you say?"

"Ay!" said the mate. "I'd heard it was much worse. This is but a roll and toss, as you might say; soothing to the nerves."

Michael left him, unable to think of a reply.

Doherty, fully dressed, was already in his bunk. "Oh, God, but it feels good to lie down, lad. Let her roll. The roll I don't mind as long as I stay horizontal. Get in the bunk. It sails easier that way."

Michael took off his boots, propping himself against a stanchion to do it and nearly falling on his face at the roll. In a moment he was in the bunk and heaved a long sigh. "Doherty, I believe you're right, man," he said. He felt himself drifting into sleep, in spite of the creaking and groaning and the rolling and pitching, so he sat up and looked over to see if Doherty was all right before he permitted himself to lose consciousness. Doherty was drinking from the brandy bottle.

"How are you?" called Michael.

"I'll make it, I think. I'll make it," Doherty replied weakly.

And then Michael lay back and instantly fell asleep. Vague, weird dreams plagued him, and he almost woke at times, enough so that the creaking of the timbers and the pitch of the vessel and the occasional ringing of a bell mingled in with his dreams and distorted them further until they became more and more fantastical. He was being pursued across a wind-swept, blasted landscape by a large, enigmatic dark figure, and he was filled with such a hopeless terror that he wondered how he bore it without flying all apart . . . and then suddenly he was in a lovely green landscape with a mirror-like Irish lake, and a harp was playing some place and a high old voice was singing a beautiful Irish song, and then, across the lake, he saw a handsome dark-haired girl drifting slowly towards him in a little cockle-shell boat that also looked somewhat like a large white swan . . . and was it Aga? . . . no, it was Catherine—and the old voice was singing the "Bride of Mourne" . . . and the dark, menacing shape was gone, and Michael felt so happy that he joined in the song, and then, strangely enough, he was in the swan-boat with Catherine, and quite effortlessly it was drifting slowly down through the mirror-dark water towards the long slender reeds and tendrils of the sandy bottom . . . but all at once the gentle swaying motion of the swan-boat ceased and the world seemed to explode in all directions as if a powder-magazine had gone up. . . .

And Michael woke beside his bunk, with his feet high against a stanchion and his head covered by a blanket and Doherty's feet in his face, and the ship was rolling and pitching like a feather in a gale, and Doherty was cursing with almost normal strength, and above them the light swung and banged and swung again, and Doherty cried: "It's like one time a hunter threw me at a five-bar gate!" and, little by little, they disentangled themselves, got back into their bunks, and held on grimly to keep from being thrown out again.

And a short while later the mate put his head in the door. "We've hit the open water, gentlemen; and she an't so bad as expected."

"You mean," gasped Doherty, "we just cleared the Lough?"

"Ay!" said the mate; then he whistled a bar or two of an Irish jig and went on: "And the crew's mighty happy, gentlemen. We was feeling maybe we'd gone too far for once for extra pay, but it an't so. 'Tis a routine blow—nothing at all. Sleep well, gentlemen. The horses are safe and quiet, and little Pedro is sleeping with them. God be wi' ye."

When the mate had left, Doherty cursed him quietly for a moment or two; then, over the creaking and groaning and the banging of the lamp, he said: "Ah, well; it's just another example of a fellow inured to his trade. The executioner hangs his man and thinks nothing of it, though he might start at the squeak of a mouse. If we'd had that towering mate with us on our ride, he'd have sung a different tune.

Do you see what I mean, lad? Other people's fears are always ridiculous. And now be damned to Doherty and his big mouth!"

The pitching got neither worse nor better, and after a while they grew used to it, and both drifted into a troubled sleep. Michael had been heartened by Doherty's manner and by the tenor of his discourse —it was the true, brilliant Doherty speaking; and he slept, more at ease than he'd been since Doherty had suddenly plunged from his horse on the back-country road near Belfast.

But at dawn it was a different matter. Doherty was delirious. He talked, talked, talked, making no kind of sense whatever, and even after Michael had got him to swallow a big draught of brandy, he still could not orient himself and kept asking where in the hell that big bitch Anne Hanna was—and why didn't she bring him his breakfast, and why was Aga not about the place, and where Princey, the dog, was . . . "the elegant little white fellow," Doherty cried. "The best friend I have in this sorry world—mark me!" And then finally he went back to sleep, grumbling about his breakfast, and Michael, feeling lost and abandoned again, sighed and went up on deck to see how the horses had weathered such a terrible night.

His first sight of the wilderness of grey pitching waters almost sent him below. Little by little, he fought off his feeling of panic, and moved forward cautiously, bracing himself against the jerking roll. Far to the northwest he could make out a black line, like a pencil mark on the misty grey horizon—land!—and immediately he felt heartened, though still nervously fearful in these bleakly alien surroundings. A mahogany-faced seaman was working at a big coil of rope, whistling as he worked, and at the sight of Michael he grinned and winked.

"Be in at nightfall, sir, with luck," he said. " 'Twas nothing at all, and half the crew praying to the Virgin before we put out. The Channel will fool a man, one way and another. I'll say this for the crew. We all admire your nerve, sir; you and Lord Doherty. You could know no more than us that the Channel was merely playing tricks."

Michael was astonished. "It's sometimes worse than this?"

"Worse!" cried the seaman. "We've been dismasted in the middle of June. The *Clementine* out of Campbelltown turned turtle once in May at a sudden nor'wester out of Iceland—all hands lost except the ship's dog. Iceland's only fifteen hundred miles to the nor'west, believe it or not. I've been there. You going forward?"

"Yes," said Michael.

"I'll come along. There's quite a roll for a landsman."

The seaman helped Michael forward. Pedro grinned at him from beyond the stanchion at the shelter. "All snug, sir," he said. "They've weathered it like drum majors."

Michael stared at the horses with wonder. They seemed clear-eyed and rested.

The seaman went back aft with him. To their horror, they found Doherty stumbling about the deck, talking wildly. The seaman crossed himself. "It's a mercy he didn't go overboard. I'll help you below with him."

"Land, ho!" cried Doherty, as they helped him down the companionway. "Ah, Fortune, thou bitch—I've done thee. I saw the strip of land. I saw it. Scotland, my home. I'm back."

"Yes, my Lord," said the seaman soothingly. "You saw land, right enough. It's the far eastern edge of Kintayre, and off ahead's Arran and the Kilmory light—and we're nosing for the Firth of Clyde."

"Home," cried Doherty with a sob, as they got him back into his bunk at last.

As Michael gave him a little more brandy, the seaman hurried to the galley to order a bowl of gruel for the ailing man.

THEY MADE port at Prestwick that night, later than they had expected, but early enough. The water was calm, and the ship was warped in with no trouble at all. Doherty was on deck, himself again, but grim and pale, and leaning one hand on Michael's shoulder. The crewmen cheered the two gentlemen after the score had been paid, and the captain came forward to shake their hands.

"Sailors is what the two of you are, not landsmen at all," he said gruffly, grinning. " 'Twas a prosperous voyage for all of us."

"Ay! Doubly so for me," said Doherty, trying to grin.

On the dock Doherty said: "I can never ride to Glasgow, lad. It's twenty-five miles as the crow flies, but longer by road. Here is what you do. Leave the thoroughbreds for collateral—they are worth all the cobs in Prestwick and Ayr—and hire us a fine calash and driver. We'll go home in style, so. After all, it's Lord Doherty you're looking at, man. You heard the seaman." And Doherty tried to laugh loudly, but began to cough.

"If it's not, it should be," said Michael, trying not to stare at Doherty, whose face had that bluish-white look again.

"Why, thank you, Michael. Thank you. Hurry. Get the calash. My body wants to take the horizontal again, and I'm master of the brute only so much longer."

It was very late when they entered the outskirts of Glasgow, and Doherty, who had been dozing fitfully and talking to himself, came round now and excitedly began to point out places and name names to Michael.

"I was a boy here, you understand," he said. "My father was prosperous; my mother pretty and adorable. It was a sorry day for me, the day she died. I was but sixteen. It was like an arrow in the heart."

The calash bowled along through the sleeping streets at a good rate. Michael was somewhat shocked at the look of Glasgow—bleak and ugly, it seemed to him, harsh and unfriendly.

"One or two turnings and we're there," said Doherty, his excitement rising, becoming feverish. "I haven't seen it—oh, it's four years now. The Master is getting quite an old man, a good seventy, perhaps more. I hope that Trim and his son, Trim II, are still about. Trim II fought at Waterloo, lost his left hand. A great fellow, Trim II—and no boy any more, since he's my age and I've just passed forty." Doherty sat thoughtful for a long time. Finally he spoke. "Did you by any chance, lad, ever hear of a Continental ruffler of the name of Casanova?"

"I did not," said Michael.

"Ah, well. No matter. I was thinking about him on the voyage over. He said a thing once that has always bothered me. He said: 'After forty, a man has no luck.' Well, I hit my fortieth birthday six months back, and I've had no luck since. 'S Faith, I've been mostly on the run since that cursed hour struck." Then suddenly Doherty gave a loud, strident shout that startled Michael badly. "Here we are—the damned old prison of my boyhood—home!"

Michael got a quick glimpse of a rundown-looking brick manor, crowded in among many poorer houses. Then Doherty fainted and fell to the floor of the calash.

IN SPITE of the ensuing confusion, the halting explanations, and the amazement of the Doherty household, Doherty was finally carried to a bedroom on the second floor by two tall, pale, heavily built, placid-looking men—the Trims, father and son—helped by the little driver of the calash and by Michael. Doherty's father, a big bald man with a touch of Doherty himself about the eyes and the mouth, looked on at the proceedings with a sort of grim irritation. "Not drunk this time, eh?" he said curtly, and Michael turned and glanced at him in surprise as they were moving Doherty around the landing. Was this a way for a father to greet a son he hadn't seen for four years?

As soon as Doherty was on his bed, with the silent Trims undressing him, Michael hurried back downstairs to talk to Doherty's father, who was pacing in the hallway.

"He's in a bad way, sir," said Michael without preliminaries. "You must send for a doctor at once."

"Ay!" said old Doherty. "As soon as young Trim is free."

"I'll go," cried Michael. "Believe me, sir, there's no time to waste. Where would I go?"

Old Doherty regarded him in silence for a moment, his shaggy eyebrows moving slightly in thought. "And who may you be, young man? By the look of you, fresh from some place, despite your fine clothes."

"My name is Martin, sir," cried Michael impatiently. "I'm your son's best friend, as I think he'll tell you."

"You don't look that wicked, lad—but perhaps your face belies you. His best friend, is it? Well, man, don't brag about it. Have you ever heard word of a friend of Lucifer's? He may have had some, but all would deny it."

Now Michael's impatience turned to anger. "A fine way to talk of your son, sir, with him lying near to death in your own house."

Old Doherty laughed jeeringly. "Him die? No such luck. He's been like this before—and he always comes home. In fact, it's the only time he *does* come home, the rogue! Though I am not complaining about that. I wish that he would stay away altogether."

Michael took him rather roughly by the arm. "Sir, where may I find the doctor? I've got the calash and the driver."

But at that moment Trim II came hurrying down the stairs, followed by the little, bewildered, flushed Scottish driver. "I must go for old Dr. Cates, an't please you, sir," he called on his way to the door. "I've never seen Master John in such a case as this before, sir."

"As you will, Trim," said old Doherty indifferently.

As Trim II went out, pushing the driver ahead of him, Michael noticed that the big servant was minus a left hand and that he flourished the stump without self-consciousness. The door slammed.

Old Doherty stared at Michael ironically, making him uneasy. "Yes, yes; you've got a nice face, lad. Doherty himself—Captain Doherty, I believe: though it's a wonder he hasn't promoted himself to Colonel by now—well, our Captain Doherty has bewitched you, very likely, as he has bewitched others, though not me. You are an ass if you listen to that ranter. He has only one object in the world: money. Gold guineas, so that he may game and have his trulls and his horses and his fine clothes, and not work for them like a proper man. His best friend, you say?" The old man laughed. "His most useful tool at the moment. They come and they go, these tools. Some to the hulks, some to Botany Bay, some to the public executioner, and some merely to six feet of quiet earth, the lucky ones!—while Captain Doherty goes merrily on." Old Doherty stared at Michael in silence for a long time, then he asked: "How do you suppose it seems to a respectable man to raise a son like that? Put yourself in my place and add fifty years. It's been the ruin of my life. I have a son in the British Army—a legitimate officer in the cavalry; he fought through the late American war and was in at the burning of Washington, the American capital—he has just been made a colonel, a fine man. I have a daughter married to a man of quality in London. That should be enough for any man, you say? But it is not. I have this graceless rogue —my eldest—and he casts a shadow over all of us."

BUT LATER, as the days passed and Doherty grew no better, the old man and Michael became friends, and after supper they'd sit in front of the fire in the little drawing-room just off the front hall and the old man would talk about the past. Occasionally, Trim II, his big, pale, placid face showing deep interest, would stand by after serving them, listening. He was quite a formidable big man, Michael thought; certainly no one's idea of an average servant.

"Ah, young Trim," said the old man reminiscently one night after the serving-man had left. "He was born in our house at Paisley and was the closest of all to John. They were reared together. In fact, he's been away with John—but was sent home for one reason or another. Lately, he fought at Waterloo and lost his hand. He will not hear a word against John, though the devil did not use him too well abroad, you can be sure."

Old Doherty had come over from Belfast, a green young Irishman of Protestant stock, and had settled at Paisley, where he had met and married a young Scottish girl of the name of Mary Moray. He had done well as a wool merchant on a small scale and then had moved on to Glasgow, after selling out his business, and had invested much of his capital in a modest manufactury, which, going with the times, had prospered unbelievably and expanded to such an extent that it grew beyond the capabilities of old Doherty, and once more he had sold out, invested his capital in consols and also in several sutlery and ship's-chandler ventures, which had also prospered—and now old Doherty, at seventy-odd, had been retired for nearly twenty years, and lived a lonely life in the old brick manor in a neighbourhood which was no longer what it once had been—his wife dead for nearly twenty-five years, and his children scattered.

"He'll not get a penny, the graceless rogue," said old Doherty; "and he knows it. I'll not see my hard-won money scattered over England, Ireland, and the Continent for horses, women, and godless living. My son James and my daughter, Nan, shall have it all. Let him lie in debtor's prison or the hulks, for all I care. He merits it. And as for you, young man, listen to what I say. Abandon Captain Doherty to his fate—it will be an ill one at last, I promise you. Go your own way— and if you've done wrong, admit the fact, take your punishment, and be a free man."

Confused, Michael tried to explain about the S.F.Y.I. Movement, but old Doherty brushed all this aside. "Nonsense, you are deluding yourself. It is merely an excuse for rebellion against the constituted authorities at Dublin Castle—a young man's excuse. Captain Doherty is one of you, you say?" The old man laughed jeeringly. "Doherty for a Cause? Oh, come now, Michael. Don't be so simple, lad. Doherty has only one grand Cause: Doherty!"

Then Michael went on to explain how open-handed Doherty was with poor people, always handing out gold guineas to the deserving poor.

"Why, yes," said the old man, "he's a lordly fellow with other people's money, and a great one for the grand gesture—has been since childhood. But it's all selfish play-acting and folderol—it's the Captain's complaint against life that he wasn't born a Lord. He has always looked down on his humble beginnings. I could scarce read or write till I was a grown man, so the Captain must read all the books and talk of Dean Swift as of a close friend. Believe me, lad, all play-acting and windiness."

Michael shook his head in bewilderment and confusion. The old man was wrong, he was certain; and yet old Doherty was an apt and persuasive speaker like his son, and Michael knew that he himself was no match for him.

"I'M FEELING a little better tonight," said Doherty, lying white and still on his big bed, "so we must have our talk, lad. Pass me the brandy."

Michael rose and gave Doherty the bottle, and after a long pull

Doherty said: "If I do not make it, Michael, you are my surrogate—you take over for me in Dublin; when I am roasting in hell, I at least want the satisfaction of knowing that my place has been filled by an adequate substitute, and that all my enemies, who have been waiting for years to see the end of Doherty, will be discomfited."

Michael laughed loudly, but Doherty merely glanced at him and continued: "It's no joke. Believe me, this time, Michael, it is no joke. It tired me to lift the brandy bottle. And the old doctor has as much as told me that my day is out. 'John,' he said last night, 'you've finally exhausted that great body. For years you've spared yourself nothing: you've lived a life of gaming, whoring, and violent excitement—you've lived ten years in one, and now at forty you are an old man, and all this bleeding of late has finally turned the trick.'"

Michael laughed again. "It is probable the old doctor is only trying to get you to lie quiet."

Doherty raised his head at once and smiled, and Michael saw such a look of forlorn hope in his eyes that he felt a great inner shock, and at that moment he began to realize what had been blank to him before —Doherty was done for.

"Ay! Ay!" said Doherty, lying back. "Perhaps, perhaps." Then after a moment: "But we will not count on that. Listen while I talk. It is tiring me, so listen and don't interrupt. If it turns out that I've got my *quietus est*, then you must return to Dublin in style. Trim II will go with you. He's been out with me before, and he's a brave and likely hand. The old man downstairs does not know the extent of Trim's commitments or he would not allow him in the house." Doherty laughed weakly, then continued: "I had to send him back. It was a rough time, and I feared he might be taken, and then I could not have saved him. Ah, well. Listen to me. I have a choice enemy who will be waiting. He's a ruffler of the name of Captain Hood. He looks bold, but is not. In truth, he's a coward, though a handy man for the knife in the back. Watch him. He has had his eye on Lady Anne and Aga for several years. He wants them. He wants Lady Anne's clientele. When you arrive back at Dublin, go at once to Nine Steps—Big Tom will protect you. All the clothes there are yours, all the appurtenances. Anne will keep in touch with Tom. She fears Hood, who is brutal with women. You must protect Lady Anne—and Aga."

"Ay!" cried Michael, "with my life."

"And there's Clagett. The rat has been the death of me and of Sir George. He has neatly trimmed us both. But he is not a present trouble because he will stay in Liverpool till word of my plight or my return reaches him. When you return alone, he'll be back. I would see him fixed, Michael."

"Ay!" cried Michael. "I'll do my best."

"I have already written to Lord Clayton and Aire's son Patrick. They are powerful protectors, but you must keep them in money, lad; and you must look after their interests otherwise. Consult with Lady Anne. And, lastly, I've written her. She will be fearful till you return." There was a long pause. "Until I . . . I return. . . ."

"Oh, but you'll return," cried Michael, feeling young and lost and appalled at all the responsibility being piled on his unaccustomed shoulders, and not understanding a good half of it.

"I believe that's all," said Doherty, his voice growing weaker. "Trim will help greatly. Go back in style, with Trim in livery. You'll find three thousand guineas and better in this drawer . . . and now to sleep. Sleep, lad . . ." Doherty went on drowsily, "sleep . . . makes us all . . . Pashas."

And as Doherty dropped off, the phrase carried Michael back to that old Norman inn, ages ago, and Doherty was in his parson's dress, dancing a jig, and he himself was a poor bewildered gossoon out of Ballymore with no idea in God's world what was ahead of him.

He rose, walked to a window, and stood looking out into the night. Where would he be in another month? Would he ever see Ballymore again and Tim Keenan and Regis Donnell and lovely Catherine, the Dream—and would he ever again pat the rough coat of Buffer, the O'Herlihy dog, or sit beside his own father's hearth in the big, beamed kitchen, listening to the Kilkenny rain falling outside and the tea-kettle singing on the hob . . . ?

Doherty was snoring faintly now. Michael turned and tiptoed down the stairs. Through an open door at the back he saw Trim II polishing silver in the pantry, deftly managing his stump. Trim bowed in his direction and murmured: "Sir . . ."

Michael went back to the pantry. "How do you think he's doing, Trim?" he asked.

The big, pale man shrugged slightly. "He is not doing at all, sir. Not at all."

"You mean you don't think . . . ?"

"No, sir," said Trim.

MICHAEL SAW Doherty again the next night. Doherty was worried about something, and Michael leaned down to listen to him. "In all the excitement and weakness and such," said Doherty, "I forgot to mention the blessed 5 – 1. What an oversight!"

There was a pleading look in Doherty's eyes now, Michael thought, and, strangely enough, the pleading look was followed by a look of such sharpness and shrewdness—almost the true look of the sound Doherty—that Michael was amazed. But in a moment the look faded and Doherty's eyes were dimmed once more.

"You understand," said Doherty, "that a man has to do many things he'd rather not for the sake of other things more important. Therefore, take my place in Dublin. It will be a great move for 5 – 1. Defiance towards the Castle, and a source of money for the poor."

"I understand," said Michael.

"Well, then," sighed Doherty, "that's all I had to say."

Doherty fell asleep almost at once, and Michael went down to the pantry and had a glass of whisky with Trim—several glasses, in fact, and they talked about Doherty, and Michael noted a very odd thing. Trim's pale face was as calm and placid as ever, and his eyes were blankly noncommittal—and yet he was crying.

IT WAS very early in the morning, not much after three, when something woke Michael and he sat up in bed with a start and looked about him, shivering slightly with the cold. The small fire had died in the room, and there was a chill wind blowing across Glasgow. The house seemed silent, and he wondered what had wakened him, and he was just lying back when he heard a thumping down the hall, cries, and then the crash of an overturned chair. It seemed that the noise was coming from Doherty's room, and that was a thing that puzzled Michael greatly, so he leaped from bed, flung on a dressing-gown Trim II had put at his disposal, opened his door, and went out into the hallway to listen. At once he heard Doherty's voice, strident as ever and strong, and immediately a feeling of relief rushed over Michael—the great man was mending, obviously, and Michael's panic at the thought of facing Dublin all alone and fulfilling a mission he but vaguely understood slid away from him like a dream: with Doherty at his side, all would be well!

And then he heard the voice of Trim II begging and pleading with Doherty, and once more there was the sound of a chair overturning and a faint crash, as of breaking crockery, and then old Trim chimed in in a cracked voice, and the struggle went on, until at last Michael began to realize that there was something shockingly unnatural and ominous about all this, so he went down the hall to Doherty's room and opened the door.

Doherty, a ghost of his former self, wearing nothing but a shirt, was in the middle of the room, swinging an old cutlass through the air and making it whistle dangerously.

Michael stared open-mouthed as the two Trims pleaded with Doherty to drop the weapon and get back into bed, but Doherty, who was making a havoc of the room, seemed not to hear them or even to see them; nor did he notice Michael. He whistled the cutlass over his head and cried: "Stay back. Keep your distance. You will find it is not so easy to overcome Doherty as you thought. What—you advance?" Doherty made the cutlass whistle and opened a huge gaping wound in the back of a brocaded chair. "Stay back. Back! Or I'll open you up like a carcass at the knacker's yard. Back . . . !"

"He fights with the phantoms of the mind," said old Trim sadly.

But Trim II said: "No. With the Dark Gentleman himself, I think. Or with another, worse."

"I'll not go," cried Doherty, on guard. "You can't take me against my will. Stay back!" The cutlass whistled again through the still air of the quiet bedroom.

And suddenly Michael understood with whom Doherty was fighting, and this shocking spectacle turned suddenly macabre for him, and with a shiver of dread he thought that he discerned an alien Presence in the room—and suddenly he crossed himself and murmured a prayer under his breath.

And at that moment Doherty's eyes seemed to clear, and turning from his opponent, he caught a glimpse of Michael and cried: "Run for it, lad. Run. This time you can't help Doherty," and the cutlass slipped from his hand and hit the thick carpet with a muffled thud, and Doherty slipped to the floor sideways, sagging suddenly like an emptied sack, then rolled over on his side.

Trim II ran immediately for the doctor, while Michael and old Trim lifted Doherty back into bed. But in reality they were not lifting Doherty back into bed at all—that strange complex of mental, spiritual, and emotional qualities known in the world as "Captain Doherty" had left them, and had now set out on another journey, a journey more hazardous than any he'd gone in the forty years before. What remained on the bed was of no use to any one, an inert puppet whose strings had been cut.

"He's gone," murmured old Trim, finally.

"Ay," said Michael, and then he went back to his room and stood at the window looking out into the gusty Glasgow morning, and he did not even stir when he heard Trim II return with the doctor, nor when he heard old Doherty's heavy tread in the hallway, nor the wailing of a parlour-maid in the back. Bustle and grief were alike useless, but it was with a pronounced shock that he recognized this.

And now what? Dublin? Michael felt a terrible inadequacy and longed for Doherty's commanding voice and reassuring presence.

AFTER THE FUNERAL old Doherty showed marked reluctance to have Michael go. "Look, lad," he said, "you're leaving two old men behind, Trim I and myself. What will we do in this house all day long?"

"I shall write you," said Michael, "and perhaps Trim II will be back one day."

"Ay!" said Doherty grimly. "But maybe one day will not be soon enough."

As they drove away in the calash with the little Scottish driver handling the reins, old Doherty stood on the curb waving and nodding till they'd turned a corner far down the street.

Trim II sighed heavily. "Well, sir, we're for it now."

Michael turned and looked at him. "How is that?"

"Oh, I talked with the Captain night after night," said Trim. "I know your plans."

After a long pause Michael said: "Oh, I'm aware I can never take his place. I can but try."

"I'm with you, sir," Trim replied. "I promised him, and that's good enough for me."

They picked up their horses at Prestwick and shipped out from Ayr on a fine big boat, the *Allen Davy* of Belfast. The green water was smooth as glass, and the day was wonderful with a mild southern breeze and a warm sun and great banks of sculptured, snowy clouds at the western horizon.

Michael could not believe that he was crossing the same stretch of water. Jewels of light danced on the surface, and the motion of the ship was so faint that he might have been in a house except for the wild, heady smell of deep water.

Trim slept throughout the passage, and Michael did not disturb him because he knew how many nights he'd been up with Doherty.

The next morning, standing in the bow, Michael saw the grey smoke of Belfast staining the greenish western sky. He felt a rising excitement. Little by little the real optimism of his nature was asserting itself. "We'll see, we'll see," he said, addressing the morning and the cloud of gulls that had flown out to welcome the ship, many of them lighting in the rigging. "I'm sound, I'm young, and I have had the tutelage of the greatest man I ever hope to meet. We'll see."

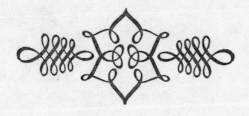

BOOK
II

Book II

AGA

The journey down from Belfast was completely uneventful—the sort of journey any gentleman and his serving-man might make along the highways of the day. Trim was not very talkative, and his long silences weighed heavily on Michael, who remembered with a sigh the brilliantly voluble Doherty and his entertaining but bewildering conversation. Michael decided that there was something a little dreary about Trim, with his big, pale, placid face and his air of melancholy respectfulness. And then the man's rusty-looking livery, his garments of servitude, bothered Michael greatly. Having none of the lordliness of Doherty, to Michael a man was just a man, good or bad, as the case might be; flunkeyism was as repugnant to Michael as it had been to the wildest revolutionary in France or the American Colonies.

They stopped at Lisburn, and Michael insisted on buying for Trim a decent black suit, and he told Trim to pitch the livery to hell and forget it. Trim obeyed neither command, but packed the livery in a saddle-bag and remained as silent, as attentive, and as servant-like as before. Even so, there was a slight change, but not for the better. Although Trim made no comment, Michael had the feeling that he had forfeited some of Trim's respect by unsuiting him. It was to be read, Michael thought, in a vague glance here and there and a slowness in replying, now and then, to some inconsequential remark of Michael's.

Little by little Michael began to realize that he might have made a blunder and perhaps given Trim a false opinion of himself, and it seemed to him that he would have to win the man over one way or another. But how? Michael was astute enough to see that with Trim you simply could not come out in the open with the matter. Servant-like, he would merely evade.

Beyond Lisburn, as they passed along the King's Highway, Michael saw the roof and chimneys of the McCandless manor, and he wondered if Alfred was still rising at sundown and going to bed at dawn, and then he remembered Doherty, a dying man but still full of fight, putting the supercilious Alfred in his place in regard to literature and languages and other matters far beyond Michael's competence; and suddenly such a powerful pang of regret shot through him that tears came to his eyes and he looked off across the fields in the opposite direction from Trim so the servant, who was sharp-eyed behind his front of melancholy indifference, would notice nothing amiss.

Ah, Doherty! With him a man did not have to do any thinking of his own. Doherty met the situation, whatever it was, head on and mastered it—you merely followed his lead.

And as the journey continued, Michael's head began to ache with thought to such an extent that at last he started to draw some sort of ironical satisfaction from his plight and said to himself: "A great one you are, Michael Martin, plaguing yourself with worries about things that haven't happened yet or may not happen at all. As for Trim! Try to imagine Doherty's face if he knew that you were racking your brain how to win him round. 'What—win Trim round, lad? Why, he's round already, and bound to you by promises and other ties.'"

And so finally Michael emerged from a cloud of worries and gloom, and as they rode along through the sunshine of an Irish summer day, he began to whistle the "Tinker of Armagh," and turning suddenly, he noticed that Trim was studying him, and in a moment Trim smiled slightly and said: "'Tis a lively tune, sir. I remember it well. There was a fifer with the Guards at Waterloo. He was from Mooncoin near the Suir. At night he'd play the fife for entertainment, and he'd always play the 'Tinker' last, and we'd all go to the blankets full of cheer."

"'Tis a good air," said Michael, greatly heartened by Trim's un-prompted comments, and then he sang it as they rode under a green tunnel of trees and over a little arched stone bridge—and beyond, there were black cattle in a field, and a lark sang, and the sun was warm, dappling the broad highway—and Michael, for the first time in weeks, felt light-hearted and free—the old Michael of Ballymore and evenings at the Bonnie Prince Charlie.

It was after sundown and misty when they reached Dublin and crossed the big bridge over the Liffey, whose water, giving off faint, dullish glints, was the colour of a pewter tankard, and along the far shore the lamp-lighter was lighting the river-lamps, one by one, and the yellow bars of light falling over the river, one after another, seemed to mark the gradual approach of darkness from the direction of the hidden bay, as if night itself came in eastward from the sea.

And now the familiar jam, rush, and clatter of Dublin streets, and the commotion of a score of red-coated dragoons riding northward on some portentous errand, their steel helmets flashing under the lights—and the eternal gigs and carts—and then the narrow streets, the masts and spars of the quays, and at long last the Dublin of Nine Steps just waking to boisterous life as the day faded.

Word of their arrival had moved ahead of them along the mysterious grape-vine of the stews, and when they dismounted at the stable behind the inn, there was a crowd of men to meet them; and Michael saw old Mahony and Big Tom himself and half a dozen other familiar faces, with Bessa hiding shyly in the background and flashing her row of ivory teeth at him. And Big Tom shouted: "By God, it's Trim." And then to Michael: "And Doherty himself? His premonition was right, then."

And Michael nodded slowly, and a great solemn silence spread at once over this group of hard-faced men, and finally Mahony said: "Ah, well. 'Tis best to leave so, still full of power. It's all downhill after forty."

Bessa brought Michael's supper, and Michael, remembering Doherty's generosity, gave her a guinea, which delighted her to such an extent that she danced lithely about the room, clapping her hands in time and showing her big teeth, until Trim, having had enough of it, eased her out, then began to serve Michael at his table by the window.

"A shilling would have been plenty, sir," said Trim. "To the blacks it's all one—shilling or guinea. Both soon gone and forgotten."

Michael ate in silence for a moment, then he said: "One time Doherty told me: 'Think in pence and you're a shoe-maker; think in guineas and you're a gentleman.'"

Trim smiled wanly. "The Master was like a black in regard to money, though he considered it to be lordliness. There is nothing in this world more shilling-pinching than your true Lord. The Master's acquaintance with Lords was confined to the sporting kind only. This warped his judgement."

Michael glanced up and studied Trim's big face. He was far from sure just how to take the serving-man's reproof. Doherty would have given him a kick in the arse, no doubt about it! But there was also no doubt at all that the reproof was well meant, and Michael was only too aware that he had a dreadful lot to learn. He lowered his eyes at last and went on eating.

Big Tom brought the coffee himself, and Michael could see that he wanted to talk, so he invited him to sit at the table, but Big Tom declined with thanks and stood near by helpfully while Michael finished his supper. Trim withdrew to an anteroom.

"It was a great thing to bring Trim," said Big Tom. "You'll need him, and he's a man to bank on."

"So Doherty said."

"Ay! And who should know better? He saved the Great Man's neck on several occasions I know of. A whale of a fellow with a cutlass, Trim. The best, perhaps, since old Mahony's eyes were ruined in a sea battle."

"An odd serving-man," said Michael, leading Big Tom on.

"Odd, indeed," laughed Big Tom. "More of a soldier, I'd say. There's hardly a ruffler in Dublin could stand up to him, stump and all. He's been in and out of the King's Army since a boy of sixteen. Ay, you'll need him. And now, Captain," said Big Tom with a change of tone, "I'd like to speak of important matters if I may."

Michael felt a kind of pride in being addressed as "Captain" but also a sort of shame at flying under false colours. Captain? Why, "corporal" itself would have been a promotion. And yet, how refuse? In the eyes of the denizens of Nine Steps and environs, he had taken Doherty's place and they would no more think of calling him "Michael" than they would have thought of calling Doherty "John." "Go ahead, Tom," said Michael, sipping his coffee.

"Well, sir, I'm in touch with Lady Anne, and she's dying to see you. The new Mansion is ready to open, but there are problems she wants to discuss with you. Could you go to see her tonight?"

"I intend to," said Michael.

"Very well. I'll have a coach ready and a driver and boot. You will take Trim, of course? Good. And the driver and boot will be men you can trust. There's trouble, Captain. Since Sir George was shot by some unknown assailant"—Big Tom brought this out smoothly—"and since Captain Doherty's departure, things have been somewhat at sixes and sevens in the sporting world. There are those who think that Captain Hood is the man to deal with, especially now that young Lord Bracken has returned from the Continent and taken Hood under his wing. Hood has been . . . well, importuning Lady Anne to join in with him. As you know, Lady Anne has a large clientele among the quality. Her name and presence is valuable."

"And what about Lady Anne?" asked Michael. "What's her attitude towards Hood?"

"She's afraid of him, I think. He is a very bold fellow—with women; and also with men—those who allow themselves to be intimidated, that is, by his size and military bearing."

"I'll go to Lady Anne as soon as I finish here."

"Good," said Big Tom. "We'll be ready."

Big Tom left and Trim came back. Michael explained about his plans, and Trim nodded; then he said: "And Aga? She must be quite a large girl now."

Michael looked at Trim blankly. "Large girl? No, I'd say she was rather a small girl."

Trim stroked his big pale face with his big pale hand, studying Michael's expression, trying to read in his eyes how much he knew. "Ay! Rather on the small side," he said.

"How did you know about Aga, Trim?" he asked.

"Oh, through the Master, of course."

This was all very puzzling to Michael, but he didn't pursue it.

LADY ANNE lived on the second floor of a huge old grey stone building that had once been the mansion of an extremely rich English ship-owner of the 1750's. The owner had died, the neighbourhood had deteriorated considerably, and the Englishman's executors had sold the mansion to real-estate speculators, who had turned it into a great warren of apartments to be rented to the shabby genteel. The address was still fairly good, and the rent was not too exorbitant.

Michael, leaving Trim below with the coach, climbed a wide curving stairway, screened off from the immense and gloomy entrance hall, and knocked at a neat white door on the second floor. After a moment a middle-aged Irish-woman with coarse red hair and a wide, flat, pleasant, homely face opened to his knock. She was wearing a neat frilled cap and a big white apron. She looked at him inquiringly, her blue eyes bright and young in her weathered face.

"Captain Martin," said Michael, rather sharply, because he was embarrassed at referring to himself so.

"Ah, Captain," said the woman, "I'm Mary—at your service, sir. I've heard so much about you."

She admitted him and took his hat. There was something about her manner of speaking that stabbed at his memory, and he asked: "Kilkenny?"

"Ay," said Mary, grinning. "Blackfountain."

"Good God," laughed Michael. "Blackfountain, is it? A town of rogues and ruffians. I've raced horses there."

"Ay. And so have all the other young good-for-nothings, I'll warrant."

Michael wanted to kiss her. Here was home incarnate, in a plain female face, a coarse mop of red hair, and a manner. Laughing, he put his arm around her big waist and gave her a bear hug. "And how is it with you in the great city of Dublin, Mary?"

Mary returned the hug with surprising strength. "Can't complain, though the place is full of jiggling foreign fools."

"Why did you come here?"

"My husband was killed dead in the Army, Captain. So what was I to do—stay a widow in Blackfountain, where the men are so scarce?"

"And the Dublin men?"

"I've married two since, neither worth his salt. And now I am wiser and live single and have my money to keep instead of spent by a drunken lout and the back of the hand for thanks."

They were hugging each other and laughing when a door opened and Lady Anne came out into the little hallway and stood staring. She was wearing a beautiful black velvet robe, cut very low at the neck and showing nearly half of her plump bosom, and her pale-blonde hair was piled high and gorgeously arranged, with a slim white plume and some glittering jewellery. She was nearly as tall as Michael and very grand and impressive in appearance.

Mary disengaged herself with a loud laugh, then composed her face. "Captain Martin, m'Lady," she said, and there were definitely ironical overtones in the manner of her speaking.

Lady Anne curtsied with studied grace, and Michael bowed as Doherty had taught him, hitting a chair leg with the end of his sword scabbard and flushing darkly because of this. "M'Lady," he said, in imitation of Mary.

Lady Anne turned to Mary. "Tell Agatha she will be wanted in the drawing-room presently—and fix your cap; it's over one eye."

Mary bowed but grinned. "The Captain was roughing me, m'Lady. Like all the boys from home, he has a rough hand with the girls."

"Very interesting," said Lady Anne, then she turned and went into a little white drawing-room, where there was a pleasant coal fire in the grate, candles in tall candelabra, a harpsichord, and several large, gold-framed pictures. Michael winked at Mary, who was regarding him impishly, and followed Lady Anne.

Michael sat opposite Lady Anne at a grand gesture from herself, carefully managing his sword this time. In the corner he saw a small wicker dog's-basket lined with padded blue silk, and remembering

Doherty's words, he asked politely: "And is that Princey's basket, m'Lady?"

"Yes," said Lady Anne. "He's with Aga. How did you know about Princey?"

"Doherty mentioned him."

"Ah, Doherty loved the little white fellow—Doherty, who loved nothing. It was a great blow to Aga and myself, Captain—Doherty's passing. We've had a note from Big Tom. It was worded most graciously. Of course, we were prepared. Doherty wrote us many letters. The tone of them prepared us. It was not Doherty writing at all. It was a worried man. Ordinarily, Doherty did not know the meaning of the word." She studied Michael languidly with her odd green eyes.

And he in turn studied her. She was not quite as he had remembered her—but then, of course, he had seen her only that once, and through a haze, a bewildered, beglamoured country boy, dazed by events, befuddled by the unaccustomed grandeur of his surroundings, trying to learn everything at once . . . no, then she had seemed like a cold, statuesque goddess, remote, unreal, of no particular age, and definitely intimidating. But now he saw that she was just a woman after all—and far from young; perhaps forty, or more. There were rather deep lines about her eyes and a faint touch of age at her throat, and her hands were not those of a young woman, and there was a definitely mature, almost matronly, expression in her green eyes, especially in repose.

"Be Gob," Michael told himself, astonished, "she's old enough to be my mother."

"You're very young, Captain," said Lady Anne, startling him by this revelation of parallel thinking. "But then Doherty had such great faith in you I'm sure your age will prove no drawback, though we have many problems. The Mansion is ready to open, but I hesitate about it."

"Why?"

"For several reasons. Captain Hood is making himself obnoxious."

"Oh, don't worry about that," said Michael airily. "I'll talk to the man."

"Of course," said Lady Anne. "But it's deeper than you think. He has gilt-edged backing now. Lord Bracken is quite rich—and also quite simple-minded, and Hood is a great one for impressing the simple-minded. Captain Hood keeps trying to make propositions to me. He wants me as a partner—and, to be quite frank, at times I've been tempted. You see, I tell you the truth, Captain. Doherty is one thing, you yourself are another. If I did not need capital, I tell you frankly, Captain, I might consider teaming with Hood, even knowing him for a soundrel. All men are scoundrels in one way or another."

Michael felt a rising anger, but managed to control it. He studied her narrowly. There was something about the way she spoke that made him think she was not telling the truth, that she was fishing, fencing—something of the kind. Was she trying to test him? Michael decided to speak his mind.

"There will be no Captain Hood," he said firmly. "Doherty would turn in his grave."

"And how can you be so sure, Captain Martin?"

"How? I'll not have it, that's how!" said Michael bluntly.

Lady Anne laughed. "Oh, you talk so big for such a young man," she said. "What makes you so sure Captain Hood will not gobble you up as he has gobbled up many others? He's a dead pistol shot. He's one of the finest swordsmen in the British Isles. And he is six foot, three inches high."

"If he were the devil himself and seven foot high, it would be all one to me," cried Michael.

"Then you won't mind speaking with him tonight?"

"I'd be delighted."

There was a long pause, and several times their eyes met, and Michael thought he discerned rather a notable softness in Lady Anne's glances now, and he felt somewhat embarrassed and confused. What did this softness portend? Was he supposed to take Doherty's place in everything? Of course, the legend of Lady Anne being Doherty's sister had long since been dissipated in his mind. Michael felt nervous. Why, the woman was twice his age. It would be an unnatural thing.

"And then," said Lady Anne at last, "there is Aga. Did Doherty speak to you much of Aga?"

"Hardly once, if that."

"I think she looks not unkindly on Captain Hood."

"That's her affair."

"It is not. She is a very headstrong girl, and might get herself into serious trouble over the Captain. You must thrash her soundly."

Lady Anne spoke calmly, and this made her statement even more startling. In fact, in spite of all he had gone through since leaving Ballymore, this was the most stunning thing of all, and Michael stared open-mouthed. "Thrash her, you say?"

"Yes," said Lady Anne. "She is eighteen and, true to that age, thinks she knows it all."

"Aga is but eighteen?" Michael was stunned again.

"Did you think her an old woman? Yes, eighteen—and she needs a strong masculine hand. Thrash her soundly at once and it may be enough."

There was another silence, then Lady Anne broke out: "Why should we keep you in the dark any longer? What Doherty was thinking of not to tell you, I can't imagine. Aga is Doherty's daughter. His natural daughter, and I've been saddled with the imp for years. Doherty thrashed her regularly, and she was frightened of him and for that reason behaved herself more or less. But since there is to be no more Doherty, you are the nearest thing to a father she has—a sort of guardian, shall we say?"

Michael was suffering one blow after another. But now he recalled the mysterious words of Trim: "She must be quite a large girl now." Obviously, Trim had known her as a child. Doherty's daughter! Michael did not know at the moment what he thought or felt; he knew only that he was confused and interested and deeply agitated. Was it true what Lady Anne had said about Aga's interest in Captain Hood? Or was it only part of the testing?

"She is interested in Captain Hood, you say? What of her father?"

"She does not care one shilling for her father's opinion, or for anybody's opinion, for that matter. You must thrash her soundly. She is too old now for me to thrash."

Michael sighed and looked about him at the pleasant little drawing-room, the discreet fire, the wicker basket patiently waiting for Princey, the many candles shedding their soft light on the white panelled walls, the faint glimmering of the gold picture-frames . . . did any one ever thrash a woman in such surroundings? Women were thrashed every day, hundreds of them, in the stews! But here?

Michael glanced up. Lady Anne was regarding him rather oddly, he thought, running her eyes up from his boots to his shining black hair, and then down again, and then studying his face as a painter might or a woman with definite ideas about how the next few minutes were to be spent. "On second thought," said Lady Anne, "there is a possibility that thrashing may not be necessary—at least for the time being."

And then she burst out laughing in a surprisingly loud and coarse manner, Michael thought, flushing; and at that moment he heard a faint commotion in the hall and the little white fox-terrier, Princey, ran into the room frisking, and then leisurely Aga followed, dressed plainly and neatly, her luxuriant coal-black hair simply arranged, her eyes demurely lowered. She hardly looked eighteen, Michael thought, marvelling. Was this really the girl who had spoken to him so boldly that night at Doherty's Castle?

"Captain Martin, Aga," said Lady Anne, and Agatha obliged with a dainty, girlish curtsy, keeping her eyes lowered as before. Rising, Michael managed a very good bow this time, and did not knock anything at all with his sword scabbard.

Lady Anne had also risen. "The Captain would like to speak with you, Aga," she said. "Then I must take the Captain away for a while, as we have business."

"I know the business," said Aga quickly, "and I'd like to go along."

"I think not, Aga."

"Please," begged Aga in a childish voice, and Lady Anne gave her a long ironical look, then turned and left the room.

"You don't mind if I go along, do you, Captain—dear one?" asked Aga, sitting down beside the fire and snapping her fingers for Princey, who was busy looking Michael over and trying to make up his mind whether to welcome this strange new man or not. The little dog came to her and was patted, then Aga said: "You forget, I see, Captain, and are a little surprised at my being so bold as to call you 'dear one.' And yet that's what you called me the very first and, in fact, the only time we ever met."

Michael sat down, flushing. "Of course I remember. But the circumstances were somewhat different." Now Princey came over to him and laid his head on Michael's knee. "Good fellow," said Michael, patting him. "I am a great friend with dogs," he explained to Aga. "One of my choicest friends is a large mongrel of the name of Buffer."

"You seem quite a kind man, Captain," said Aga. "Your face is kind, and Princey took to you at once. Princey runs howling from

Captain Hood. I think the Captain kicked him once when there was no one else about."

"A man who will kick a dog will kick a child," said Michael, his anger rising. "And such a man I would love to kick."

"Oh, but not Captain Hood. I cannot see you or any one kicking Captain Hood."

"Let him kick a dog in front of me once and you'll see, Aga."

After a pause, Aga said: "It would be a pity to have you die so young, Captain," and then she burst out laughing, and suddenly the demure schoolgirl air disappeared entirely and her bold black eyes danced, and Michael was sure that he saw something ruthless and Doherty-like in the set of her sturdy small chin. He sat studying her face, noticing the delicately made but turned-up nose, the rather harsh line of her Kalmuck-like cheekbones, the small, thick-lipped, sensual mouth, the stormy-looking black brows, the long lashes. In colouring she was somewhat similar to Catherine, but there the resemblance ended. Aga was no great beauty like Catherine. But there was a subtle animal force in her face entirely lacking in Catherine's, a suggestion of rough weather, sleeping danger, Michael thought.

Her manner was beginning to irritate him. "Aga," he said sharply, "we'll have no more of the Captain Hood business."

"Is that an order?" laughed Aga.

"That's an order. What kind of an unnatural daughter are you, girl —when you know how Doherty felt?"

"I am no kind of unnatural daughter whatever, Captain. I am a *natural* daughter. A bastard, if you prefer. And my sainted father did nothing to legitimize me. So you think I should care about his opinions, do you?" She snapped her slender fingers. "That's what I care about his opinions, or yours." Now she jumped from her chair and confronted him, her black eyes sparkling with vitality and malice. "An order, is it? You think you can order me, you bog-trotter dressed as a gentleman? Why, you can't even manage your sword." She threw back her head and burst out into loud, maddening, ironical laughter. "What—order me? Why, you puppy! I laugh at your orders. Do you understand? Fill Doherty's shoes? Not even one of them half as far back as the instep. No more Captain Hood, is it? He will eat you, do you hear what I'm saying? Eat you for supper with a French sauce."

Michael rose suddenly and hit her a hard blow on the cheek with the back of his hand, and she fell to her knees and hid her face and burst into tears, and with a yelp Princey bared his teeth and made a leap for Michael, and there was a great commotion of weeping, cursing, and barking—and at this inauspicious moment Mary came in, glanced about her calmly, and announced:

"Captain Hood is asking to speak with you, Miss Agatha."

Aga glanced up at Michael through her fingers, but made no reply. Michael said: "He will speak to me, Mary. Not Miss Agatha." Now he turned to Aga. "Go to your room at once and take this poor bewildered animal with you."

Mary stared open-mouthed as Aga grabbed up Princey and ran out through a side door, weeping loudly.

"Well," said Mary. "You waste no time, I see, Captain. A Blackfountain boy you should have been."

But Michael was furious and in no mood for joking. He said curtly: "Show Captain Hood in."

Mary pulled a comical face and bowed low: "Yes, sir, an it please Your Honour, sir." Then she went out chuckling.

In a moment there was a faint rattling as of accoutrements, and Captain Hood stepped in, followed at a distance by Mary. He was dressed in the uniform of a Prussian captain of Uhlans and was wearing a heavy cavalryman's sabre. He loomed tall in the doorway, dwarfing Mary, who looked up at him with mock awe, pulled a face behind his back for Michael's benefit, then disappeared.

"Captain Martin, I believe," said Hood, banging his heels together with a loud rattle and clank of heavy spurs, then bowing with clockwork stiffness like a tightly wound-up toy. He was black-avised, and there was a certain theatrical fierceness about his bearing which, taken together with his tremendous height, made him feared on all sides.

"Captain Hood," said Michael, jerking his head slightly. "Now, since we've met, it would please me very much, Captain, if you would leave."

Hood was plainly taken aback. "Leave?"

Michael walked past him and opened the door wide. "Yes, leave," he said harshly. "And don't come back."

Hood looked Michael over carefully, noting the wild glare of icy blue eyes. "But, my dear fellow," he said, "this is preposterous. Correct me if I'm wrong. Isn't this Lady Anne's domicile?"

"It is."

"Heretofore, I've been a welcome guest."

"Maybe," said Michael. "Women with no men in the house are apt to be foolish. Good-bye, Captain."

Hood smiled slightly. "You have me at a loss here, Martin. A lady's apartment is hardly the place for a quarrel."

"Should I step downstairs with you?"

Hood considered this for a moment. "No, on the whole, I think not. This is all very unfortunate. I was hoping perhaps we might see eye to eye about several matters, Martin."

" '*Mister*' Martin, if it's not Captain," said Michael, remembering Doherty's quarrel with Alfred McCandless.

Hood looked at Michael, then laughed. "These boys learn fast nowadays. They no sooner turn the handles of the plough over to their brothers than they are taking on titles. Well, *Mister* Martin . . . Captain Martin, I doubt if there is room for both of us in Dublin."

"Ah, well," said Michael, "you're used to living on the Continent."

Hood's eyes flashed; then he bowed stiffly, jingling, and turning abruptly, left the room. In a moment the outer door slammed.

Michael stood gritting his teeth in rage. Farm boy, was he? Bogtrotter? They'd all see before time ran out. He heard a loud giggling, then the side door burst open, Princey ran into the room, barking, and turning, Michael saw that Lady Anne had surprised Aga listening at the keyhole. Now they both came into the drawing-room.

"Well, that was short and sweet," said Lady Anne. "What a very rash young fellow you are! Why, he could split you in a moment with that sabre he wears."

"He was dressed to fight a war," said Michael contemptuously. "Why didn't he fight one, then?"

"Oh, he's subtler than you think."

Michael glanced at Aga, who was looking at him rather strangely, he thought. "Subtle, is it? I'll leave subtlety to women."

Now Aga spoke in her little-girl voice again. "Captain, dear," she said, "please let me go along with you and Anne. I want to see the new Mansion. I haven't had a peek yet. Please, may I go?"

Michael studied her as if he'd never seen her before. Had he actually slapped that intriguing feminine face? Yes. There was a noticeable red mark on the cheek. He glanced at Lady Anne, but her expression was blankly noncommittal.

Aga came over to him quickly, raised his right hand, and kissed it. "May I go please, Captain?"

Then as he still said nothing, she went on: "Captain Hood might come back, and I'd be here all alone with only Mary to protect me. Please, may I?"

"Very well. Very well," said Michael stiffly. "Though I doubt he'll be back."

He glanced at Lady Anne, but her bland face still showed nothing. He shrugged in irritation as he escorted them out into the hallway. So many things all at once for a man to make up his mind about!

THIS TIME Michael took Trim with him and left the two boys from Nine Steps with the coach and horses. As they went up the broad stone steps of the new Mansion, Aga skipped along beside Trim, holding his arm. "I couldn't have been more than eleven at the time, Trim," she was saying, and Trim replied: "Hardly that, I think, Miss."

"And we rode in the pony cart," cried Aga, "and the wheel came off, and you kept shouting: 'Oh, that bloody great wheel!'"

"Did I now?" said Trim. "Maybe I did. But don't repeat such words, miss. It's not quality to do so."

"Not quality!" cried Aga. "Oh, I've heard the quality say worse, when losing at the tables."

The Mansion looked as gloomy as a mausoleum in the flickering light of a few tall candles; all the furniture and pictures were sheeted; and a couple of Doherty's old card-men with blunderbusses were on guard.

Michael was overwhelmed at the size of the place. It was even larger than Doherty's Castle. Lady Anne took him aside.

"We must open at once, or lose it," she said. "The rent's ruinous, and I have less than two thousand guineas for the stake. What will we do?"

"I have three-thousand-odd more," said Michael. "Why, we'll open, of course."

"It's a slender stake. We could be wiped out easily by two o'clock."

"Or rich," cried Michael, laughing.

Lady Anne studied his handsome young face in the flickering light cast by the candles. "He's taught you well, Michael," she said. "Or else you are him reincarnated. He would have spoken exactly so." Now she leaned forward and kissed him on the cheek. "I feel so much better. We'll open, and be damned to Hood and Lord Bracken."

"Ay," said Michael.

On the way down the front steps, Aga came up beside him, took his hand, and held it. "You were a beast to hit me," she whispered in his ear.

"You wanted it."

"I needed it, you mean?"

"What else?"

"Sometimes I don't quite comprehend your countrified way of speaking, Michael, me bhoy!" Now she drew away, pinched him hard on the thigh, and ran for the coach.

The boot helped her in respectfully.

In a moment Lady Anne came up with Trim. "You may drop the three of us off, Trim," she was saying. "The Captain's room is ready."

"Yes, m'Lady," murmured Trim.

Michael said nothing. He was not sure that he liked this arrangement at all—and yet it was no doubt expected of him.

On the way home, Aga went to sleep in the coach with her head on his shoulder. This he found rather pleasant.

When they arrived back at Lady Anne's, they found Patrick Clonmel, Aire's fifth son, waiting for them in the little white drawing-room. Michael felt his usual stiffening and freezing at the presence of a Lord. Nevertheless, he managed a very good bow, did not hit the furniture with his sword, and even forced a rather truculent smile as Aire's son insisted nervously that he was immensely relieved that Michael was back in Dublin.

"There's trouble afoot," Aire's son went on. "It's this dastardly, bold fellow Hood. And now that Monty's backing him! I'm sure I don't know what Monty's thinking of. Monty's not a bad sort."

"Monty?" Michael inquired, puzzled.

"Lord Bracken," Lady Anne put in quickly, and Michael thought he heard a faint giggle from Aga in the background.

But Aire's son paid no attention to the interruption and went right on complaining about conditions in the city. He was a self-absorbed, dandiacal young man, short, thin, with straw-coloured hair, a large hawk nose, blue eyes, and a narrow hatchet face. His more literate contemporaries referred to him as "Sir Andrew Aguecheek." He was mincing, affected, and posturing, and yet there was a certain expression at times that Michael found rather attractive. What was it shining out of those odd, opaque eyes? Courage? Michael couldn't tell, and yet he felt a certain trust in Aire's fifth son.

"He's the devil, this Hood fellow," Aire's son was saying. "Great swordsman. Pistol duellist. What is a man to do? He's surrounded by bravos from the Continent. I said to Monty: 'My dear fellow, if you must cut your throat at last, why, do it privately.' Imagine, encouraging a ruffian like Hood. He will grow more and more arrogant. Binny's sick about it. Says the happy old Dublin is perhaps no more."

"Binny?" inquired Michael.

"Lord Clayton," said Lady Anne, and again Michael heard that faint, muffled, derisive giggle.

"I've half a mind to set out for Paris," said Aire's son. "But one doesn't like to be chased from one's own playground by a Captain Hood. You're not teaming up with him?"

"Of course not," said Michael bluntly.

Lady Anne laughed. "Captain Martin threw him out of the house earlier this evening."

Patrick Clonmel's eyes lit up, and turning to Michael, he put a small, thin hand on his shoulder. "Ah, good man! So then I'll sleep easy tonight. Are you opening the Mansion, then?"

"Tomorrow night," said Lady Anne.

To Michael's astonishment, Aire's son did an odd little dance, waving a large white silk handkerchief in time, and at the conclusion of it he bowed low to Lady Anne, who curtsied.

Now Aire's son looked thoughtfully at Michael. "Aren't you rather young, Captain? It comes to me all at once that you are a very young man despite the size and swagger. I am not old myself, but I think you have the advantage of me."

"I'm old enough," said Michael bluntly.

Aire's son laughed, throwing back his head. "A good enough retort. You know, pleasure is such a problem. All we ask, Binny and myself, are pleasant surroundings and freedom to indulge. But there are always these contretemps. With Doherty, no; except for an occasional brush with the constabulary, and that is always exhilarating. But with a man like Hood . . . well, if he comes to power, I shall leave for the Continent—or"—Clonmel waved his handkerchief—"slap his face."

Michael stared hard at the little man, then he smiled widely. Aire's son meant it, and Michael was pleased that he had recognized this something in Clonmel's glance earlier. A slap in the face meant only one thing: a duel. Captain Hood was a good foot taller than Aire's son.

"You'll do neither, I hope," said Michael, still smiling. "I think Captain Hood has plans in regard to myself. He told me Dublin was too small for the two of us."

"Ah! And what did you say to that?"

Michael explained what his reply had been, and Aire's son broke out into hysterical laughter. He couldn't stop. He leaned forward with a hand on his stomach. Finally Lady Anne brought him a glass of brandy. When he had recovered, he asked: "Do you mind if I repeat that about town, Captain?"

"Not at all," said Michael.

"Splendid! And now, good night. I shall see you tomorrow. I've had rather a good run lately and am laying for your faro box, I warn you. Good night, all."

Lady Anne showed him to the door, hovering over him like an anxious mother with a small, unpredictable son.

Michael turned and glared at Aga. "You will conduct yourself in a more ladylike manner after this, my girl—or you'll get the back of the hand once more."

But Aga was all innocence. "What do you mean, Michael? Patrick is so amusing. How can I help laughing?"

Michael did not pursue the point, but neither was he taken in. In a moment Lady Anne returned.

"Lord Clayton's waiting in your bedroom to see you, Captain," she said. "Mary put him there because he wanted to avoid seeing Patrick. Will you go to him?"

Michael froze. Aire's son was one thing, the great Lord Clayton another. "Yes," he said, "I'll go at once." Turning, he saw Aga's mocking black eyes on his face. Setting his jaw, he left the room with a swagger.

The old Lord was sitting in an armchair by the fire, looking at a book he'd found on the night-table. "Ah," he said, glancing up as Michael entered, "Casanova's *Memoirs*. I find them most spirited reading, Captain, and, I might say, a perfect bedside book." Lord Clayton laughed, shaking his shoulders.

Michael stood frozen. Through tight lips he said: "That would be Doherty's book . . . sir . . . Your Excellency."

Clayton looked at him narrowly. "Now, now, lad. No formality. A simple 'sir' will do, if you like. Sit down."

Michael, handling his sword with great care, sat on the opposite side of the hearth from Lord Clayton and tried to compose himself. He remembered one time in Ballymore as a boy hearing how the great Lord Clayton's coach had broken down on the King's Highway near town, and what a great to-do and bother there had been, with people being turned out of their rooms at the Bonnie Prince Charlie in order to make space for Lord Clayton and his retinue.

"You are a singularly silent young man," said Lord Clayton. "Not much on the order of Doherty, a very amusing fellow, by the by. We'll miss him greatly."

"Yes, sir," said Michael.

The old Lord sighed and sat looking into the fire. His face was covered with a network of fine wrinkles, and his dyed hair made him look older than his years, which were sixty-odd. Once a force politically, he'd fallen out with George III and his ministers, and was now without office, as well as heavily in debt, though his prestige was still great. His pouched dark eyes were world-weary and his body was shrunken with age and dissipation, but nevertheless there was still something jaunty and commanding about him.

"Captain," he said, after a long silence, "I find myself in a great embarrassment for the temporary want of a hundred guineas." He turned and glanced at Michael now. "Don't you find that a comical pass for Lord Clayton, lad?"

"Not at all," said Michael, jumping up at once and going to his desk, sighing with relief that he was able to do something, anything, rather than sit there opposite the great Lord Clayton, frozen with awe. He counted out the guineas quickly, returned, and with a bow offered them to the Lord.

"Ah, thank you," said Lord Clayton offhandedly, taking them and slipping them carelessly into the outside pocket of his coat. "Money, money. The root of all evil, they say, and yet a man is helpless without it." Sighing, he rose, having considerable trouble with his knee-joints owing to long sitting. They cracked one after the other, and Michael looked away in embarrassment. "You will note I avoided Sir Andrew, Captain."

"Sir Andrew?"

Lord Clayton laughed. "Aire's airy son. We call him Sir Andrew in jest—a character in a barbarous play by one Shakespeare. Well, he is too disturbed for my taste. I am too old to be disturbed by anything but the want of money. This Captain Hood—it's an obsession with Patrick. He will challenge him yet, and that will be the end of poor Sir Andrew. You must prevent it, Captain."

Michael once more repeated his conversation with Hood, and it had as great a success as before.

After he had stopped laughing, Lord Clayton said: "I begin to discern the lineaments of another Doherty, God be thanked. May I tell this about town, Captain?"

"Yes, sir," said Michael, feeling a slight bit easier now.

He saw Lord Clayton to the door and managed a very fine bow, he thought. The old Lord waved carelessly: "Night, lad. Read a chapter of Casanova before retiring. It is full of the most extraordinary ideas. Night."

Michael glanced into the drawing-room, but most of the candles were out and it was deserted, so he started down the hallway to his bedroom. A door opposite his own opened noiselessly, and Michael glanced into a large, dimly lit boudoir. Aga was standing a few feet inside the doorway, wearing nothing but a scanty lace French shift. Michael gave a start at this lovely sight, and then, with his blood pounding, he made at once for the doorway. But with a sudden and unexpected movement, Aga slammed the door in his face and locked it. Michael drew back to kick the door open, then hesitated. He heard muffled mocking laughter. Making up his mind at once, he turned on his heel, went to his own room, and shut and locked his door.

Play games, would she? Such antics could be two-sided.

Much later, after he had—with stark amazement—read a chapter of the *Memoirs*, undressed, blown out the candle, and got into bed, he was certain that he heard the slow and gentle turning of the outer door-handle.

He was laughing as he fell asleep.

THE BIG NIGHT had arrived. It was nine o'clock, and the new Mansion was blazing with light. Only a scattered few had arrived as yet, and there was but one small card-game going in the front salon. But the card-men, the footmen, and the women had been ready for hours, and a French orchestra was playing in the immense entrance hall, its presence partly hidden by large potted palms.

Lady Anne, beautifully dressed in a revealing gown of gold gauze, was everywhere, giving orders, and Aga, no longer the young schoolgirl, nor yet the mocking minx, amazed Michael by her cold efficiency and attention to business. This was a many-sided female, not the slightest doubt about it.

Shortly before nine thirty, Trim took him aside. "There is a man from Ballymore to see you."

"From Ballymore!" shouted Michael.

"Ay! I put him in the little private card-room under the stairs and gave him supper and a bottle of whisky."

"Then he's happy," laughed Michael.

"Will you see him now or later?"

"Now," cried Michael, and he hurried down the hallway as if going to a fire and banged back the door with a cry.

A little slim dark-haired man raised himself up awkwardly from behind a table loaded with food.

"Brady!" shouted Michael. "What in God's name . . . !" And he hurried round the table, grabbed the little man in his arms, and almost suffocated him with his embraces.

Brady, the quiet little harness-maker from Ballymore! A solid man!

"Leave off, you great ape!" cried Brady, intimidated neither by his surroundings nor Michael's elegant clothes. "You're killing me with your kindness."

Roaring with laughter, Michael sat opposite him, and Brady returned to his meal, ate placidly, and drank straight Dublin whisky. "'Tis a fine light whisky, like wine," he said. "Not like our own rough country stuff. A man can drink a power of it with a steady head. For everyday consumption, I'd say it was for girls."

"What the devil are you doing here, Aloysius?"

"I came to see you. What else? You're the only common Ballymore man who has any money, and from the looks of things, you have plenty."

"Money, is it?" said Michael, his face falling.

"Ay, money. We've been having these rent riots, and the S.F.Y.I. have got themselves in a devil of a lot of trouble. We need money for bail and for fighting the cases. You are one of us. The only one with real money. Shell out."

Michael was so relieved that it was not to be just a personal touch that he jumped up and began to pace the floor excitedly.

"And how much would you need, Aloysius?"

Brady shook his head dolefully. "A big sum, Mick. A big sum. I hesitate to mention it. One hundred round guineas, man. A stunner."

Laughing, Michael took the money out of his pocket and gave it to Brady at once. Brady stared in amazement—Brady, who had the Ballymore ideas of money that Michael himself had once had—and now Michael remembered how he had offered Doherty his three pounds and how the great man had said it was no more than a tip for a doxy.

"Why, you must be a millionaire," cried Brady, "carrying a hundred guineas in your clothes. A man in Ballymore might spend five years working for it." Brady pocketed the money with a grin of satisfaction.

Michael sat down again. "Tell me what's happening in Ballymore."

"Oh, it's not just Ballymore—it's all of Kilkenny. The wild ones have got the upper hand over Regis and have taken to rioting. Windows are broken in the manors, stock is run off. Rents are refused to absentees. There is merry hell to pay—and the gaols are full. You know Regis, Mick. There's a man, if you like. He has taken the whole thing on his own shoulders, as the leader, and is being hunted like a stag by the dragoons. But he's well protected. He sleeps at a different house every night, and the dragoons are very, very careful. It is one thing to hunt a common malefactor, and another to hunt a man beloved of all the country people. Dragoons have been stoned along the roads. Regis is known all over Kilkenny now, and the people are looking to him for guidance. If he is not caught—and I doubt he will be—he will have things quieted before he's through. But many of the boys are not so fortunate. However, the authorities are going slow and are holding them only for disturbing the peace and destroying property—not for treason. Even Regis himself is not wanted for treason. Only for inciting to riot. Dublin Castle wants no more public executions, I take it, with things in this state. Oh, it's a grand affair, and spreading all through Leinster. Mick—Regis will be a big man yet, a great man. They will send him to Parliament next. And he will speak his mind to the bloody Saxons and be damned to them."

After a pause, Michael asked: "And Catherine?"

"Oh—as to be expected. Worried about Regis. A brave, brave girl. The loveliest 'Owl' of all."

There was a tap at the door, and Trim came in. "Excuse me, sir," he said. "People are arriving in droves. The great English actor, Grantham, is here, and many others. Lady Anne was wondering . . ."

"Right away, Trim," called Michael, and Trim shut the door. "Brady," Michael went on, "enjoy your supper, and I'll see you later."

"No. I must slip away at once, back to Ballymore. Thank you, Michael. There are those who say you have gone to the devil and are no more than a common bravo. Be damned to them. You've saved a lot of fine lads from rotting in gaol till tried. And we must get them out at once. There is a movement among the British to rescind the Habeas Corpus Act once more. Go about your business, Michael. May I come again when necessary?"

"Ay! Whenever you like, and if there's money, you'll have it. How did you find me, Aloysius?"

"Why, the boys are everywhere. I was directed to Tom at Nine Steps."

"Good. Always see Tom. He'll know where to find me."

Michael shook hands with Brady and hugged him, then he turned and went out. He could hear the hubbub and chatter of many arrivals and the bawling of the footmen and the pleasant sound of violins and hautboys, but all this came to him as through a mist. He was lost in a dream of Ballymore . . . Catherine . . . pebbles against a window . . . and herself in a country night-dress kissing him frankly in front of her father and her brothers . . . and Buffer licking his hand good-bye. . . .

He was clapped gently on the shoulder, and a high-pitched voice said: "Why, it's far grander than Doherty's Castle, Captain. What a rout! What excitement!"

And he woke from his country dream and saw little Patrick Clonmel smiling up at him. "Why, thank you, sir," he said.

"I'm for the faro bank," said Aire's son. "I intend to win a great sum from you tonight."

"Good luck," called Michael.

The Mansion was jammed by eleven thirty, and equipages were standing at the curbs for three blocks round. There was heavy play at the faro banks and much dancing in the great entrance hall, which was lit now by hundreds of tall candles.

Michael wandered here and there and was bowed to by all the quality gaming or dancing, and he began to feel like a very wonderful and important fellow indeed—until he overheard a lady say: "Yes, handsome. But just an ignorant bravo from the back country, after all." For a moment Michael experienced a terrible deflation, but then finally he was able to laugh at himself, and after a while he was honest and level-headed enough to think: "By God, the lady's right. I'm ignorant and from the back country (if that's anything to be ashamed of, though I doubt it), but I'm learning, ladies and gentlemen, I'm learning."

Shortly before midnight he went into the little room under the stairs, had a bite to eat and three good stiff shots of Dublin whisky, and listened to a report from DeLane, the French head card-man. "The play is heavy, sir," said DeLane. "Table one is losing, but that's all to the good, I believe, because Lord Clayton is winning. Lord Clonmel has lost five hundred guineas at table two, but is now recouping somewhat. The house at present is a good two thousand guineas ahead, and the heaviest play is generally after midnight. I am not counting the withdrawal from the small private games, which should net by now a good three hundred guineas more."

After DeLane had gone, Aga slipped in for a moment. She'd been dancing with some of the gentlemen and was a little out of breath.

"And so," she said, as Michael neither greeted her nor made any comment at all, "our friend Michael, of the blue-black locks, has become a great man overnight. Or at least is thought so. But I know better. May I have a drink?"

"Help yourself."

Aga poured out quite a stiff shot of Dublin whisky and tossed it off neat. "Ay—as my father always said," she went on, "I know better. Did you ever yet hear of a great man stopped of his desire by a little wooden door?"

Michael laughed curtly. "It was not my desire. If it had been, I would have kicked the lock off."

"Oh, yes, yes," cried Aga, aping Michael's rather forceful way of speaking, "quite so, quite so. He's getting to be such a great fellow, and with all the ladies running after him—how could one expect him to be interested in a little Scottish girl of dubious origin?"

Michael laughed easily. "And I locked my own door, as you found out, eh, Aga?"

Aga's eyes flashed, and she burst out violently: "You are an impossible jackass, and I hope Captain Hood cuts your silly head off with his sabre." She stopped suddenly. "No, I don't, really. But it would serve you right."

And then, almost as if on cue, there was a light tap at the door and Trim stepped in. "Captain, I thought you'd like to know. Captain Hood has arrived with Lord Bracken, and they are playing faro bank at table two. Lord Clonmel is also playing there, and losing."

"Thank you, Trim. I'll be out at once."

Trim bowed and left. Michael turned to Aga. "Well, here's your Captain Hood."

Aga glanced at him, her pretty mouth working; then she said in a low voice: "Be careful now, Mick. They say he's dangerous and very tricky."

"Tricky, is it?" cried Michael. "Girls are tricky. Cowards are tricky.

Men are not tricky. So much for Hood." And then suddenly he stopped, realizing that Aga's whole attitude had changed and that she was warning him.

But before he could make capital of the situation or even speak, her attitude had changed again. Her black eyes were snapping angrily. "You talk like a ninny, a great baby!" she cried. "What would you be —a dead hero? Men not tricky? Doherty was the trickiest man in Dublin, and the bravest."

Michael was astounded by this outburst. "I thought you hated Doherty."

"I hated him, and I loved him," cried Aga. "Can you understand that? No, I think not. You are a woodenhead, Mick. You will be buried young."

Michael was not particularly angry with her, but for the sake of future peace and to teach her the dangers of vituperation, he did what he thought the situation called for—struck her smartly on the cheek with the back of his right hand, and she fell to her knees again and began to weep loudly.

"You're a beast, Mick," she wailed. "A dirty Irish beast out of a bog. He'll cut your head off sure."

Michael went out, slamming the door. Aga rose at once, completely composed, poured herself a glass of whisky, drank it down at a swallow; then she danced about the room gracefully, humming to herself.

"He will not cut Mick's head off, I think," she said aloud, then she burst out laughing.

DeLane spoke to Michael in the entrance hall. "There is trouble at table two, sir. Captain Hood and Lord Clonmel have had words. It seems Hood is cheating."

Michael flushed darkly and started away, but DeLane stopped him by laying an urgent hand on his arm. "Pardon me, sir. Correct me, please, but I don't believe you are entirely familiar with all the ins and outs of faro bank."

"That's right, man. But if he's cheating—"

"There is always trouble with rogues such as this. He is slipping the counters off when the card is turned. It takes dexterity; and he has it, I assure you. Sir, it's an almost impossible thing to prove, and it is very, very bad for the house to accuse a patron."

"I could ask him to leave."

"That would be even worse, sir, if you will excuse me," said DeLane. "We can't set such a precedent. What would we do then if some true gentlemen of quality became obnoxious and . . ."

"I see. Has Clonmel accused Hood of cheating?"

"Oh, no, sir. That would mean fighting—a duel. But he's vaguely implied it, and I think there will be trouble."

"In that case," said Michael, "I'll go look on."

"That is the best thing, sir," said DeLane, smiling with relief.

Michael moved quietly and unobtrusively into the main salon and stood near an anteroom doorway, looking on at table two. The dealer was cold and impassive in his demeanour and paid no attention to the squabbling at the table. Lord Bracken was not playing, but merely watching. He was a rather pompous young man with somewhat the air of a self-satisfied pigeon. He was dressed in the most extreme French fashion and from time to time touched his nose with a lace handkerchief. Clonmel was red with annoyance, and again losing heavily. Captain Hood bucked the box with practised aplomb—and Michael saw him doing something swiftly with his hands. Clonmel lost again and danced with rage, then he turned to Hood.

"Sir, would you mind keeping your hands still while the card is being turned?"

A hush fell over the upper end of the room in the vicinity of table two. This was the thing itself. Michael moved over swiftly to the table and was just in time to prevent Clonmel from being slapped with a glove. Pivoting on his left foot with the speed of a professional boxer, Michael hit Hood squarely on the jaw with his left fist, and Hood, with a look of wild surprise, went down, clashing and clanking, his long legs comically kicking the air.

There was a horrified gasp. "Ruffian!" cried Lord Bracken, raising his hand as if to strike Michael with his handkerchief, but Hood rose quickly, moved Bracken gently back, and stood confronting Michael.

"It's against my principles to fight with riff-raff," he said coldly. "But my seconds will wait on you, sir."

"Good," said Michael shortly.

"You struck me, sir, unprovoked, so no doubt you will allow me choice of weapons?"

"Suit yourself, Hood."

"Pistols at ten paces."

There was a gasp, but Michael ignored it. "Good," he said.

Hood eyed him carefully, but got nothing but a cold blue-eyed glare. "This is for blood, Martin," said Hood. "No gentlemanly nonsense, you understand."

"I understand," snapped Michael; then he turned his back on Hood and motioned for the dealer to continue.

Lord Bracken turned and left, followed in a moment by Captain Hood, who swaggered considerably now, looking about him fiercely.

The gambling went on, but Lord Clayton and Clonmel took Michael aside. "At ten paces he can't miss, lad," cried Lord Clayton.

"Nor can I," said Michael bluntly.

Aire's son laughed quietly but nervously. "He's right, Binny. In a way, it's to his advantage."

"And then," said Michael, "the man was already beginning to crawl, trying to terrorize me. I have the word on him, and from the best authority I know, John Doherty."

"Well, well," said Lord Clayton, "time will tell. We'll act for you, lad; both of us."

"And with delight," said Clonmel. "If you fall, Martin, I'll challenge him at once. Why, the man was cheating!"

"You'll do nothing of the kind," said Lord Clayton. "I'll challenge him. I'm fifty years old. You're young."

Aire's son could not restrain a smile. "All of fifty, Binny. All of fifty."

Lord Clayton flushed darkly, but made no further comment.

"Do you think Monty will act for him?" asked Clonmel, after a moment.

"I've no doubt of it," said Lord Clayton. "The fellow has bewitched him."

Clonmel smiled reminiscently, a look of intense pleasure in his eyes. "Oh, the way he went on his back and writhed his long legs! What a punch, Martin!"

"It was only my left," said Michael solemnly, and the two Lords burst out into loud laughter, and many turned to look at them, wondering at their levity at such a time.

After the laughter had died down, Lord Clayton said: "It will be at dawn behind the University, I have no doubt, Martin. So prepare yourself."

Michael nodded slowly.

At two Michael went into the little room under the stairs for a quick drink. Just as he was pouring it, Aga came in.

"Why did you hit him like that, Mick?" she demanded. "Did you think you were at one of your country fairs among the pigs and cattle? It's a disgraceful thing to hit a man so. A tap is enough."

"Mind your own business. A tap was all it was. I did not even split a knuckle."

"Well," said Aga, "at least you will not have to worry about the sabre. Are you a good shot?"

"Good enough. Your father taught me pistol-handling."

"Glory!" cried Aga, suddenly excited. "It's the talk of the place—of the town, I'm sure."

And then all at once Michael, seeing her so warm and excited, felt a strong desire for her and, reaching out, pulled her into his arms. She struggled vainly, laughing.

"God, you're strong, Mick," she whispered in his ear.

They kissed at length and then finally, taking him off guard, Aga pushed him back suddenly, tripping him, and laughing triumphantly, she ran out, slamming the door. Michael just barely saved himself from falling by grasping the edge of the table.

Furious, he rushed out and searched for her, but she had disappeared. No one had seen her, apparently.

IT WAS an odd tableau at the foot of the great staircase, Michael thought, as he and the Lords Clonmel and Clayton descended from an upper room where they had been discussing the duel. The last patron had left only a quarter of an hour ago, many candles were still burning in the deserted public rooms, and roustabouts were covering the tables and sweeping the floors. Grey was showing faintly at the windows.

Yes, an odd tableau. Lady Anne, pale as death and with a look of agonized suspense. Little DeLane, collected and correct but unusually flushed. Trim, as placid as always, effacing himself. A strange gentleman of the name of Mr. Shanley, very drunk but very polite, a strayed reveller, who insisted that they use his big coach, which was waiting at the door. Various hard-faced, cool-eyed card-men, whose looks of admiration were tempered with scepticism. And Aga! Her black eyes were dancing with excitement, but she seemed no more concerned than if she and Michael were leaving for a ball.

"Take me with you, Michael," she cried, grasping his forearm.

Before he could speak, Lord Clayton thrust her gently aside. "It's no place for a female, girl. What are you thinking of?"

Michael merely looked at her disdainfully. Clayton had spoken for him. Aga glanced from one to the other, then she turned on her heel suddenly and, running, disappeared into the back of the Mansion.

"A fantastic young lady," said Clonmel. "That's always been my thought."

Michael gently refused Mr. Shanley's offer of his coach, and bowing with drunken gravity, Mr. Shanley said: "Would you allow me to attend on you, sir? Not as second, of course—as you have admirable seconds. But merely as a friend. You see, it is my firm opinion that the air of Dublin will be so much easier to breathe once Hood has been eliminated."

Michael grinned. "Why, yes, Mr. Shanley. Follow us if you like."

As they were leaving, Lady Anne took Michael aside. "This Mr. Shanley, Michael—he's rich as sin. His father and his uncles own the big distillery: McWorth's. They don't use the family name because it's not genteel, the making of whisky."

"But very profitable, eh? Very well, m'Lady."

"For the love of God, be careful," cried Lady Anne, on the verge of tears. "Michael, we've got the town in our grasp. It's greater now than even with Doherty. Don't get killed."

Michael looked at her steadily. Now here, if you like, was a frank woman. No nonsense about her. "I'll do my best to stay alive for your sake, m'Lady," he said with a laugh.

Lady Anne hugged and kissed him, half smothering him with her large matronliness; then he turned and went out, followed by Clayton and Clonmel. The old Lord was carrying a large rectangular duelling-pistol case he'd had brought to him from his rooms. He was taking no chances with strange weapons.

Trim had gone ahead and was now waiting at the coach with the driver and the boot from Nine Steps.

Day was showing palely as they drove off in the direction of the University, followed by the great gaudy lacquered coach of the polite and drunken young Mr. Shanley.

HOOD HAD arrived first. He was attended by Lord Bracken and a gentleman of the name of Mr. Benchley, who, from his attitude, had been dragooned. He did not seem to approve of the proceedings at all. In the background was a small, stocky, dark-faced Italian bravo, known as Arrigo; he had narrow, slitted black eyes, and a huge sabre scar on the right side of his face, from cheekbone to chin. He did not seem to like the proceedings too well himself.

Hood tried to fix Michael with a glare, but Michael turned his back and stood looking off across the quiet precincts of the University. Strangely enough, he felt not the slightest nervousness or doubt. Doherty had prepared him, given him the measure of his man. Hood's heart was not in the right place. Michael felt vastly superior to him, contemptuous of him even. He was certain that no such man as Hood could overcome him.

Behind him, Lord Clayton was speaking: ". . . and now, gentlemen, I must perform a routine duty. I call upon you, Captain Hood, to withdraw your challenge temporarily and submit your quarrel to arbitration by the seconds of both sides."

Michael turned. Hood, who seemed nervously truculent, was wetting his lips before he spoke. "Quite out of the question," he said, but his voice did not sound nearly as steady and harsh as he had intended, and Michael noted that Lord Bracken threw him a puzzled look.

"Well, so much for that," said Lord Clayton abruptly. "Now, gentlemen, I have here, if there are no objections, two of the finest duelling-pistols in the British Isles. They were made to my specifications years ago by Bruter, the best gunsmith in London."

Lord Bracken spoke up at once. "I brought my own. But I have no objection to the use of Lord Clayton's if the Captain has not."

"I must see them loaded," said Hood in a low, surly voice.

"Naturally," said Lord Clayton.

And then began the business of the loading, and Michael turned away again. The sun was just rising, and he could see Mr. Shanley's huge coach gleaming on the roadway like a great block of coal. Shanley's smart grey cobs were tossing their manes restlessly, and a liveried boot got down, as Michael watched, and stood at their heads. Just as Michael was turning away, he saw a small public calash driving at a smart pace up the road behind the University. It drew past Shanley's coach and stopped, and Michael wondered who it could be, but Lord Clayton spoke to him and he turned immediately, forgetting the calash.

"And now, Captain Martin, if you are ready . . ."

Michael stripped off his coat. A few paces away, Hood was doing the same. Then they were handed the pistols and placed back to back.

"Lord Bracken, will you count?" asked Clayton.

"Yes," said Bracken, fanning himself languidly with his handkerchief. "The damned gnats are out early today, I see."

Clayton ignored the comment, the irrelevancy of which shocked both himself and Clonmel, who looked narrowly at Bracken. "The count," Lord Clayton went on, "will be as follows. One, pause. Two, pause. And so on to five. At five the gentlemen turn and fire. Is this as you see it, Captain Hood?"

Hood nodded grimly; then in a low voice, without turning, he spoke to Michael. "You are a dead Irishman, boy." Michael merely laughed contemptuously.

After a long, steadying pause, Lord Clayton dropped a handkerchief, cried: "Now!" and Bracken began the count. As the men paced to the count, a crow flew over them, perched in a tree, and began to caw hoarsely, as if trying to recall the odd creatures below him to their senses. This was the only sound except the inexorable counting of Lord Bracken.

Whirling suddenly, Hood beat the count of "five" by a split second, raised his pistol, fired, and Michael, taken completely by surprise, heard the sour whine of a pistol ball and felt the clammy wings of death brushing his forehead.

"Coward!" cried Lord Clayton, exploding with outrage.

"Ah, *sacré!*" sighed Arrigo in the background. "He missed." Arrigo turned his back on the proceedings and walked slowly towards Hood's coach. As far as he was concerned, it was all over. Hood had signed his own death warrant.

Lord Bracken screamed at Hood. "You beat the count, you scum! You've disgraced me for life. I'll never be able to hold my head up in Dublin again."

"Wait!" shouted Clonmel, coming suddenly to life. "Captain Martin still has his shot to take. Captain Martin, Hood is at your disposal."

Hood's face was greenish, and he was having great trouble keeping his long legs from trembling. "I protest!" he cried. "The count was incorrect. You threw me off balance, Bracken. I demand another try."

"Reload his pistol," said Michael.

"No, by God!" shouted Lord Clayton. "There will be none of that, lad—not with my pistols. This man deserves hanging. He tried to murder you."

Michael raised his pistol suddenly and fired it into the air. "I'll shoot no man in cold blood," he cried. "I'll fight him with sabres, clubs, or bare fists, but I'll not kill a helpless man."

Hood was in a state of near collapse, but now his eyes lit up and the colour began to return to his face, and he made a move forward as if to clasp Michael's hand, but Michael turned his back on him.

Bracken was dancing with rage. "Get out of Dublin, Hood. Tonight. Or I'll see you locked up in Dublin Castle for one reason or another."

Arrigo had hurried back and was now helping Hood on with his coat. "How could you miss?" he was hissing in a whisper. "This man was a pigeon. *Sacré bleu!*"

Hood was staggering slightly as Arrigo led him off. "We catch a boat, I think," said Arrigo sadly.

Clonmel respectfully held Michael's coat for him. Lord Clayton was still in a state, his face an apoplectic red, and he was puffing and blowing. Lord Bracken, with tears in his eyes, seemed on the point of abasing himself. Mr. Shanley stayed respectfully in the background, smiling with drunken gravity; while Mr. Benchley, Hood's reluctant second, was already moving towards the shelter of Bracken's coach.

"I hope," said Lord Bracken, "you will accept my humble apologies, Captain Martin—and I have a further hope that in the future you will allow me to refer to you as a friend."

"Why, certainly, m'Lord," said Michael, bowing and shaking the hand offered him.

Beyond them there was a soft thud, and they turned. Mr. Shanley had collapsed on the turf, and Trim was already running to his aid. Bracken, Clayton, Clonmel, and Michael all burst out laughing at once. They roared. They held on to each other in their hysterical mirth.

"Ah, by God!" cried Bracken. "What a morning!"

As THEY walked to the coaches, Michael noted with a start of remembrance that the calash was still in the roadway. Struck by a sudden suspicion, he excused himself and ran towards the calash. The driver went to work at once furiously, hitting his horses, cursing them, trying to get away fast, but Michael grabbed a bridle, and the driver, looking scared, subsided.

Aga put her head out of the window and shouted fiercely: "Let my driver alone, you ruffian! This is the King's Highway, free to all."

Michael walked back and stood looking at her. "Well," he said, "here I am, you see. He did not cut my head off."

"No, you fool," cried Aga, "but it was close. Now maybe you will listen to me. I warned you he was tricky. But, no, you knew better. Men are not tricky, you say. Only women and cowards. Well, you must deal with women and cowards. You were lucky. Just lucky."

She was right and Michael knew it, and this made him furious.

"Go home. You had no business here. I'll deal with you later. What I need for you is a dog whip."

"Ho, ho, ho," jeered Aga. "What a big brave fellow it is!"

Michael controlled himself with difficulty. Stepping back, he motioned for the driver to go ahead, and in a moment the calash bowled off. Aga leaned out and laughed jeeringly.

The three Lords had been looking on with amazement, and when Michael came up to them, Clonmel said: "Fantastic, that girl! I've always said so. She puts me out of countenance no end. I don't understand her at all."

"Nor do I," said Michael thoughtfully.

MICHAEL WAS very glad to be in his own room now with the door locked. He was dead for sleep and was already sick and tired of the to-do about the "duel" with Captain Hood. Lady Anne had cried over him and kissed him and danced about the apartment like a wild young girl; and although it was but a little after eight in the morning, Bracken, Clayton, and Clonmel were drinking champagne in the drawing-room and downing one toast after another: to Michael, to Doherty (God rest him!), to various ladies of their acquaintance, to the Darby winner of that year, to the King, and even to Lord Castlewood, the Lord-Lieutenant of Ireland, though Bracken referred to him as a "rum customer enough."

In regard to Lords in general, as far as Michael was concerned, quite a bit of gilt was off the gingerbread, and while he liked both Clayton and Clonmel, he no longer felt that terrible awe that had unsettled him so at first, particularly with Clayton. "What is a man but a man, after all?" Michael told himself, as he slipped into bed with a long sigh of relief. "Lord or no, he eats and excretes. He gets wet when it rains, and he shivers when it's cold. He falls in love, gets old, dies. Six foot of earth suffices for him as well as for Doherty—or for myself, for that matter."

Michael was amazed at his own thoughts, considering them to be starkly individual. There was no way for him to know that millions of men all over the globe had been thinking along the same lines for some years now, and that an old world was crumbling to dust and a new world being born. Michael had never heard of Bobby Burns, and he had heard but vaguely of the French Revolution (just the Frogs at it again!) and the American War of Independence.

In short, Michael was one of the New Men in a New World—but completely unaware of the fact.

Yawning widely, he turned over on his side and fell into a doze, but of a sudden he woke with a start. Aga! Where the devil had she got to? The last he'd seen of her, she'd been jeering at him through the window of the moving calash. Cursing, Michael got out of bed and began to walk about, pulling angrily at his hair. She hadn't come back to the apartment or he would have heard about it. Crazy, the girl was; a loon. Only eighteen, yet running around alone in a calash like a strumpet. But what was there to do? He'd only make himself ridiculous if he went out inquiring for her. "To bed, Michael," he ordered himself.

But just as he was kneeling on the edge of the bed, he heard a faint scuffling sound in the hallway, then a giggle. He went to the door and listened.

Lord Clayton's voice: ". . . but it was naughty of you, child. Duels are for men."

Aga's voice, after a laugh: "Oh, I like excitement, Your Excellency."

Lord Clayton's voice, insinuating, a tone Michael had never heard him use: "A pox on Excellencies! Why won't you call me 'Binny'? And as for excitement, what about a kiss, you lovely?"

Aga's voice, impudent: "You call that excitement, Your Excellency?"

Lord Clayton's voice, hurt, gruff: "Oh, I know I'm just an old buffer, nearly fifty. But please call me 'Binny.' That would give me great pleasure."

Aga's voice, very formal: "As you wish, Lord Binny. Now, please, you must go back to your champagne and your companions." Then the little girl voice: "I haven't slept. And I'm so-o-o drowsy. I think I shall take off all of my clothes, and rest."

Michael gritted his teeth. A dog whip was clearly the thing.

Lord Clayton's voice, after a whinnying laugh: "Ah, yes. That is the way to rest. But lock the door, little one, lock the door."

Aga's voice, faint outrage: "Why, Lord Binny! What do you mean?"

Lord Clayton's voice: "Oh, a mere jest, dear. You are but a child after all, you know."

Aga's voice, childish again: "Of course, Lord Binny. There are many, many jests I do not understand. Now, bye. Bye, bye, Binny."

Lord Clayton's voice, sickeningly coy for a man of sixty-odd: "Bye, bye, little dove. Bye."

Michael waited until Lord Clayton's rather unsteady footsteps had died away, then he opened his door cautiously and peered out. Aga, with her own door open, was looking over at his with a calculating eye. Michael smiled broadly. He'd caught her.

"Bye, bye, little dove," he called.

With a curse, Aga pulled off one of her shoes and flung it at him, missing by many feet.

"I dare you to come out in the hall," Aga shouted, her face twisted with rage.

"I can't," said Michael. "I have nothing on but my shirt. I dare you to come here."

Aga gave a snort of derision, went into her room, slammed the door, and shot the bolt ostentatiously.

In a moment Michael closed his own door and went back to bed. "We must have a talk," he said, "the little one and me."

AND THE TALK came about rather abruptly and in a strange way.

The Mansion had prospered unbelievably, and as a result of this, Michael and Lady Anne had decided to keep the apartment and use it for living-quarters, rather than move to the Mansion as was the custom in Doherty's day. It was very comfortable and roomy, and they were well suited servant wise, as the apartment itself furnished a valet for Michael and a maid for Lady Anne and Aga, and this in addition to Mary, who was left free to do the cooking, and Trim, who now acted as butler but slept out.

Michael liked to come home to the fire Mary had waiting in the drawing-room grate, to Princey sleeping in his basket, and to the cozy privacy after the vast halls and crowds of the Mansion. He liked to have Aga sleeping across the hall from him, in spite of her mad antics. And he liked breakfast in bed at noon, with Trim drawing the curtains, handing him the morning paper, and helping him with the tray. Princey usually jumped up on the bed to greet him, and then Lady Anne would come in in a beautiful dressing-gown, her hair already arranged for the day, sit on the edge of his bed, and hold a postmortem on the doings of the night before. Aga might look in also, with her long black hair hanging and tied carelessly with a ribbon, schoolgirlishly.

Be Gob, it was the life of a Lord!

And then, one night, suddenly it was all changed!

Aga disappeared from the Mansion. Lady Anne mentioned the fact to Michael at about midnight, but they didn't really begin to worry until past three o'clock. At four they sent Trim out to look for her. At five they went back to the apartment, and Lady Anne said calmly: "Well, I've done my best for the girl out of regard for Jack Doherty. But I can only do so much. She's eighteen now and a woman, God knows. I can't keep her locked up any longer. I'm going to bed, Michael. I'm tired. I've never been so tired before in my life."

Michael, sitting by the fire, stroking Princey's ears, nodded without looking up. Lady Anne went to her room.

And now the time dragged past, and Princey went to sleep in his little basket, and the coal fell in the grate, and the clocks ticked on in staggered time, and Michael fumed and fretted about the room and wondered why in God's name he was so upset over the disappearance of that little black-haired, thoughtless, heartless, mocking baggage. And finally he found the reason—at least, the reason that satisfied him and made him think somewhat better of himself. Doherty, that was it! He'd promised to protect her. That was it, clearly. Well, what was to be done? Comb all of Dublin, street by street?

Michael heard a soft tapping at the window and went to look out. A misty rain was falling over Dublin. It was after nine o'clock. The town had a silvery-sad look about it, the melancholy of an old, old city dating back a thousand years in time. Vaguely Michael wondered if the rain was falling on the fields of Ballymore, but, much to his surprise, the memory of Ballymore did not have its usual soothing and quieting effect—as a matter of fact, before he could stop the thought, he was thinking: "Oh, damn Ballymore. That's the past. This is the present." And then he was as horrified as if a sacrilege had been committed in a church, and he asked himself: "How is it with me when I damn my birthplace?"

Shortly after nine thirty, Trim came into the front hallway, dragging Aga by the wrist. Her dress was torn, and she was crying and fighting at the same time. Trim's pale face was harsh in the wan light of the rainy morning.

"What's this?" cried Michael.

"Why, she run off to marry a drunken gentleman of the name of Shanley, and he jilted her, slipped out the back of the chapel. Sobered suddenly, I think."

"It's a lie," screamed Aga. "It was all a game. I had no intention of marrying the fool. But I was tired of all of you. All, all, all! Your smug faces—the gold guineas. The idiots at the tables. The stupid Lords. Is there nothing in the world but gold and Lords?"

"And she's been drinking," Trim added.

"What will you do?" cried Aga. "Beat me? All right, beat me. I don't care. Lock me in my room? I'll climb down the pipe, if there's a pipe. I've done it many times, always to spite Doherty, who thought to beat me was enough. No kindness, just beating. Ship me to a reformatory? Oh, you needn't look so startled. Doherty threatened me with it. No, damn you. I don't care what you do. Any of you. From putty-faced Anne—to you, you big beast of a bog-trotting peasant. I hate all of you!" She burst into wild sobs and kicked at Trim.

"Such talk!" said Trim in a pained voice.

Michael felt tears at the back of his eyes. For the first time he was certain that he had gained at least a vague insight into the motives behind Aga's strange actions. "Aga, dear," he said in his kindest voice, "will you do something for me?"

Aga raised her head and stared at Michael in amazement. "What . . . Michael . . . ?"

"Go to bed. Get some rest. Sleep. Later we'll talk. If you want to go away, it's all right. I'll give you the money."

Aga blinked rapidly. "But I don't want to go away, Mick. Why should I want to go away?"

Trim was staggered, and stared at Aga as if she'd taken leave of her senses.

"Well," said Michael patiently, "you might. If not, fine. We'll talk later. Aren't you tired?"

Aga began to cry. "I'm exhausted." Her knees seemed to buckle, and Michael caught her just in time, lifted her, and carried her to her room.

The whole house was awake now. Princey was frisking in the hallway, thinking the entire business a lark. Lady Anne appeared in a robe with her monumental blonde hair in curlers, looking somewhat old and very exasperated that her rest had been disturbed. Then Mary appeared with the expression of an outraged monkey, her coarse red hair bristling, holding a dirty old flowered robe about her thick body.

Michael deposited Aga carefully on her large canopied bed. "Undress her, Mary," he said. "She wants sleep."

"*Needs* sleep," whispered Aga, then she kissed him lightly on the cheek.

"Well," said Lady Anne, laughing. "So it was only a runaway, east by north."

Trim threw up his hands and disappeared. He wanted and needed a hot grog at Nine Steps. It had been a rough night and morning.

. . . And now it was not quite ten o'clock. And yet the row was completely over and everyone asleep, even Princey in his basket, though he cocked one eye from time to time as the last coals fell in the grate.

MICHAEL WOKE about two the next afternoon, rang for his breakfast, then rose and dressed, and as he was combing his hair at the mirror, he observed to the image: "Sleeping till the middle of the afternoon! What would Seumas Martin be saying of his son if he knew!" And then he laughed and walked about whistling, but his actions were all mechanical because he did not feel lighthearted at all. He had a problem, a serious problem, and he had slept ill because of it.

Trim brought his tray and raised his eyebrows at the sight of Michael already up and dressed.

"Was I that long with the food?" he asked, and there was more respect in his voice than ordinarily, and Michael looked at him in mild surprise.

"Wasn't that, Trim. But the day's so mixed up I thought I'd better dress and get started about my business. It will be evening before I finish my food and paper."

Trim put the tray on a table by the window, and Michael sat down and began to eat, glancing at the front page of the morning paper meanwhile.

Trim lingered, unnecessarily moving dishes about and stalling. Finally Michael glanced up at him. "Well, Trim . . . ?"

A broad smile spread across Trim's big face. "You should hear the talk about town, Captain. Nine Steps is buzzing with it. I can hardly get away from Big Tom and Mahony. They want to hear all the details over and over. Why, you're a hero all over town."

Michael snorted derisively. "Just luck, Trim. I was a quarter of an inch from being a dead man. He almost outtricked me."

"That's as it may be," said Trim complacently. "Nevertheless, you are the talk of the town, and they say that Hood shipped out for Liverpool with a sorry lot of Continentals he's had in his pay."

"The man gives up easy."

"Oh, he's through, and smart enough to know it. You see, you broke his bubble, Captain. He had the kibosh on the rufflers about town. Had them terrorized. But after you finished with him . . . well, they knew he was just a man after all and could be had. They would have made his life a misery. A man can't fight every day. It's not only dangerous, but monotonous."

"Trim," said Michael, "Doherty gave me the man's measure. That made the whole thing possible."

"Ay," said Trim, "Hood was inclined to avoid Captain Doherty. The devil himself would have had difficulty tricking the Master."

"The kippers are excellent," said Michael rather pointedly, and Trim, taking the hint, bowed and withdrew.

LATER, Michael found Lady Anne sitting by the fire in the drawing-room, concentrating on her needle-work. Every time Michael saw her so occupied it was a shock to him. It seemed so incongruous to see this queenly-looking woman engaged in such an ordinary feminine activity. Michael felt that she should be playing a great gold harp, or contemplating the day from the balcony of a high tower. He often speculated on what she must have looked like twenty years before. Overwhelming, no doubt about it. Trust Doherty.

He sat down opposite her, and Princey came over to be patted. "You knew Doherty quite a long time, eh, Lady Anne?" he asked.

She glanced up at him and smiled slightly. "Between ourselves—though I'd never admit it to others—eighteen years."

"Why, that's indeed a long time," said Michael, surprised. "What was he like that long ago?"

Lady Anne laughed sadly. "The same. Doherty was never one to change. I met him at a ball. Lord Havenhurst—dead now many years—had Doherty with him for protection. There'd been some trouble or other. I was singing there."

"Oh—not a guest?"

"Neither of us. Doherty was a bravo, pretending to be a Lord. I was an entertainer pretending to be a Lady. And I'm still pretending, though not really. The name's good for business now—and it's not like it used to be. Lord or no Lord, Lady or no Lady—it's all one. I saw it change." Lady Anne sighed and contemplated the tablecloth she was working on.

After a moment she went on: "I was singing, and a little Frenchman of the name of Monsieur Anatole was playing the harp. He was drowned later, poor man. Fell from the end of a quay, or was pushed —we never knew. Well, I looked up, and here was this big, brawny, dark-eyed young man staring me out of countenance. He looked rough. I said to myself: 'They are breeding a new kind of quality in Dublin these days.' Later, Monsieur Anatole told me that Doherty took him aside and gave him a couple of guineas and asked: 'And who is the large, grand, golden-haired bitch, my man?'"

Lady Anne spoke with the true accents of Doherty, and Michael laughed. "Doherty was not one to waste time," he said.

"He was not," said Lady Anne. "I drove off with him that night, and I remained with him. I did not even go back for my clothes.

Doherty sent someone. He couldn't bear to have me out of his sight for a moment. He was wild jealous—that is, at first. Of course, that never lasts. But the miracle was—one way and another—we were together for eighteen years and might have been for eighteen more." Lady Anne sighed and went on with her work.

"Aga, then," said Michael, "was just being born about that time."

"Yes," said Lady Anne. "But that affair was nothing at all. Just one of Doherty's side-blows. Aga's mother was a little sad-eyed actress of the name of Alison McDonald. She took poison, finally."

"What!" cried Michael.

"Oh, that was much later. It had nothing to do with myself and Doherty. Alison was just a weakling, couldn't make a go of it in the world. She drank heavily. I'll say this for Doherty, he paid for Aga's keep from the first, though he wasn't even certain she was his own. With a woman like Alison McDonald, how could you be certain? Or with any woman, for that matter?"

"*I'm* certain," said Michael bluntly.

"Oh, there is no doubt about it now. All you have to do is look at her. She's a pocket-sized female Doherty—a devil on wheels. She's got that dark look of anger, and the mockery. You can bank on it, she's a Doherty. But when I first took her to rear, there was doubt in my mind. Her little face was round and fat. She was quiet as a mouse—but sly as a fox. But I didn't discover the slyness till later."

"How old was she then?"

"A little past four. Doherty brought her in one day, turned her over to me, and said: 'Rear her!'—just that! But . . . I always found that arguments with Jack were very unprofitable. So . . . I took her. I was much younger then and much more restless and silly. It was a drag, having a helpless young child on my hands. But I made out. Trim helped for a year or two. The trouble started when she was about eleven. She'd run away. She'd get in fights with boys and girls both. She tore the nice clothes Doherty bought her. The other children did not like her, and I think they found out some way that she was a left-handed child. You know how children are—sweet but cruel. Well, Doherty, as you know, was not a patient man. He whipped her soundly, time after time. I whipped her. Trim talked to her with tears in his eyes. Then Trim whipped her. It made no difference. Lock her in her room and she'd escape. She'd lie, steal money, sell her school books.

One day Doherty said he'd had enough, and that he was either going to drown her, apprentice her off to a dressmaker, or send her to a house of correction. She was making his life a hell. He'd be gone for months, as you know, and when he got back to Dublin, he'd want to relax and enjoy himself—and here'd be this young she-devil, baiting him. Well, after Doherty threatened her with the house of correction, she improved considerably, and she's been improving ever since—but there's plenty of room."

Michael sighed. "I think Doherty was too rough with her, Lady Anne. That's my opinion. I may be wrong."

"Perhaps," said Lady Anne placidly. "But she was enough to drive a saint to brutality."

"The fact that she was nobody's child," said Michael, "made her wild, I'm sure. Nobody's *anything*. There was a girl in Ballymore like that. A large red-haired girl. Her mother was a farm servant. She had no father. She was the wildest girl I ever saw in all my life. When she was sixteen, she ran away and never came back."

Now Lady Anne raised her green eyes and studied Michael's face for a long time. "I'll say this," she said after a moment. "Aga's lucky to have you taking Doherty's place. Very lucky."

After a while Michael went back to his room and sat lost in thought. He had a very difficult decision to make, and his smooth young brow was puckered with worry. It was a very hard thing to say good-bye to Ballymore for ever, but, realistically, all dreams and aspirations aside, what else was there to do? He was wanted in Kilkenny. There were bills out on him. He'd robbed Lord Devereaux's steward on the open street—a capital offense. He was a known member of the S.F.Y.I. And there were the rent riots and all, and even fine, respectable Regis Donnell was forced to hide from the dragoons.

As for Catherine—well, Catherine was a dream. In fact, he had always thought of her that way and had even called her in so many words "the Dream." He could never go back to Ballymore and lead a respectable life now, and Catherine would never leave. The O'Herlihys had been in Ballymore for countless generations; they were like the dark soil and the trees and the little streams, always there. Yes. Catherine was merely a dream—the Catherine of the swan-boat and the dark, legendary, mystical, mirror-like lake.

Regis was the man for her. Regis, who would one day be a big man in Ireland.

Michael rose and walked to the window. Dublin lay before him, old, calm, misty, eternal. Michael cried quietly for a while, as he hadn't cried since he was a boy of ten; then, absent-mindedly fingering his chin, he discovered that he'd neglected to shave. "And with a blue beard like that," he told himself. "Why, you're getting as forgetful as old Jimmie O'Hare, who used to go out of a morning without his pants." And Michael laughed loudly, and then, of a sudden, Bally-more rose before him, misty and still in the early morning, with the chimney-smoke rising straight as a string, and the faint tinkle of cow-bells in the distance—but he thrust this image rudely from him, got out his new razor-case (a present from Clonmel) and began to shave at a window, whistling.

After a moment he heard Aga romping in the hallway with Princey, and a wide smile spread across his face.

MICHAEL SPENT what remained of the afternoon at the Mansion, checking with DeLane, then he had a light supper alone in his bed-room at six o'clock, and when he was through, he told Trim he'd like to see Aga in the drawing-room right away. He'd hardly sat down beside the fire when Aga appeared, her black eyes shining with curi-osity.

"Sit down," said Michael.

With a laugh, she tried to sit on his lap, but Michael pushed her gently away and motioned for her to take the chair opposite him.

Aga sat down, composed herself, clasped her hands on her knees, and finally said: "That is the first time in my memory that a man has refused to take me on his lap—except Doherty, of course. When I was small, he'd brush me aside, afraid I'd ruin his fine clothes."

"Aga," Michael began, then he stopped and sat stroking his shining blue-black hair.

"Oh, you like yourself, don't you?" cried Aga. "You pat yourself as if you were a little dog."

Nervous, Michael lost his temper. "Hold your tongue, girl; I'm trying to think what to say."

"What?" cried Aga. "An Irishman thinking before he speaks? I don't believe it."

"Did it ever occur to you," shouted Michael, "that you are a damned irritating girl?"

"No, it never occurred to me. But it must be true. People always end by shouting at me." Then with a change of tone: "What is it, Michael? I thought you'd changed towards me. You were ever so nice when I came home roaring drunk, like Doherty himself."

"What was this business with Shanley?"

"He wanted me to go to Paris with him. Offered me a thousand guineas and expenses. . . ."

"What!" cried Michael, rising.

"Oh, sit down, hero. I've had better offers."

Michael sat down with a groan and took his head in his hands. Was he going to persist in being an idiot as he had intended?

"Michael," said Aga slowly, "will you stop thinking of me as some eighteen-year-old girl from the bog country who swoons at a kiss and winds herself in her crucifix beads for safety's sake? I was raised round whores, to be blunt. And Doherty was an obscene talker, and when he was going good, you could hear him all over the house, or a block away, if you like. And God knows, Anne's no nun. Yes, I was raised round whores, and it was an education. What is cheaply bought is cheaply held. That's one lesson I learned. Whoever gets me pays heavily. And no one has got me yet—and it's not because of any of your damned virtue."

Michael stared at her in astonishment, but made no comment.

"Yes," Aga went on, "I'm held in great esteem by Patrick and Binny and the lot because they can't have their way. A thousand guineas? I laughed in Shanley's face. So he said: 'By God, I'll marry you, girl'—drunk as a Lord, and me drunk as an old bawd with a rich client. I thought: 'You will not, you drunken fool!' If there is one thing I can't stand, it's a man who is too weak to hold his liquor. I have seen Doherty drink a quart at a sitting and only get a little louder in his talk. . . . After the second quart, of course, there might be trouble. But it was roaring trouble. It was not silliness and falling down in a stupor. So I made a game of the business with Shanley, and got him as far as the chapel, where he finally fell through a door, he was so drunk, and scandalized the clergy. I drank him down."

Michael sat staring at her as at a monster.

She studied his face for a moment, then asked: "And what did you think I was like? What would Doherty's daughter *be* like? You knew Doherty well."

"Why did you never call yourself 'Doherty'?"

"Because," cried Aga, her black eyes gleaming, "he never asked me to. It was always 'Agatha McDonald, a Scottish girl'! Later he could have begged me and I wouldn't have taken his name."

There was a long silence, then finally Michael asked: "You've had better offers than Shanley's, you say?"

"Far better. There was a young Lord Allen about for a while. This was over two years ago. He offered to buy me a big house of my own and make a large settlement if I'd go to London to live."

"You were sixteen?"

"Not quite, I think."

"Musha, and what are the men in Dublin thinking of!"

"One thing," cried Aga, and then she laughed loudly and threw herself about in her chair. "Musha, and phwat a wurrrld it is, at all, at all!"

Michael flushed at the mockery, and then he rose and stood looking into the fire. Aga took Princey on her lap and talked baby talk to him, stroking his silky ears.

"I am like Doherty in one thing certainly," she said. "I prefer animals to men. They are more noble, more faithful, and cleaner."

"God," said Michael at last. "You should have been reared in a convent."

"Pity the poor Sisters!" cried Aga. Then she sobered and went on: "There is nothing wrong with the Sisters. I love them all, and perhaps they have the right of it at last. It's a dirty world, Doherty says."

"He seemed to enjoy it."

"It suited him," said Aga calmly. "He was a dirty man."

Michael collapsed back into his chair. This girl was fantastical!

There was another long silence. Then finally Aga spoke in a sweet, coy voice: "Michael, you were thinking heavily to say something. What was it?"

And Michael, taken by surprise, and like the countryman he really was, blurted out: "I was thinking we might be married, the two of us. But with all these offers . . ."

Princey turned and looked at his mistress in surprise. She had stiffened and frozen. He tried to slip his head under her hand, but she paid no attention to the gesture at all, so he got down indignantly and went over to Michael, who, much to the little dog's surprise, was just as unresponsive. Grunting, Princey got into his basket and looked at the two of them reproachfully.

All at once Aga burst out into wild laughter. It sounded like mockery to Michael, and he was just rising to clout her when she bounded out of her chair and disappeared. Michael stood stunned. And then he heard a ho-lo-boloo all through the apartment, and first Mary appeared, staring wildly, then Trim in an apron, then Lady Anne, half-dressed and owing to her voluptuousness somewhat obscene, on the order of a naughty French drawing—then Aga, like an actress making a great entrance, pushed them aside and re-entered the drawing-room wearing Michael's hat cocked over one eye.

In all his life Michael had never before seen a girl look so cute and attractive. She took off the hat and made a deep masculine bow, sweeping the floor with a gesture reminiscent of Doherty in a gala mood.

"Your servant for life, sir," she cried.

"Aga!" shouted Michael, grinning all over his face.

And now she rushed into his arms and burst out into loud, childish sobs.

"A brave man, that one," said Mary, turning back to the kitchen with a sigh. Later she said to Trim, who seemed stunned: "I've had three meself. Not one of them worth the powder to blow him up. And look what that God-damned fool girl gets!"

After a long, contemplative silence Trim said: "The Master will sleep quiet now."

But Mary roared with laughter, and cried: "That's more than you can say for Michael, begor!"

ABOUT MIDNIGHT, at the Mansion, Lady Anne took Michael aside. "Would you and Aga like to keep the apartment?" she asked.

Michael stared blankly. "Naturally. Of course."

"Fine," said Lady Anne. "It's too large for me alone anyway. There's a small apartment across the hallway and down a bit. I've looked at it several times. It's a little gem, with a lovely Louis Quatorze boudoir."

"But—you mean you're leaving us, Lady Anne?"

"Michael—you're young. You'll learn. Aga and I would soon be pulling hair. You see, shortly she'll be a young matron instead of a girl, and she will want to run her own establishment. And she can do it. I think I've taught her well."

Michael was used to big families and a clutter of female relatives all in one house. He had the idea that Lady Anne was hurt about something, or angry. "I don't take this well, Lady Anne," he said. "I thought we'd all be cosy. But if you want to go, go."

Lady Anne laughed easily. "You'll thank me later. Besides, it's time I had a little privacy. After all, I'm not exactly decrepit. There's quite a lot of life left yet in the 'large, grand, golden-haired bitch'!"

Michael couldn't resist this, and laughed. Then he took Lady Anne in his arms and kissed her. "Well, since you will be right across the hallway . . ."

They were in the little card-room under the stairs. He glanced up. Two eyes were glaring at him from the darkness of the doorway: eyes such as you would see on a hungry lynx in a forest.

"Aga," he called, "Lady Anne wants to move out. Thinks she might be in the way."

Michael noted the effort it took for Aga to compose herself and revise her ideas. "Oh? Well, perhaps it is best," she said, coming into the card-room. "May we keep Princey, Anne?"

"As long as I can see him from time to time."

"Oh, certainly," said Aga, one woman to another now. "I'll bring him over to visit in the afternoons."

"Good," said Lady Anne, then she patted Michael's cheek, carelessly embraced Aga, and went out.

"What were you glowering at in the doorway, girl?" asked Michael.

"You and your sloppiness," said Aga.

"I was but kissing Anne. She's no more to me than my Aunt Mag in Ballymore."

Aga snorted delicately. "I detest this promiscuous kissing," she said. "There's no point at all in it."

Michael grabbed her into a strong embrace and kissed her passionately. "That's what I call a kiss," he said. "All the rest is mere politeness."

"Where politeness is concerned," said Aga, "I prefer a bow."

"Ah, God, what a girl!" exclaimed Michael. "Not married yet, but already taking the married line."

Aga recoiled slightly, and Michael saw an odd, unfathomable expression in her eyes. "But it's soon, Michael," she said. "Don't forget that."

"Soon, is it? Gob, I forgot to tell you. It's not soon, girl; it's Saturday. Lord Clayton will be back on Friday evening. He's to be best man."

"Saturday!" Aga flushed, and a look of wild joy appeared in her black eyes; then suddenly she turned abruptly away. "I don't know if I can be ready. It doesn't give me much time."

"You'll be ready, damn it," cried Michael. "Do you want to be disrespectful to Lord Clayton?"

"Well," said Aga slowly, "perhaps if I hurry things a little."

It was one of the oddest marriages on record. The groom was pale as paper and smelled like a breeze from a distillery; the bride fainted at the conclusion and had to be carried from the chapel by Trim, who handled her as if she were a small, sleepy child.

Later there was a great supper at the apartment, and Lord Clayton fell down with a thump dancing a coranto with Lady Anne, and Bracken broke a musician's fiddle over the mantelpiece just for the hell of it. And Clonmel insisted on dancing a Highland Fling ("My mother was a Macbeth, by God!") and making a gruesome noise with his lips which he took to be a perfect imitation of the bagpipes. And Mary grew so drunk and maudlin and obscene in her remarks that Trim had to put her to bed. And then Lady Anne took too much champagne and developed a crying jag and went on and on about how lonesome she was now that himself had died far away in the mists and rain of Scotland. And suddenly Clonmel began to cry with her, to everybody's astonishment, and kept saying: "Ah, Scotland, thy lakes!" till Bracken laughed so hard he had hysterics and had to be patted on the back by Trim and given some brandy.

The French musicians looked on in awe at the "brutal drinking and carousing of *les Anglais!*" What barbarians! Drink was for pleasure. You took it lightly, lightly. You did not stupefy yourself with it. Above all, you did not *pour it into the harpsichord . . . !*

Finally, Michael and Aga escaped and locked themselves in.

"Darling, I'm scared," sobbed Aga. "I know nothing. Absolutely nothing."

"You'll learn," said Michael gently.

AND so the days passed, and then weeks, until finally it seemed to Michael and Aga that they had always been married, and that Lady Anne had always lived down the hallway from them, and that Doherty had always been dead and yet not really dead, but like someone who had moved permanently to a remote corner of the earth—like India or Australia—and was still very much alive owing to their memories of him and to the vivid impact he had made upon their imaginations.

Aga was a constant source of amazement to Michael—she was indeed, as he had thought earlier, a many-sided girl. The marriage had settled her beyond all belief, and Michael was deeply pleased to see that he had been right in regard to her and her wildness. She had never really belonged to anybody before, had never had any bona-fide status in the community. She'd had no mother and no real father, and no authentic name. But now she was a legally married woman, Mrs. Michael Martin, and the rebel in her had been replaced by the housewife. If at times it seemed to Michael that she was merely "playing house," like a charming little girl . . . well, there was nothing wrong with that; in fact, it was amusing and in a way touching. She always took a high hand with the tradesmen, like a true-born lady; and furthermore, she had no compunction whatever about bargaining and trying to get a good price. Michael, who was careless with money, was somewhat irritated at times by what to him seemed like "market haggling," but he didn't interfere; and he couldn't help noticing that the tradesmen treated Aga with deep respect.

And she had stopped drinking except for wine at dinner, and more and more she avoided going to the Mansion at all, and finally fell into the habit of referring to it contemptuously as "that place!" until Michael began to feel like a workman with a bucket in his hand setting out for his job in the coal mine.

Trim was amazed at the change in Aga and allowed her to order him about without a word of protest or even an ironical smile, and Mary, tippling more and more in the kitchen, and tearful in her praise of the "dear young lady," would often say: "And now I'm beginning to wonder if she's really Doherty's daughter at all. He was a great brawling, drunken ruffian, Doherty was. And this little girl is clearly quality. And what was her mother but an acrobat or tumbler of the halls?"

"She was an actress, you auld scut!" Trim protested mildly.

"Actress, me arse!" cried Mary. "You think I did not know Allie McDonald? She was an actress, yes, if you call walking on and smiling at the stalls an actress. She played the parlour-maid and such great parts—and that was only after she took up with that silly Frenchman, what's his blasted Frog name? Why, she was a tumbler on the high wire at Sadler's Wells, and also Dublin, showing her legs in tights like a strumpet. Actress, is it? And look at this angel of a girl, running her house like the finest lady. She is clearly not the child of such parents."

"One more drink," said Trim, "and she'll be the Lost Dauphin, at least."

And then perhaps Mary would weep a little and say: "And what can a poor lonely woman without folks or man of her own do but soothe her feelings with a small nip now and then?"

"It's a fine thing for you, Mary," Trim would reply, "that the Captain is not the type of gentleman who counts his bottles."

And Michael found Aga to be as loving at night as she was efficient in the daytime. But there was a difficulty about that—Aga's jealousy. She was violently—you might almost say, madly—jealous of him, and

sometimes when they were lying quietly together in bed, after pro-
longed love-making, she would try to pump Michael in regard to all
the girls he had known before he had met her. Now Michael, a proper
Irishman, had a divided soul when it came to sex; warring tendencies
pulled him in opposite directions: one moment he was all for libertin-
age like that rum fellow Casanova, and other times he was remorseful
over his looseness and was inclined to turn prude. He had none of
Aga's frankness in regard to sex. He did not like to talk about it. It
embarrassed him deeply. And laughing, he would brush off all of Aga's
queries, till one night she cried heatedly: "The big brawny lad arrived
in Dublin a virgin; there's no doubt of it."

And Michael said: "I have a great friend, Tim Keenan. He has a
loose-mouthed brother, Francis, who is always talking about his nightly
forays. And one night Tim clouted him and said: 'Do it; it's natural;
but shut up about it.' "

Much to Michael's amazement, this story hurt Aga's feelings, or
made her angry, or something, and she burst into tears and ran into
her old bedroom across the hall and locked herself in and wouldn't
speak to Michael or open her door until supper-time the next evening. As he was eating, she came into his room, dressed beautifully,
sat opposite him, and began to talk as if nothing had happened. Sighing, Michael let it pass.

But several nights later she was after him again with questions about
his love-affairs of the past, and in exasperation Michael cried: "I was a
stud, girl; a stud. Does that satisfy you?"

And Aga laughed lightly, much to his surprise, and said: "At last
he begins to tell the truth." And that was the end of the matter, except that Aga began to appear suddenly and at odd hours at the Mansion, dressed in her best and attended by Trim in livery.

Michael would look up from a conversation with one of the patrons,
or one of the card-men, and there would be Aga, fanning herself
grandly and looking about her as if she were the daughter of the
Earl of Aire.

And one night (it was two in the morning, actually) when she
arrived in the entrance hall, Michael was dancing a coranto with a
somewhat drunken and *déclassée* lady of quality—and there was hell
to pay!

Lady Anne managed to drag Aga into the card-room, where she and

Trim held her until Michael appeared, smelling strongly of Dublin whisky and grinning. Aga fell down into a chair and wept, and Trim and Lady Anne left hurriedly.

"And what is this nonsense?" cried Michael, high as a kite and exhilarated by his frolic with the amorous Miss Dawson.

Aga looked up at him, her eyes like jet buttons. "Oh, that horrible French perfume," she cried. "You stink of it."

"I noticed it was somewhat strong," said Michael, grinning.

"Take a bath before you come home. I don't want that whore smell in our nice bedroom."

"I will not," cried Michael, laughing. "Because I'm going home right now."

And then, to Aga's utter amazement, he broke into a wild country jig, making the music for it with his mouth, and the chairs flew over at his kicks, and Aga, half hysterical, almost collapsed with laughing; and a short while later they ran out of a side door, whooping, and Trim, chuckling to himself, drove them home through the sleeping streets of Dublin.

MICHAEL HAD become quite a figure in the sporting life of Dublin, and his rise had been so sudden, so abrupt, that there was much speculation among the quality in regard to his origins. His intimates among the quality, Bracken, Clayton, and Clonmel, were feverishly sought out by hostesses, and all three of them, night after night, held tables spell-bound with highly coloured accounts of Michael's duel with the formidable Captain Hood, and Michael's silly, country-boy words: "Reload his pistol!" were made famous by constant repetition and became a sort of watchword all over the town. Nothing like it had ever been heard of before in the whole history of duelling in Dublin—or in England or on the Continent, for the matter of that.

Full of champagne and grouse or venison, Lord Clayton would lean back in his chair and talk for half an hour without a stop about the bravery of the very young Captain Martin, of his handsomeness, his gaiety, his wit, and his daring, while refined and sheltered ladies of quality of the conservative set listened with shining eyes and moist lips and wondered why it was that they could find no such man among the gentlemen of their acquaintance: only fops, drunkards, imbeciles, self-absorbed politicians, and military careerists.

One night Lord Clayton was extremely flattered by the interest shown in his recital by Lord Glen. Glen was a rising young man in Ireland, and already first secretary to Lord Crewe, the Lord-Lieutenant's chief adviser. He was tall, elegant, with an affable manner but a cold grey eye.

Politically speaking, Clayton was an "out" and Glen an "in"; and as a rule, the two classes avoided one another; or rather the "ins" disdained the "outs" and had little or nothing to say to them, but plenty to say *about* them behind their backs. So Clayton was doubly flattered by the young Lord's interest, his attentive silence; and later, when they retired to the smoking-room, Lord Glen monopolized Clayton and they sat in a corner for nearly an hour talking about nothing but Captain Martin and his exploits, with a touch here and there of the late Doherty and the vanished Hood.

Now Lord Clayton was, in some ways, a foolish old man. He'd squandered an immense fortune on gaming, race-horses, and young girls; he was neither well read nor a philosopher; he could not do simple problems in arithmetic, and his geography, once you eliminated the British Isles and the Continent, was exceedingly shaky—for instance, he was never quite certain whether Philadelphia was in the Americas or Egypt: in short, Clayton was not brilliant. And yet politically he was far from a fool, and as the effects of the champagne and the flattery began to wear off somewhat, he started to realize that Lord Glen's interest in the affairs of Captain Martin was not a polite, dinner-table, dilettante interest—it had sinister overtones. In other words, Dublin Castle, slow but sure, was beginning to recognize the presence of one so-called Captain Martin.

And old Lord Clayton was very pleased with himself for having told the probing Lord Glen nothing that might harm Michael in an official sense. Gambling was almost never interfered with unless there were "public nuisance" complaints by irate prominent citizens. The late Sir George Bracey had dishonestly made just such a complaint against Doherty's Castle, and had eventually paid with his life for it. The higher branches of prostitution likewise were seldom harried, though the harrying was a daily—you might say, hourly—thing with the drabs of Nighttown and other unsavoury neighbourhoods. Besides, what went on at the Mansion could hardly be called prostitution in the strictest sense. Dinner and dancing-companions were provided for lone males by Lady Anne. What they did after leaving the Mansion was their own affair, but there was no nonsense allowed on the premises. The Mansion was a definitely respectable place of entertainment and refreshment.

As for duels—they were illegal, it is true, but any official who tried to interfere with one or who insisted on prosecution afterward would have been jeered out of Dublin, or, worse yet, sent to Coventry; certainly ruined politically.

So Lord Clayton smiled inwardly and went on chatting with the cold-eyed young Lord. And finally Glen laughed and said: "A wild young Irishman, by all accounts. One of the disaffected, no doubt, from the back country. A rebel. A member of one of those everlasting societies they manufacture in the bogs."

"Oh, I think not," said Lord Clayton mildly. "Completely nonpolitical would be my observation. Just a young ruffler with ability and ambition."

"Well," said Lord Glen, "in all my experience—which, of course, is meagre compared to your own, sir—I have never heard so much talk in such a short time about one lone man."

"It's incredible," said Lord Clayton, and then he rose stiffly, his joints cracking, and asked in a purring voice: "Shall we join the ladies?"

But this was not the end of the matter, as Lord Clayton knew it would not be. One midnight a large party appeared at the Mansion: a score of men and women, obviously of the highest fashion, and yet they came by way of public conveyances—an odd thing in itself; odder still, they all wore black lace Venetian masks, such as Doherty had worn at the robbery of Sir George Bracey. Michael was for excluding them unless they unmasked, but Lord Clayton quickly persuaded him that this would be a terrible mistake. He had recognized the powerful Lord Crewe—also Glen.

Michael was presented to the masks by Lord Clayton, and the old Lord was pleased by Michael's manners and by his unexaggerated courtesy. God, how the boy was learning! And Michael found himself surrounded by politely chattering and laughing, delicately scented women, looking like dressed-up elegant cats with their slitted black masks. And Michael kissed hands all around, and even permitted himself a mild heel-click or two.

And later the masks ate supper, after gambling desultorily for a while, then they danced in the entrance hall, and a lovely tall blonde female mask motioned Michael to her with a commanding gesture and galloped off with him in a coranto, but finally had to stop for want of breath. There was still a good deal of the jig in Michael's dancing, and he was a strenuous partner.

And then, towards two, Bracken came in roaring drunk, gave a wild start, and cried: "Good Christ! It's Crewe!"

And there was tremendous confusion, and the masks melted away, except for the tall blonde, who pressed Michael's hand suggestively at the door and raised her mask for a moment, showing slanted blue eyes, a small, plump, sensual face, and a large, lovely, insinuating red mouth. She fluttered her eyes at him and gave him an overpowering, ummistakable intimate look—then a grumpy male mask hurried back, grabbed her roughly by the hand, and pulled her away. "What—now it's a vulgar ruffler, my dear? Aren't play-actors enough?"

Clonmel arrived in time for the explanations. He had a red-haired girl with him nearly a foot taller than himself. She seemed dazed, disappeared into the back of the Mansion, and was found asleep in the third-floor hallway by the roustabouts when they cleaned up at dawn.

"Good God!" shouted Clonmel. "Crewe! What is it—a matter of state?"

"Mere curiosity, I think," said Lord Clayton, though he was far from sure, and he took Michael aside and warned him that he was now a marked man. The Castle was interested in him. He must avoid anything at all that had the faintest smack of illegality.

"It was the Hood business," cried Bracken, weaving about with a glass of champagne in his hand. "Good God, it's all over Paris, I hear. We know that Hood was laughed out of London. I understand he is headed for Rome. Now what in the devil does a man do in Rome?"

But Michael was immensely elated and could hardly wait to get home and tell Aga all about it, omitting, however, any account of the rather crude advances of the tall blonde woman. But Aga was more wary than himself in regard to this matter, and she said: "We must close the Mansion for a time. Doherty would. I don't like the sound of this."

"Why, it will be Castlewood himself next," cried Michael.

"Castlewood's dragoons, you mean," said Aga. "Listen to me, Michael. We must close the Mansion now."

"No, by God!" cried Michael, and then he shook a lively leg in a crude parody of the coranto, thinking of the tall, scented blonde lady of quality with the face of a prostitute, and then he shouted: "And what in the hell is there to eat in the house? I'm hungry as a wolf-hound."

"Please, Mick. Listen to me," cried Aga.

But Michael wouldn't listen.

BOOK
III

Book III

LIGHTFOOT HIMSELF

Winter passed, then spring, and finally it was summer again, and as Michael sat in the little card-room under the stairs, checking the sheets with DeLane, he could see through the window a thin, gentle, mist-like rain falling on the well-trimmed trees of a little park across the street from the Mansion. The trees were lushly green, the atmosphere was silvery, and there was something unreal and melancholy about the look of things as the afternoon waned.

Michael went over DeLane's figures on the last sheet hurriedly, paying little attention, then he pushed the stack aside. "DeLane," he said, "are you married?"

"Oh, no, sir," the little Anglicized Frenchman replied with a startled look. "Not me."

"You don't approve of marriage?"

"For others. Not for myself, sir. It's like possessions. I never own anything. Only the clothes on my back. No furniture, no pictures, no books: nothing. I can lock the door of my room and leave—in five minutes' time. Go anywhere I like. No burdens, no protests. Are we through now, Captain?" DeLane seemed in a hurry to leave, as if afraid of further questions and possible embroilment.

The Captain had become rather surly of late, and it was very easy to displease him and quarrel with him. Carrington, the floor-manager, had quit only the day before, and he'd confided to discreet little De-Lane: "If he was George III himself, I wouldn't stay. Oh, I know he's a great hero in the town, and it gives a man prestige to work for him. But he doesn't know the gaming business as Doherty did, and there's always the possibility of a row. He's got a look in those blue eyes—I don't know . . . like ice, at times. And then he's taken to drinking that damned whisky at all hours! And he's generally wrong in his arguments with me, but I keep giving in more and more. One day I won't, and then I'll get a crack on the jaw from the brawny fellow, and I'm brittle. On the whole, I think I'll ship for London."

So DeLane had taken on Carrington's responsibilities as well as his own, and was actually the only go-between now for Michael and the rest of the gaming help. DeLane did not fear the "crack on the jaw." That sort of thing was outside his experience. He was suave, diplomatic, practised in his relations with other men, hardly ever attracting anger or dislike to himself. Even so, he was in a hurry to get away now that the business was finished.

"You may be right, DeLane," said Michael, brooding, as the little Frenchman moved unobtrusively towards the door, carrying the sheets. "Yes, you may be right. A man can clutter himself up to such an extent that he's trapped, like a pony in the bog—and the more he pulls and struggles, the deeper he gets."

"Yes, sir," said DeLane at the door. "Now if that will be all, sir . . ."

Michael turned and glanced at DeLane, wondering why the fellow was in such a hurry to be on his way; then he gave a curt, surly nod, and DeLane went out, bowing slightly and noiselessly closing the door. Always business, business, in Dublin, thought Michael with a curse. Not like Ballymore, where business always waited while men talked their fill, as proper men should do. None of your dirty grubbing there. A shilling was something you bought whisky with; not something you entered in a little book and then said: "Now if that will be all, sir. . . ."

Michael got a bottle out of a cabinet and poured himself a drink. He knew that he was drinking more than he should. But what in God's name was a man to do? He had no familiar; there was no Tim Keenan to sit and laugh with him while the clock ticked on unnoticed and someone else thought of the shillings. Could a man, cold sober, sit at a table and look at a wall?

Aga? She was smothering him with her care and the petty intricacies of daily domestic life. "I've been an ass, an ass!" cried Michael, banging his fist on the table and nearly upsetting his drink. "At Ballymore I was like a colt in an unfenced meadow, roaming at will. Why, there was Catherine the Dream, even! And did I think of marrying her? I did not. I wanted only to love her. I told her so. And now look!" Michael drank in silence for a moment, then he went on: "It's not that Aga doesn't mean well! But, by God, the wild girl's turned into a grinding Irish housewife who thinks of nothing but welfare, welfare. 'Oh, alack, the fish is not of the best quality tonight!' Or: 'Michael, it's raining out and there is a chill wind off the Liffey—put on your heavy coat, bundle up, and don't catch cold.'

"Catching cold, is it, for the love of God! Did I catch cold riding a four-day journey in two with Doherty? Or crossing the North Channel in a damned hurricane?"

Michael rose and began to pace the floor. He felt swamped by worldly problems, he who had always been free to do as he liked and go as he pleased!

The Mansion itself, what was it but a gilded manufactury? And expensive and difficult to run, even with the help of DeLane and Lady Anne. There were card-men to pay and footmen and roustabouts and cooks and waiters and maids and musicians; and there were rent bills and food bills and liquor bills and bills for flowers and floor wax and candles (my God, the candles!) and green baize for the tables and new counters and new cards and other equipment; there were bills for livery, for horses and coaches, for drivers and boots—there were bills, bills, bills; and then there were the nights when the house lost, the largest play always being at the faro-bank tables, where the house prospered the least, percentage-wise.

Many times he'd been tempted to close the Mansion, at least for the time being; but that was exactly what both Aga and Lady Anne wanted him to do, out of caution, and so, perversely, he would not do it.

And then there was the protocol. Different men had to be treated differently. Michael allowed himself to be guided by old Lord Clayton in this, but it was very, very irksome to him—a further chain, binding and suppressing his natural instincts. There were nights when he could just barely refrain from kicking some boring nincompoop of a Lord down the front steps.

And then there was the business of the Honourable Rosalind Henly-Dex. She was the tall blonde mask with the small, plump, sensual face who had come to the Mansion with Lord Crewe's party. She was a descendant of an old Norman family originally called Des Aix, and she was a wild, crazy woman, nearly thirty and not yet married, running loose with play-actors and boxers—her activities cynically overlooked by relatives because she was an heiress and they stood to profit, and also by the man she had been promising to marry for three years, Lord Blackton. She began to come to the Mansion alone, masked. Michael danced and frolicked with her, and after two or three times it grew to be a scandal. And finally Lord Clayton took Michael aside and warned him that under no circumstances was he to let anything serious happen. "Am I a schoolboy, Lord Clayton?" cried Michael, furious. And the old Lord replied: "There are too many eyes on this establishment now."

And so Michael fenced with Miss Rosalind Henly-Dex, and she grew furiously angry at him and then vindictive, and then one night Lord Blackton came in and made a great scene, and Michael would have hit him on the jaw except that Clonmel succeeded in tripping Michael just in time and, with the help of Trim and some others, got him into the little card-room. "A duel with Blackie?" cried Clonmel. "Oh, no! He's an utter clown. You'd kill him, Michael; and he has the ear of Lord Glen and Crewe himself. Lightly, lad, lightly."

It was just one more thing added to all the others. Michael did not enjoy the taste of his pride as he swallowed it.

Some time later he had a great row with Aga over nothing at all, and after a few moments of it Aga cried: "Then why did you marry me?"

Like a fool, Michael replied: "Because you are Doherty's daughter and wanted settling."

And Aga's castle fell down in one moment, and she was a wild, footloose, unwanted girl in her heart again, and she contemplated flight for a long time until she looked about her and saw this lovely habitat she had created, with everything in its place and Princey in his little basket looking worried over the loud voices, and dinner to be arranged, and Mary to be spoken to about her drinking, and a new rug to be bought for the drawing-room, and the big bedroom's curtains to be cleaned and aired—and suddenly she realized that she was trapped, as trapped as Michael himself. And instead of sliding down a drain-pipe or getting good and drunk with a ready fool like Shanley, she ran across the hallway and put herself at the mercy of Lady Anne, who was the nearest thing to a mother she'd ever had.

To Aga's great relief and delight, Lady Anne laughed at her comfortably and said: "Aga, this is nothing, nothing at all. Pay no attention to what he says in anger. He's a wild-headed young man. Loosen the rein on him and take off the curb bit. Listen to me. I kept Doherty for eighteen years, and a man was never kept yet by a gradual tightening of the reins; or if kept, he was a poisoned soul, and not worth keeping. Stop going to the Mansion at odd hours. It makes him furious. Doherty would have smacked me soundly in like circumstances. Michael's a man, Aga, not a child. Stop mothering him."

Aga listened carefully and finally said: "Then you don't think he meant . . ."

"Men never know what they mean," said Lady Anne. "They just lash out at times—like tied-up bulls. Perhaps I could take a lesson myself. If we both stop talking about closing the Mansion, maybe he will close it. It's time, Aga. Believe me. It's time. Doherty wouldn't have thought of running it this long at one stretch. And Doherty wasn't nearly as much in the public eye as Michael."

And so in a sense Lady Anne and Aga conspired against Michael; but it did not work out quite as they had expected.

Michael misunderstood. It could be raining pitchforks and still Aga made no mention of his wearing a heavy coat. She no longer appeared at the Mansion at odd hours; in fact, she no longer appeared there at all, and never spoke of it at home. She did not even notice his drinking at table, which had seemed to annoy her so at first—wine, yes; but not raw spirits. Michael, perversely, felt abandoned.

And then one night Big Tom appeared at the servants' entrance of the Mansion and insisted he must have a hurried word with Captain Martin. They went into the card-room together.

"Captain," said Big Tom, "I know I shouldn't be coming here, but I took every precaution. I'm afraid you're being watched."

Michael brushed this aside. "Watched? For why? It's no secret we're running."

"These are bad times, Captain. Trouble, trouble in the back country, and even in Dublin. Dragoons were stoned along the quays last night in Nighttown."

"What has that to do with me?"

"You're a member, Captain. I'm a member, and the Castle has hired a new flock of narks, some from the Liverpool Irish. And that's why I'm here. I was hoping you'd come to me. I sent you a note."

"I know," said Michael wearily. "But I've been so damned busy buying candles."

Big Tom stared at him in amazement. "Candles?"

"Oh, everything," cried Michael, waving his arms in a violent gesture. "I've been busy, Tom; too busy to think, or even live, you might say."

"I know, I know," Big Tom replied, understanding finally. "With me it's the same, running Nine Steps. Well, Captain; we have a rumour that Clagett has crossed over with a Hunyok bravo of the name of Villona, a real murderous fellow. . . ."

"Clagett, is it?" cried Michael, bristling, remembering Doherty's words.

"It's only a rumour as yet," said Big Tom, "but I wanted you to know. He's the smartest and slipperiest of narks, and the Castle's used him many times when the troubles got bad. He must have expected great difficulty or he wouldn't have brought Villona with him. Villona would cut Clagett's throat for a guinea or two. I've got Tuer O'Brien and Willie the Goat searching the stews for word of him, a couple of lovely fellows of the Clagett stripe, but with us heart and soul. And Mahony's seen the light."

"Mahony?" cried Michael.

"He's given up his singing, his harp, and his caution. Clagett is a man he really hates, since the doing in of Doherty. Mahony will be a help. He's a great swordsman, in spite of his age and bad sight. But better yet, he would not be suspected like O'Brien and Willie. If he finds Clagett, good-bye to our nautical friend. And now I must go."

Michael reached out and shook hands with him, and Big Tom was mightily pleased by the gesture.

"At your service always, Captain," he said. "I hope I was not twigged coming here. Dublin is swarming with narks. Good night, Captain."

Big Tom bowed awkwardly and withdrew. Michael fell down into a chair and poured himself a drink. He felt restless, dissatisfied, not himself at all; and as he sipped his whisky, he wished to God that Doherty had not died and left him with all these unaccustomed problems on his hands.

IT WAS only a few nights later, about eleven o'clock and raining very hard, when Michael was called to the card-room because of visitors. As he opened the door, there was Aloysius Brady in a wet greatcoat, and Michael let out a yell of welcome that could be heard in the front salon, and noticing an odd, sly expression on Brady's face, he turned . . . and there, big as life, was Tim Keenan, grinning all over his loutish face, his straw-coloured hair on end as usual and a good familiar smell of home-made Ballymore whisky about him. Michael yelled louder than before, and then he pummelled poor Tim about the room till finally Tim fell over a chair and sat on the floor laughing. Roaring with laughter, Michael rang grandly and ordered supper for two and champagne for three.

Tim rose to his feet now and stood staring at Michael as if seeing him for the first time, and he stared at him and stared hard, his big mouth open slightly; and then he fell down into a chair and said: "Why, the Master himself—Devereaux—never looked more lordly. Is it really you, Mick?"

"It's him right enough," said Brady, "and don't let the fine clothes and the lordly air put you off—it's still Seumas Martin's son Mick."

But Tim was overawed and had an attack of embarrassment, and when Michael looked at him, he grinned feebly and flushed. But Tim soon thawed.

And Michael felt so happy that he whistled in between talking and jumped up a dozen times and sat down again, and clapped both Brady and Tim on the shoulder; and there was a great, mad clamour as they all talked at once and nobody listened, till Brady finally said: "No one would think we were here on serious business, to hear us. We are more like Lords waiting for our supper. One point, Mick. I came here directly. I didn't consult with Big Tom. Was that all right? I knew where to find you, so . . ."

Michael waved him to silence. "Of course. Of course. Don't give it a thought. And now here's supper, and dive in, and I'll drink the champagne with you as you go along. I've eaten."

Two liveried waiters arranged a table for three, and Tim's eyes grew to saucers as he stared at the beautiful china, the silver, the candelabra with the tall candles, the napery, the frosted silver wine buckets, and the crystal goblets. And he stared open-mouthed as the foreign waiters moved about with "*Oui, monsieur,*" and "*Ah, ah, allez!*" and "*Bon appetit, Capitaine et messieurs. . . .*"

And then he looked at the food set before him with true country suspiciousness, and noticing this, Michael began to laugh and said: "Eat, eat. It's all French food here, and sauces, sauces, till a piece of undisguised fat pork seems like the greatest treat in the world."

"Just so there's no frogs nor snails," said Tim, pushing his food about with a fork.

Brady roared at him: "Eat, man, eat. It's poor manners to look a gift horse in the mouth."

Finally Tim began to eat, and at the first bite a look of wonder spread over his wide face, and he tasted again with the same result, and then he dove in with a will and the food disappeared from his plate as if by trickery, and he said: "Be Gob, it's not the Bonnie Prince Charlie, but it's stranger, Mick, stranger." But the champagne was something else again. At the first sip he gave a jump, tried it once more, then put down his glass. "Why," he said, "it's weak beer that tickles your nose. This is a temperance beverage, Mick?"

Brady, grimacing, told Tim the price per bottle, and Tim almost fell off the chair in surprise. "Yerra, when you drink this stuff, you could say: 'Now I drink my red cow. And here goes my new black shoat, and old Charlie, the plough horse—and there goes the money in the crock for the rainy day.' It's sinful," he cried, grinning broadly, and drinking a glass down at one swallow.

Michael poured him another, and Brady said: "Bubbly, the bloody Saxons call it, and be damned to 'em. I'll take whisky."

So Michael got a quart of Dublin whisky from a cabinet and put it on the table within easy reach, and they drank one noggin after another, using the champagne for a chaser, and pretty soon, as the waiters were clearing away the remains and bringing dessert, Tim groaned: "Musha, that Dublin whisky's stronger than a man would think."

Brady loosened his collar and remarked: "My own thought, Tim. Seemed like wine the last time I drunk it."

And Michael, laughing to himself, kept urging them to drink more whisky with champagne chasers until Tim's mouth began to take on that familiar look of looseness, and Brady grew more and more punctilious in his behaviour.

And finally Brady got down to business and said: "Mick, we need more money."

"Good," said Michael. "How much?"

Tim lowered his head and held his hands over his ears as Brady replied: "We are deep put. We need two hundred guineas."

Without a word, Michael rose, took the amount from a drawer in the cabinet, and handed it to Brady, who tucked it away with a bow, and Tim stared open-mouthed again at Michael, and his awe returned, and he could not bring himself to say a word for some time.

"It's bad, Mick, bad," said Brady, "and the gaols of Ballymore and Blackfountain are full again. A dragoon fired into a crowd with a pistol near Blackfountain, and there was a woman shot, and a bloody riot, and the barracks at Killeen was rushed and burned to the ground. Even Regis himself is mad as a horse with a bur under its saddle. There was no use at all in the firing of that pistol; just a crowd of country folks yelling at the Lobsters. So Regis wrote a proclamation, and it's up in every market-place with his name signed to it, and now he's wanted for treason, and it's touch and go in Ballymore. The boys have got muskets hid at the monastery. Oh, it's a grand row!"

"And me *here!*" cried Michael, jumping up.

"Ay, ay," said Brady, "but you're doing a great part, Mick; though a lot of folks will not understand. Even Regis. Mick, me boy; I don't tell him where the money's from. I tell him I collect it. For why? Once

I broached it to him, and he shouted he'd have nothing to do with the wages of gaming and whoring."

Michael laughed easily. "Always the same—Regis." Nevertheless, he felt some hurt and humiliation.

"A st—st—" Tim began, but broke off. He had intended to say that Regis was a stiff-necked fellow, but he couldn't get the words out, and in surprise he picked up the whisky bottle, stared at the label, and remarked carefully and slowly: "This Dublin whisky sneaks up on a man, begor!"

Michael laughed loudly, then suddenly he sobered as a wave of melancholy swept over him and he fell to thinking of Ballymore. Was it raining there tonight? Was the peat smoke rising slowly in the damp air? Were the streams high and muddy with the rain and singing softly as they moved through the low fields? Was the moss still on the old stone wall by the Bonnie Prince Charlie? Was the old town tramp-dog, Wellington, still looking for his morning hand-out at Keogh's butcher shop? Did old Jimmie O'Hare still light the lamp at the corner at sundown? Was Buffer still roaming the fields and guarding the O'Herlihy cattle from harm?

And suddenly he blurted out: "And how's my Catherine?"

There was a perceptible, jarred silence. In a moment Tim Keenan's big mouth opened for a word, but Brady stamped on his foot under the table, and Michael did not miss this.

"Well? Well?" cried Michael impatiently. "And what the devil is this?"

"We're under oath to say nothing," Tim said quickly. "Hand of God! We're under oath, Mick. We swore, and swore."

"Imbecile!" snapped Brady.

Michael looked from one to the other angrily. "I'm good enough to take money from, is that it? But not good enough to trust."

Tim stammered incoherently as he saw that familiar look in Michael's blue eyes, but Brady said: "Man, man, we're under oath. The oath is not against you, Mick. But against everybody. Everybody except those who know—a mere handful. It's an iron oath. You could cut my heart out."

"Not against me, then?" asked Michael, somewhat mollified, but worried.

"Against the world, you might say," said Brady with a drunken gesture that took even himself by surprise, and like Tim he looked narrowly at the whisky bottle.

"But tell me this," Michael insisted. "Is she all right?"

"Ay," said Brady. "Worried about Regis, but all right otherwise."

"In health?"

"Ay, ay."

"No troubles in the family? No deaths?"

"No, no, Mick," cried Brady. "Now let up, for the love of God!"

There was a tap at the door, and Lady Anne came in, and Tim almost swooned at the sight of this queenly woman with the plume and the jewels in her golden hair, and then he jumped up and tried to efface himself in a corner.

"Oh, excuse me, Michael," she said, "I thought you were just with one of the men. I'll not bother you."

"What is it, Anne?" asked Michael.

"Excuse me, gentlemen," said Lady Anne graciously. "It's Clonmel. He's in for two hundred guineas, and is strapped, he says."

"There is no limit to Clonmel's credit," said Michael.

"All right," said Lady Anne. "Sorry, gentlemen." She went out, closing the door quietly.

Tim stared, stupefied.

"Clonmel, is it?" cried Brady. "Why, that's the rascally Earl of Aire's son."

"Yes," said Michael.

"And you associate with such?"

"He games here. He's a friend of mine."

Brady was drunk. He rose so abruptly he almost overturned the table. "A bloody ruffian is what the Earl is, and I have a thought his son's no better. Friend, is he?"

"Aloysius," Tim put in meekly.

But Michael waved him to silence. "Patrick is not political. He has nothing against the Irish people. You are bailing out the boys with the money of Clonmel and others worse, you ass, Brady. Do you want me to pitch you through the window?"

Brady thought this over for a while, running his hand through his curly dark hair, then he said: "Mick, it's that damned Dublin whisky and the foreign bubbly! Man, what am I thinking of? It's a great joke on the Saxons to bail the boys out with their bloody money wrenched from the soil of Ireland. Ha! Ha! Ha!" And he dissolved into laughter, then had a choking spell.

While this was going on, Tim asked meekly: "And the great Lorelei who was just in?"

"In a sense, she's my mother-in-law," said Michael indifferently.

"Then I'd love to see the missus," said Tim.

"All right," cried Michael. "Come home with me."

"No, no," said Brady quickly. "We must leave at once. Take advantage of the night. We'll be well on our way by dawn."

They drank a toast to Ireland and joined arms all around, and then they shook hands and slapped backs profusely at the door.

"And Catherine's all right?" asked Michael.

"Ay, ay," said Brady, quickly, and rather furtively, Michael thought, and he wanted to detain them, but they got away from him at last, and he stood looking after them until they had disappeared at the back of the Mansion.

"There is something wrong," Michael told himself. "Something very wrong."

At two o'clock he took Lady Anne aside: "Anne, we're closing tonight. I've got business to look after."

"And it's about time," she was going to say, but thought better of it, fearing that such a statement might change Michael's mind, as his perverseness was growing more noticeable every day. "Very well," she said indifferently. "Just as you say, Michael. DeLane will tell the help."

"Ay," said Michael absent-mindedly.

LADY ANNE went home first, Michael staying to make a final check with DeLane. When Michael got home, Aga was waiting for him, beautifully dressed and smiling, and he noted that Princey was wearing a new collar, and that Mary was almost sober for once, which was more than could be said for him.

What he did not know was that Lady Anne had primed Aga. "There is something on his mind, Aga. Two strangers came to see him, countrymen by the look of them. One of them smelled of cow-stables.

I'm certain he made up his mind to close after talking to them. He's in a bad state. Don't oppose him."

And Aga, though it was a great wrench to her, did not oppose Michael in his plan to go away for a few days; in fact, she seemed rather indifferent, and Michael studied her ironically as she sat fondling Princey, and displaying the little dog's new collar she'd bought that day, and talking of nothing at great length.

And as Michael fell wearily into bed, he said to himself: "Ah, God, it's time I got away from this prison for a while, not that anybody cares!"

No, Aga did not oppose him, but she cried quietly into her pillow after he had fallen asleep, and she knew in her heart that this was the end of the first phase of their relationship. What the second phase would be she was unable to guess, and the mystery and uncertainty upset her so that she couldn't sleep all night and only pretended to sleep for fear Mick might wake and wonder what was wrong.

But Michael found a great amount of opposition from another source: Big Tom.

"Begging your pardon, Captain," he said, in the presence of Trim, who would not commit himself, "this is the wrong time to leave Dublin. You're safe here. The Devereaux business is still a local matter, and with all the trouble in Kilkenny it will no doubt remain so. What—go to Ballymore? It's like putting your head in the lion's mouth."

But Michael, pacing impatiently, would not listen. "There's something I've got to find out," he insisted stubbornly, "and the only way I can find it out is by going back to Ballymore. It's not as if I was going to stay, for the love of God! I'll be in and out in one night."

Big Tom looked to Trim for help, but got none. "Couldn't it wait, Captain?" he begged. "New horse troops have been sent to Killeen, where there's a great bivouac to protect the men rebuilding the barracks. You might just run into one of the patrols. They tell me they're all over the countryside now, Lobsters enough to people the Irish Sea.

Please, in the name of God, wait, Captain! Maybe in a month or two—"

"A month or two?" shouted Michael, losing his temper. "Good God, Tom, can't you see how eager I am to go? I'd eat my heart out in a month or two! As for the patrols, if they jump us, Trim and I will outrun them with the horses we've got—true thoroughbreds. Doherty taught me that trick."

Big Tom groaned. "And the ambush?"

Michael snorted. "Doherty and I were ambushed. We got away clean."

Big Tom shook his head in despair. "But, Captain, times are different. There are a thousand narks in Dublin, and—"

But Michael cut him off. "Well, then, it seems that I must look for help elsewhere," and he turned on his heel and made for the door.

But moving with surprising swiftness for a man of his bulk, Big Tom intercepted him. "No, Captain. No. I only say these things for your welfare."

"To hell with my welfare!" shouted Michael, thinking of Aga.

"Will you listen to me, Captain, please?" Big Tom insisted. "If you must go, be guided by me. Two men riding cross-country at the present time will attract a lot of attention, particularly two men on thoroughbreds. You must go by coach. I'll supply the boot, the driver, and the coach. Let Trim ride as postilion, and use the two thoroughbreds for lead horses. You ride the coach, Captain. You are a lawyer, going to Waterford for the coming assizes. Dress plainly. I doubt anybody will bother such an equipage. Travel the Dublin Road openly. If there's trouble, it is no problem to unharness the thoroughbreds for you and Trim, and that will leave an innocent four-horse coach with two accredited liverymen."

"Done," cried Michael impatiently, and both Big Tom and Trim heaved sighs of relief.

"If you are not twigged by narks," said Big Tom, "all will be well."

But Michael was no longer listening. "We leave tonight," he said, then turned for the door, but at that moment a knock interrupted them and Bessa put her head in and flashed a smile at Michael.

"Well, Bessa?" called Big Tom impatiently.

"It's Mahony, sir, and two others. Could they step in for a moment?"

Big Tom glanced at Michael, who nodded; then Bessa opened the door wide, and old Mahony, wearing a cutlass, stepped in, followed by two dirty, villainous-looking fellows, who were deeply abashed in Michael's presence and touched their forelocks and jerked their heads in nervous, slavish bows. They were Tuer O'Brien and Willie the Goat. Tuer was a big, bulky man with a big, pale face, flat as a plate, and a broken nose; his oddly shaped head was bald on top but ringed round by a thick fringe of grizzled hair; his right leg was off at the knee, and he wore a sturdy, padded peg. He had been in and out of the King's Navy since his fourteenth year. He had once been a pirate, it was said, and he had a great reputation in the stews as a bloody ruffian. Willie the Goat smelled like one. He was a short man with wide shoulders, a barrel chest, and bandy legs. There was something shaggy, wild, and animal-like about him. His hair was fire-red, coarse as the stuffing of a sofa, and grew to a point not over an inch and a half above his eyebrows; he had little, squinting, pig-like eyes, and when he laughed he showed a row of big, strong, yellow teeth with sharply pointed canines. In comparison with these two, Mahony looked like a tired, clean, aristocratic old eagle.

"Well, Mahony?" said Michael.

"It's about Clagett," said Mahony, as the other two men, still abashed, moved into the background. "We ran him down, in a manner of speaking. He's been living in a basement in Blackpool Alley with the foreign fellow, Villona. We near had him. But he's fled—maybe back to Liverpool, maybe to another alley, which is more likely. Jimmie Wren is still looking while we come here. We'll have him, Captain, unless we've scared him away for good."

"It's all one," said Big Tom, "as long as we're rid of him."

"Oh, no," said Mahony. "It's not all one, begging your pardon, Tom. The man must be sliced, then Doherty will sleep quiet."

"Ay! And I'm the boy to slice him," cried Willie the Goat with sudden boldness. "I'll slice him for cat-meat." He laughed loudly.

"At least he's on the run," said Big Tom, "and that will interfere with his narking mightily."

"Ay," said Mahony. "But he's very slippery and acute. I'll breathe easier when he's done in."

And both Tuer O'Brien and Willie agreed with loud, savage cries.

Michael took a purse from his pocket and handed the three men some guineas. Mahony pocketed his calmly, with perfect self-possession, but the other two men grovelled and clutched at the money. "Why, it's gold, Tuer," cried Willie, chuckling. "Gold guineas—and I an't seen one in ages. Oh, we'll slice him for you, sir. Never fear." Willie pulled out his cutlass and flourished it. "Death to all Castle narks!" he shouted hoarsely. "And a hip, hip, huzzah for the people of Ireland!"

Tuer gave a loud cheer and stumped about nervously on his peg. Mahony, a little embarrassed by the loudness of his companions, at last ushered them out.

Big Tom hurried over and threw open the windows. "The place needs air after that twosome," he said, chuckling. "But they're the boys for it. Narks themselves, of course, but double-duty narks, as you might say, robbing Peter to pay Paul. They've never twigged a man important to us yet; only the drifting riff-raff of the quays."

Michael, Trim, and Big Tom settled on their plans, then Michael shook hands with Tom, and he and Trim went out and moved towards the stairs. Trim stared at what he saw, then turned to look at Michael. The stairs were packed with men from top to bottom. They were all pressed back against the wall, making room for Michael to descend, and at his appearance they all uncovered and began to cheer for him. Loud cheers rang out all through the corridors of Nine Steps.

Michael felt both embarrassment and exhilaration, and as he went down the stairs, he smiled and nodded and shook a dirty hand here and there to wild cheers. At the foot of the stairs Mahony, Tuer, and Willie were waiting, and when Michael reached the lower level, Willie waved his cutlass and screamed: "And hip, hip, huzzah for Captain Martin himself!"

Trim had his lips compressed and showed deep concern as they crossed the back courtyard to their coach. "It was not Doherty's way," he said as if to himself.

Michael turned to glance at him. "What was not?"

"Captain," said Trim, "it's too open. You're too well known. It makes talk in Dublin, the talkingest place on the face of the earth. It gripes the Castle to hear such talk."

"Oh, damn the Castle!" said Michael as they got into the coach.

MICHAEL AND AGA said good-bye in the entrance hall at the apartment. Trim and Lady Anne had gone outside to leave them alone together, and Mary had disappeared into the kitchen, weeping. Only Princey looked on. Sensitive, like all pet dogs, to the emotions of the humans nearest him, he knew that this was not just an ordinary leave-taking, and he was worried, and he moved about restlessly at their feet, trying to attract their attention.

"I should be back in a week," said Michael, feeling more than a little awkward with Aga, who, very much upset, was overdoing her attitude of indifference.

"Oh?" said Aga. "It's not much of a trip, then."

"No, nothing at all. A mere jaunt."

But Aga was remembering "mere jaunts" of Doherty's that had extended to months, and almost a year once. He'd set out for Scotland, and the next they heard of him, months later, he was in Antwerp and wrote sparely in a maddeningly uninformative letter that he intended going on to Paris, then Rome. There had been a "little difficulty."

"Just a week, you say?" she inquired as if making conversation to fill in a gap of silence. Actually, she wanted to weep and fling herself into his arms and beg him not to go, or, if he must, to take her with him.

"Two at most," said Michael, who was finding it much more difficult to leave Aga than he had thought. But on the other hand, the girl seemed to make nothing of the parting at all. It was as if he were setting out for the Mansion of an evening, as he'd done for so many months.

"Well," he said vaguely; then he bent down and patted Princey on the head. At least the little white fellow seemed distressed.

"Well," said Aga, wishing he would go at once so she wouldn't break down and cry and make a bothersome fool of herself. "We . . . we've never been apart before, Mick," she couldn't help saying. "Not even for one night. It will seem strange."

"Yes," said Michael, glancing at her hopefully. "Very strange."

"But then," said Aga hurriedly, "it will probably be good for us.

I . . . I sometimes think perhaps we were seeing too much of each other . . . I mean, constantly. Sort of getting on each other's nerves."

"Yes," said Michael, freezing. "You are probably right. Now I should go."

They stood looking at each other for a moment, and during the silence Princey got up on his hind legs and did his only trick, walking about with awkward little hops, trying to get them to pay some attention to him.

"Well," said Michael, then he leaned forward and kissed Aga on the cheek, then the mouth.

Aga's lips were cool and unresponsive.

"Well," said Michael, drawing back; then he turned quickly and went out, slamming the door.

Aga stared at the door for a long time, struggling for control, then she picked up Princey and ran with him to her room, where she locked the door, burst out into wild sobs, and flung herself across the bed. At first Princey was appalled, but finally he lay down beside her and kept glancing about him warily as if some danger threatened his mistress and he was resolutely prepared for it.

AT DAWN the next morning the coach was a long way from Dublin and rolling southward easily over the King's Highway. Michael, in dark blue, well but conservatively dressed, a little bored at being alone in the coach, kept looking about him for landmarks, remembering his uneasy journey northward more or less along this route with Doherty, a stranger to him then. God, how far back in time that seemed now; another age. And then, all at once, he recalled himself as a staring, befuddled country boy watching a great Lord passing northward in his coach as he himself was now passing southward. How he had envied the man dozing carelessly in a corner, leaving the normal worries of travel to the help and the horses, and probably dreaming of his mansion in Dublin. And now Michael laughed at his own innocence. The fellow was probably no more a Lord than himself, and was dozing from exhaustion or drink, and was dreading his return to Dublin and to the responsibilities he'd left behind him earlier. If Michael had learned nothing else, he had learned at least two excellent things: not to trust appearances, and not to envy any man. Gold braid did not mean a full pocket; and a smiling face often hid a troubled spirit. Little by little, he was acquiring Doherty's scepticism—but not his contempt for others: that he would never acquire, if he lived to be a hundred.

He heard a shout and looked out. The country up ahead seemed to be swarming with steel-helmeted, red-coated dragoons. It looked like a full regiment of cavalry crossing the King's Highway along a side-road. Long horizontal clouds of dust, raised by hundreds of hoofs, lay over the tree-tops in the windless day. Even over the rattle of the coach and the hoofbeats of his horses, Michael could hear the sinister clanking of accoutrements. The driver, a little monkey-faced man from Nighttown, leaned down and shouted:

"And what do we do, Captain?"

Michael replied: "We go through. Tell Trim to shout for a path."

Trim, who was riding postilion, turned at a shout from the driver, then smiled grimly and nodded.

Michael leaned back, chuckling to himself. Boldness! That was Doherty's way. What was the phrase Doherty was always repeating in Frog? Ah, yes. Toojoors lowdass! And how had he translated it? Always be reckless! And he'd gone on to explain: It either takes them by great surprise, or puts them to sleep. Either way you've got the jump.

He heard Trim hollering and put his head out. "Make way for the Lord Advocate. Make way!"

And an officer outrider came clanking sideways on his horse and bawled out a string of orders, and the silly Lobsters made a path for the coach, which tore across the side-road with Trim still bawling, and the little driver flourishing his whip, and the boot saluting smartly from his stand in back; and then Michael leaned out and waved his thanks, and the officer saluted briskly with sword hilt at chin, and then the coach and the great moving body of cavalry were lost to each other in a cloud of dust.

A little later the driver almost lost control of the horses from laughing; and the boot was doubled up on his stand and in danger of falling to the road; and Trim's shoulders were shaking as he whipped up the horses to put as much distance as possible between the coach and the soldiers just in case one of the officers might begin to wonder why the Lord Advocate (whatever that was!) was in such a thundering hurry in broad day.

"Ah, Doherty!" cried Michael, roaring with laughter.

Toojoors lowdass!

It was almost night—gloaming, you might say—with lights in the farm windows and a heavy stillness over the countryside when Michael, now riding up ahead with Trim on the thoroughbreds, guided the coach to the old ruined monastery a short distance from Ballymore.

The owls, the real owls, were hooting mournfully in among the great fallen moss-covered stones, and the bluish will-o'-the-wisp was flicking across the dark bog just beyond, and Bennett, the driver, and Moore, the boot, city men both, looked about them uneasily at this obviously haunted spot, and crossed themselves, muttering.

They drew the coach back inside the shelter of a standing wall, and then the horses were fed and watered, and finally the men sat down to eat the food they'd brought with them. Michael sat by himself on a fallen stone. He had long since stopped trying to make a democrat of Trim. It was useless, and it made Trim nervous and unhappy. Trim sat a short distance off, eating and occasionally inquiring in a respectful voice if Michael wanted anything. Bennett and Moore sat by themselves quite some distance off, talking in low tones and looking over their shoulders as the owls hooted among the ruins.

At a little after eight, Bennett saddled Michael's horse, and Michael mounted and talked to Trim, who stood at the horse's head.

"Be saddled and ready, Trim. We'll be leaving as soon as I'm through, which shouldn't be long. If there is a change in my plan,

I'll let you know right away. I'd put the horses to the coach now, and have the boys ready."

"Yes, sir," said Trim. "We'll be ready."

"If there's any trouble," said Michael, "not that I expect any, let the boys look after themselves and the coach. It's nothing one way or another if they're taken, and there is no sense in getting them killed. Don't worry, Trim. I am only following Doherty's lead, trying to think of contingencies. I expect no trouble."

"Ay," said Trim. "And a very wise way to look at things, sir. It was indeed Doherty's way."

Michael rode off in the darkness with a gesture of au revoir.

AT EIGHT THIRTY Tim Keenan went out to see why his two old dogs were barking so, and started back wildly at the sight of a shadowy man on horseback in the dooryard. He had heard no one. Ghoulish stories of riding phantoms and headless horsemen flashed through his mind, and he was on the point of running back into the house when Michael spoke in a low voice.

"Tim! It's Mick."

Tim was trembling. "I know no Mick hereabouts who rides a tall horse such as that."

"It's Michael Martin."

"Oh, God!" cried Tim. "Have they killed you, then, Mick—and you come back to haunt me?"

"Damn it, man—I'm more alive than you are."

But Tim couldn't take it in. "I saw you sitting in that beautiful house only a day or two ago. Mick, Mick—go away. Go to your father. He will know what to say to you."

Michael reached out suddenly and slashed Tim with his whip, and at that Tim began to laugh and dance about in glee. "That's Mick. That's my boy. He's alive."

"Keep it down, for the love of God, man. I had to see you. I'm only here for an hour or two."

Tim came over now and rested his hand on the stirrup. "An hour or two? What are you doing back here, Mick? You're wanted bad by the Lobsters. There are new posters up. Just put up yesterday, fresh from the printers."

"Damn the Lobsters. I must see Catherine."

Tim was near to crying now. "Oh, no, Mick. No. You can't do that. Stay away from the O'Herlihy farm. I beg you, Mick."

"What's wrong, then? Tell me what's wrong?"

"I can't. It's an oath I've taken. I'd fry in hell if I broke my oath. Just don't go, Mick. Don't go."

"I came all the way to see Catherine, Tim," cried Michael, "and I'll see her in spite of the devil. I have a feeling there's something wrong, mighty wrong. I must see her. Good-bye, Tim."

He wheeled his horse and rode off into the darkness, the sound of the hoofbeats almost inaudible in the springy, damp ground.

Tim stood there blinking and rubbing his hand across his face. "Did I see him? Did I hear that? Or am I dreaming? It was a ghost, I think, and poor Mick's dead in Dublin—and his spirit has wandered back home to Ballymore." And then suddenly he remembered the harsh lash of the whip. "Oh, God!" he cried. "He mustn't go there." Then he set off at a run through the Keenan orchard towards the O'Herlihy farm.

MICHAEL DISMOUNTED in the O'Herlihy dooryard and led his horse around to the back of the house. All the lights were out—it was like that other time, ages ago, and his heart was pounding loudly. But where was Buffer? He looked about him for a long time, and listened. But there wasn't a sound in the night.

Picking up a handful of pebbles, he tossed them at Catherine's window, then he waited. Far off now he could hear the jug-jug-jug of the frogs and the whirring of insects in the grass. And then his heart almost stopped beating as a white form appeared at the window and a blurred white face peered out into the night.

Catherine!

He put his face close to the window and tapped on it with his forefinger. It was Catherine, all right; he could see that lovely forehead and the dark hair in braids as before. But she shrank away in horror and waved violently for him to go away. Michael couldn't understand this, and kept tapping gently and gesturing for her to raise the window. She seemed to be crying now, and she kept motioning for him to go away.

Then Michael heard a dog barking some distance off in the direction of the cow-barns, and then the sound of a man running frantically towards the house came to his ears, startling him—and then all was confusion as the front door opened and slammed and Buffer came rushing at him across the grass and Tim Keenan appeared, puffing and blowing, through the trees of the O'Herlihy orchard and fell gasping at his feet.

Buffer stopped suddenly and began to sniff.

"Buffer, Buffer, old boy," called Michael. A dim flash of candlelight showed somewhere in the O'Herlihy house, and Michael wondered with a curse if old John was going to show up again with the blunderbuss—and then Buffer licked his hand, and Tim gasped: "Oh, God, Mick—you may have ruined everything."

And at that moment the window was banged up, and Michael saw that there was a man inside Catherine's room and it wasn't her father, nor yet one of her brothers—and then he started back and stared. Regis Donnell!

"Go away, Martin," cried Regis angrily. "Go away."

Martin, was it? What was this cold formality all of a sudden? And why in the devil was Regis Donnell in Catherine's bedroom, and her in her night-dress?

"What in God's name are you doing here, Regis?" he cried.

"I'm where I belong. Mind your own affairs, you meddler, and go back to Dublin and leave us in peace."

"Catherine, Catherine," called Michael, all at sea. "Where are you? What's going on?"

Catherine appeared for a moment beside Regis, a vague white figure. "Go away, Mick. It's a secret. Please, for my sake, go away!"

And then Regis blurted out angrily: "We're married, man! And I'm hiding here—and that's the secret, and now are you satisfied, you swaggering Dublin bravo?"

Michael was stunned, then angry. "Dublin bravo, is it? A low fellow not up to your mark, eh? All right, then, why do you take my money?"

"What money, you ass?" shouted Regis.

"Why, the three hundred guineas I gave to Brady. Three hundred guineas, Regis Donnell. That's a lot of gold."

There was a blank silence, then Tim, still on the grass, groaned in the darkness.

"Ah, Brady," said Regis in distress. "I thought his collecting was a bit too much on the easy side."

There was another long silence, then Michael called out: "Are you happy, girl?"

And Catherine's voice came from the darkness: "Yes, I'm happy, Mick. Very happy." All the same, it sounded to him as if she were crying.

"I owe you an apology, Martin," said Regis quietly. "Yes, I apologize. Good God, where did you get three hundred guineas?"

Michael laughed contemptuously. "Three hundred guineas, is it? I could put my hand on ten thousand if you need it. But you wouldn't take my money, would you, Regis? It's not good money. You'd rather take it from a tenant farmer or a shoe-maker or maybe a poor tinker, wandering the roads."

"Mick!" Catherine protested from the darkness.

"Oh, you're a stiff-necked fellow," Michael went on. "It's all principle with you, if you hang for it; you and the others. And what of those you're fighting? Are your enemies so high-principled, then? You know the answer. But you'd rather go down to defeat and keep your soul clean and to hell with everybody else."

"Yes, Mick, I would," said Regis quietly.

"And he's right," called Catherine from the darkness.

"Yes, yes, he's right," cried Tim, only to mollify Michael, as Tim was hardly aware of what was being said.

Michael put back his head and laughed loudly. "Oh, to the devil with all of you!" he said vehemently. "I'm going back to Dublin. That's where I belong. And not with the likes of the two-shilling lot of you. Good-bye, now."

He turned, mounted his horse, and rode off towards the orchard and a short-cut he knew back to the monastery. Tim ran along beside him and grabbed the stirrup. "Mick, Mick; I'm coming with you."

"Get up behind, then," called Michael, and Tim flung himself up onto the horse and wrapped his long arms about Michael's waist.

"Why didn't you tell me he was hiding there?" Michael demanded.

"I couldn't, Mick. I couldn't. It was the oath."

"Oh, damn you and your silly oath. Wait!" Michael pulled his horse up abruptly and sat listening. "Did you hear something? I thought I heard a cry or a shout somewhere back there through the trees."

"I heard nothing," said Tim, weary, confused, wanting to be home in bed and to hell with all this ho-lo-boloo!

Finally Michael rode off, reassured by the throbbing silence, carefully picking his way through the narrow aisles of the orchard.

"When did this happen, Tim?"

"What, Mick?"

"The marriage, you fool!"

"Not more than ten days ago. It was Catherine who insisted. You see, John O'Herlihy has always been a solid, conservative man, a friend to Angus Desmond and to Lord Devereaux. What better place for Regis to hide?"

"Yes—but what about old John?"

"The shooting at Blackfountain changed his mind. He's as rabid as you like now, Mick; though he keeps it to himself and is still considered solid by the gentry. They fixed a place for Regis out by the cow-barns, with Buffer to guard him. He never leaves the place now, biding his time."

Michael groaned. "If you'd only told me! Letting me walk into the hornets' nest. Are you sure you heard nothing awhile back?"

"I heard nothing."

They were emerging from the utter darkness of the orchard now. The moon was not up yet, but stars were winking warmly in the velvet blackness of the sky. Spurring his horse suddenly, Michael took a low fence just beyond the orchard, and Tim, cursing, almost fell off backward when they landed.

"Yerra!" cried Tim. "What a horse you're riding here, Mick; takes two over the jumps with no effort at all—although you near lost me at the hurdle! Tell me what's coming, man."

But there were no more fences, and in a short while Michael rode into Tim's dooryard and let him off; then he reached down to shake hands. "Good-bye, Tim," said Michael. "And it may be for good. I doubt very much I'll ever be back."

"Aren't you going to see your family, Mick?"

After a moment of thought, Michael said: "No. It would be too painful all around. Explanations, explanations. It's best, I think, to leave Seumas and the others in peace. The place has never been home to me, in any case, since the auld patch, Kathleen, died and was planted in the Ballymore churchyard."

"Well, then," said Tim, feeling very sad and disturbed, "good-bye to you, Mick, and good luck. I'll pray for you, Mick. It's the best I can do."

Michael laughed curtly, not liking the sentimentality, particularly as he was feeling very low and sentimental himself. "Pray for yourself, Tim, and for Catherine, the poor girl! She's in trouble."

"We're all in trouble," cried Tim. "It's not like it used to be here, Mick, in your time. We are always hearing there are informers about, and it's making people suspicious of each other—and most people keep to their houses unless there's urgent business to look after. The Bonnie Prince Charlie's half empty at night, and there's no singing as in your day. Old Angus never comes near town now, but shuts himself up in the manor and sends one of the English flunkeys. Bad times, Mick, bad times. The monastery used to be fun, chasing the 'Owls' among the rocks while the orators made their damned silly speeches. But now it's all serious, like a Mass, and the 'Owls' are the most serious of the lot. There's muskets hid and powder and God knows what! I'd ship out for Liverpool if I had the nerve and the money, but since I've got neither . . ." Tim waved a despairing hand in the darkness.

"Well, then, good-bye, Tim," said Michael, "and we'll all pray for each other if it's as you say. Good-bye again."

He rode off into the darkness with a heavy heart, and Tim stood watching him go with his two old dogs beside him and at his back the whitewashed cottage with its dark windows and its look of abandonment in the night.

Michael felt a sudden presentiment of evil as he rode back towards the monastery, skirting the northern edges of the great bog. There was a marked hush over the whole countryside, a sort of waiting stillness that bothered Michael to such an extent that he took out a handkerchief and mopped his brow. "Acting like an auld woman afraid of the devil at night," he muttered, and then he felt tears in his eyes, and suddenly, in spite of all he could do, he was weeping. "Oh, God above!" he cried; then he tried to laugh. "If Doherty could see me now! I hope he's not looking, but is busy enjoying himself wherever he may be."

But the laughter was wry, and he stopped trying to force it, and finally wiped his eyes with a curse. Ah, well! It was a difficult thing to say good-bye to your birthplace for ever, and to Catherine—gone, gone . . . a worried woman now, and no longer the laughing, teasing girl he remembered. She belonged to Regis and had taken his problems on her slender shoulders. Catherine, good-bye!

And as he rode along, he began to hum the "Bride of Mourne," and then suddenly he stopped humming, remembering all at once Aga, Lady Anne, Princey, the comfortable home in Dublin . . . the thousands of guineas in the strong-box . . . Lord Clayton, Clonmel, and the dancing and gaming and merriment. . . .

And so he took off his hat and bowed in the direction of shadowy Ballymore, sleeping its nightly sleep—all dark except for Jimmie O'Hare's lamp at the corner and the pleasant yellow glow from the windows of the Bonnie Prince Charlie—and into the darkness he called: "Good-bye, all. And now good-bye. It's Mick Martin speaking, and I'm going back where I belong."

And then suddenly a pistol was fired beyond the monastery, and Michael saw a faint red glow in the night, and without a pause to reflect, he leaped his horse into a gallop and rode off at right angles to his former course, skirting the back of the monastery and avoiding the bog by skilful riding in a district familiar to him since childhood. No one could follow him here, and yet almost at once he heard some fools on horseback plunging after him, and then cries of dismay and the soggy sound of a horse falling on the treacherous soft ground, and then more cries and clanking, and suddenly a ragged volley was fired after him, and Michael felt a sledge-hammer blow in the back part of his right thigh and nearly fell from his horse.

"Hit like Doherty, damn it," he cried, and then he spurred his horse into a wild gallop, took a low hedge cleanly, and was free at last on the far side of the monastery in open flat country which stretched for miles sloping easily down towards the Dublin Road.

And now over the tall trees to the eastward the moon rose big and white, and far away across the flat meadowland Michael could make out a lone horseman riding all out in his own direction and along a parallel course. Was it to head him off? He cleared his coat-skirts so that he could get at his sword if necessary, and wishing to God he'd brought a cutlass, he reached for his pistols, one by one, and slipped them into the pommel holsters, ready for action—spurring his horse from time to time to keep him going.

Now, all settled at last, he leaned forward over his horse's neck and talked to him, urging him on, trying to outdistance the rider far to his left, but his endeavours were useless; the other horseman kept his place, and finally Michael said to himself: "And what the devil kind of horse is the fellow riding!" and then a thought struck him. Trim! It must be Trim on the big roan hunter, a devil for eating up distance even with a man of Doherty's two hundred pounds on his back.

Drawing his left-hand pistol, he veered off towards the other horseman and little by little got close to him, and finally the man rose in his saddle and waved one arm violently. Trim! By the grace of God!

And then shortly they were riding side by side across the meadow and Michael's spirits had risen to fever pitch in spite of the painful throbbing of his leg, and when they took a tall hedge without a bobble, he yelled loudly and waved his hat.

And now they settled down to the long pull, leaning over their horses like jockeys in a terrible, whipping, kicking Darby finish, and the countryside rolled away from them like a huge saucer while the big white moon went effortlessly along, peering, showing the features of its great face, placidly amused; and at last Trim shouted in a lusty voice completely foreign to his normal everyday self: "We've lost 'em! We've lost 'em!"

And wildly exhilarated, Michael stood up in his stirrups and shouted: "Lobsters, how do you like the colour of me arse!"

And Trim stared blankly in the semi-darkness. Was it Doherty himself come back?

THEY WERE riding at a walk now, following the line of a tall hedge which screened them from the Dublin Road.

"You saved me with that pistol shot, Trim. I would have walked right into their arms."

"Ay," said Trim calmly. "As soon as you left, I had a feeling—I don't know what. I've been on patrol in the Army and had such a feeling. How can you explain it? So I sent the boys back to Dublin with the coach, then I hid out beyond the old buildings—and glad to get away from that creepy place—and then I heard them coming. They searched the place, Captain, and I heard a lot of clatter as of arms."

Michael groaned, but made no comment.

"The country got brighter before moonrise," Trim went on, "and I could see a little. A big party moved off, but a small one stayed, and I says to myself: 'The old ambush.' And that was it, sir. I saw you coming along the edge of the bog, and I fired the pistol. And here we are, safe and sound."

"I have a ball in the thigh, Trim," said Michael, "but it was spent when it hit me, and it's not much bother."

"Let's get it out."

"No. Dublin will be soon enough. Doherty had one in his calf for weeks. I took it out for him at last one night in an old Norman inn. He was dancing a jig, and it hurt him."

Trim nodded slowly and smiled. "Ah, Doherty!"

AT EIGHT of the clock the next morning they were moving easily along a back road which ran roughly parallel to the Dublin Road. It was a grey day with low, dark clouds and a threat of rain in the air. They had stopped, supped, and rested just before dawn, and the horses now seemed in good shape and ready for the journey ahead.

"How is the leg, sir?" asked Trim respectfully.

"Oh, I'll make it," Michael replied. "But it's as Doherty said. The ball's gnawing at me like an uneasy conscience."

"Did you bleed much?"

"Not so much. I feel fine after the rest."

They rode on at a moderate pace, and a man drinking from a jug waved gaily to them from a field, and now and then big farm mongrels ran out into the road to inspect them and jog along with them for a while, and a white-headed farm boy drove some cattle across their path impudently, but grinned and lost his dislike of Michael's gentleman's clothes when Michael waved to him and asked him how he did and made a country remark about the cattle.

And so the morning and afternoon passed. And finally, for the first time that day, the sun showed itself low in the western sky, sending out long vague beams, such as fall from windows in a great cathedral, and for a short while there was a dim golden glow over everything, and gold dust seemed to be dancing along the sunbeams, and the road was golden, and so were the walls of the whitewashed houses they were passing; and then at last the sun went out like a snuffed candle, and a pleasant violet light spread over the countryside, and evening began to fall. The first lights winked at them across the fields, and all the chimneys began to trail long plumes of grey smoke from the supper fires, and there was the sound of cowbells as the cattle moved towards the home barns.

And Michael assured himself that never before in his life had he seen such a charming and peaceful prospect; and just as he was thinking so, there was a wild thunder of hoofs, a rush of wind, a sinister clanking of weapons and accoutrements, and at least half a dozen dragoons tore out behind them from a hiding-place screened by a ravine and came at them full tilt. Michael and Trim, without a word or a look, jumped their horses into a gallop and were off down the peaceful country road at a pace at least as fast as the last quarter-mile of the Darby. Behind them, there were loud explosions, and they heard the sour, crazy whine of pistol balls. But in spite of their almost standing start, they pulled away at once, and leaning far over their horses' necks and riding all out, they drew away from their pursuers at an astounding rate, losing them in a cloud of dust at last.

But their escape worried Michael, and he shouted to Trim: "Take to the fields eastward. They may be driving us into an ambush."

And they leaped a fence effortlessly and were off across an immense meadow which seemed to stretch as far as you could make out in the gloaming, with neither house, barn, nor hindrance of any kind. The country flew past, and the wind whistled about their ears, and then finally, far off down the road, they heard loud cries and ho-lo-boloo-ing, and the damp banging noise of muskets.

Michael had been right. They'd escaped a trap, and now it was very doubtful that they could be caught, as the dragoons' mounts were not much faster than cart horses. Nevertheless, they kept riding at breakneck speed towards the vague shadows of mountains eastward—the Mountains of Wicklow, as they both knew; and lights began to wink at them far off, and then they noticed in the distance a dull, pewter-like glimmering—a large stream, and right in their path; and Michael called: "Turn south, Trim. South. When they come to this stream, they'll turn north or cross, as they know we're making for Dublin."

· And they turned south along the reedy bank and kept up their breakneck pace until finally the glimmering lights were gone and the mountains had been swallowed by the descending night—and then, all at once, it seemed to Michael that there had been a tremendous explosion, not so much of sound as of concussion, and he found himself sailing through the air, and then he landed with a crash on the back of his neck and lay stunned, unable to figure out what had happened or where he was. Trim had torn past him and was having a hard time pulling up his mount. Michael rolled his head from side to side, trying to clear it. Not ten feet away he could hear the faint liquid murmuring of the stream; and then his eyes began to clear, and he saw his mount rising from the spill off towards his left, and the mount seemed as stunned as himself and stood stock-still for a moment, then hobbled towards him on three legs.

"Ah, God," cried Michael, "I hope the poor devil has not broken a leg."

"Ho! ho!" cried Trim as he pulled up his lathered horse and dismounted.

Michael was rising now. Trim glanced at him, then went over to examine Michael's mount.

"How is he, Trim?" called Michael, wincing away from the thought of that lovely black being finished off with a pistol.

"No bones broken," cried Trim, "but he's wrenched himself badly, and he's through for the journey. Stepped in a hole, likely."

"What luck!" groaned Michael, and then all at once he remembered Doherty's "Fortune, thou bitch!" and smiled sadly—ah, well; that was the way of it, and no one knew it better than Doherty. An exposed root, a sudden movement of the arm with the blunderbuss nails flying, an innocent hole in the ground—and there you were. Fate, accident, predestination—who knew?

"Captain," said Trim, "we'd better swim the river and swap this horse for a sound one on the far side. The patrols are out tonight, probably all over the countryside."

"No," said Michael, "I intend to get the black back to Dublin. He saved me in the north with Doherty, and he brought me safe home from Belfast. We'll swim them over, if you like, but we'll not abandon this horse."

A foolish sentiment, no doubt; but it suited Trim completely. "Ay. Then what do we do, Captain?"

"It's me they want, Trim; not you," said Michael. "We'll swim the river, then you walk the horses into that big town where we saw the lights and rest them up—as long as you like. Get the black into Dublin. I know a trick or two. I'll get in all right. I wasn't with Doherty all that time for nothing."

Trim thought this over for a while, then he said: "Not a bad plan, Captain. The truth is, it's better for us to separate. But why don't you take the roan? And I'll walk the black in and rest him."

"No," said Michael. "I'm better off without a thoroughbred at this point. I'll get in safe and sound. Don't worry."

The river was shallow, and they had only one bit of trouble crossing it, and that in midstream when the roan balked at the swiftness and pull of the current and wanted to go back; but Michael cut at him hard with the whip and yelled at him ferociously and finally got him moving forward.

They said good-bye on the far bank. Michael gave Trim his sword and retained two pistols and some ammunition.

"See you at Nine Steps, Trim," called Michael.

"Ay, Captain, and good luck to you, sir," called Trim.

But it was not quite as simple as Michael imagined it would be. Long before dawn he was as lame as the black horse had been and ached all over as if he'd been beaten with clubs; and the ball in his thigh was giving him fits, and he had no food and no brandy, and he noticed at last a strange weakness coming over him and a touch of dizziness in his head, and finally he fell down on a bank in the darkness and lay panting and unable to continue. He fought hard against sleep, but finally it overcame him, and it was more like coma than true sleep, and he did not wake until the sun was shining in his face.

He sat up with a start. There was a thicket just beyond him, and he saw eyes peering through the brush, regarding him as a hawk regards a rabbit. And then he looked down at his mud-covered gentleman's clothes, and he noticed that his pistols and his ammunition were gone, and then he grabbed for his purse and found that it had disappeared also. He looked at the thicket again and heard a jeering laugh, and then a big rough head was thrust out at him and he saw that it was the head of a huge man in old patched country clothes. The man had a thatch of thick, curly black hair, and his fat, rugged face was almost as dark as an Italian's, and, strangely enough, he was wearing steel-rimmed spectacles. He jeered at Michael and showed the pistols he was holding in his huge, hairy, powerful-looking hands.

Michael was almost bursting with rage. "Who the devil are you?" he shouted belligerently.

And the man jeered back: "Who the devil are you?"

"Sneak-thief," shouted Michael, "robbing a sleeping man. You're like a trull plucking a drunkard in a Dublin alley. Scum!"

"Yes, me Lord," jeered the man. "We are all scum to the likes of you, Your Excellency. Oh, it was a patriotic horse that pitched you over his head and down the hillside from the road."

Michael stared at the man in bewilderment, then glanced up above him, where there seemed to be a road of some kind. And then before he could speak, a strange look came over the man's face and he seemed to be listening, and all at once he ducked back into the thicket, and Michael felt a vibration along the ground, and then he heard the noise of a cavalcade, and in a moment he caught the flash of a steel helmet, and with a sudden twist of his body he rolled into a little hollow which was screened from the road by a low bush.

A score of dragoons thundered past overhead, and when the hoofbeats had died away, the big shaggy man came out from his hiding-place and stood staring strangely at Michael.

"Lobsters, they was," called the man. "Why didn't you cry out?"

Michael had a sudden thought and called: "How many buttons on your coat?"

To Michael's surprise, the man leaped into the air and gave a loud shout, then he bellowed: "Why, five minus one, sir!"

And then, laughing, he came up to Michael and handed back his pistols and his purse. "I took you for a Lord, sir," he said, touching his cap respectfully. "I see it was not a patriotic horse that pitched you off."

"And what the devil is this about a horse?" Michael demanded irritably.

"Why, sir, you've got a lump like a goose egg on your head, and you're covered with mud, and what would you be doing laying there below the road otherwise?"

"What's your name?"

"Kevin White—and they call me Kev, and sometimes the Black One because of my complexion."

"Did you ever hear of Captain Martin?"

"I did, sir. The one who is in Dublin, and is friend with the quality, and is doing them. We've all heard of late."

Michael took two guineas out of his purse and handed them to Kevin, whose eyes were growing bigger and bigger behind his steel-rimmed spectacles.

"Yes, sir, and thank you, sir," he said, taking the guineas and bowing. "And what can I do for you, sir?"

"Where do you live?"

"Not more than a quarter of a mile back beyond those trees. I have a shack of my own, though it's not much. I was working at the Hall till the trouble. I've been sacked. Will you honour me by coming?"

MICHAEL WAS an ill man, and the knowledge of it irked him so that he wanted to curse his fate and damn his luck, but did neither and contented himself with sitting in front of Kevin White's small peat fire, wrapped in a blanket, sipping a hot grog. His head pounded and thumped, and his swollen right thigh was as sore and bothersome as if it had been covered with boils. Remembering Doherty, Michael had forced the Black One to cut the ball from his thigh, and it had been a long, tedious, painful procedure with the Black One crying from time to time, with a terrible grimace, that it was no use and he couldn't do it, he was no barber-surgeon, for the love of God! At last it was out, and the bleeding staunched, and then Michael fainted, and the Black One's big, ungainly, black-haired daughter put him to bed and looked after him with a mixture of familiarity and awe which kept her alternately flushing and paling. The Captain was such a lovely young man, with his blue-black hair and his white skin! Perhaps he would be very ill indeed and stay with them for months!

But Michael had risen from the bed as soon as he'd come round, in spite of the protests of Kevin and his daughter. "I've got no time to be lying around in bed," cried Michael irritably. "I've got to get back to Dublin at once."

"Easy, man, easy," said Kevin. "I'll get you back, but there is no sense in fainting dead on the way. You must rest."

And so Michael was trying to rest, sitting by the fire, sipping his grog, while Kevin was away some place and his big daughter, Maureen, puttered about in the cabin, too timid to make conversation with the great Captain from Dublin, but moving near to him from time to time, hoping he'd notice her.

Towards evening Kevin came rushing in, slamming the door, making a great breeze and to-do in the cabin. Michael, still at the fire, wrapped in a blanket, turned to look at him.

"Captain," cried Kevin, violently agitated, "it's a disaster, a great disaster."

"What? What?"

"It's all over the countryside, Captain." Kevin was almost incoherent with excitement and shock.

"What is all over the countryside, man? Don't yell. Explain."

"They've taken him. They've taken him."

Michael jumped up impatiently, but his right leg buckled and he just barely saved himself from falling by grasping the chair-back. He roared: "Taken who, for the love of God?"

"Why, the Leader. The Lobsters have taken him."

Michael of a sudden felt cold as ice. "They've taken Regis Donnell?"

"Ay," cried Kevin. "They've taken him, and he's on his way to Dublin Castle and hanging. It's high treason he's wanted for."

Michael fell back into his chair and sat staring blankly into the fire; finally he spoke, as if to himself: "Oh, I've done a great thing, no doubt about it."

"What is that you say, Captain?" asked Kevin.

Michael turned. The Black One and his big daughter were standing side by side staring at him, puzzled, worried. He ignored the question and cried: "We've got to get to Dublin. Now! At once!"

Kevin and his daughter both protested, telling him he was too weak to be moved about, but Michael would not listen.

And so Michael rode back to Dublin on a battered old cart with Kevin and Maureen. He was dressed in patched country clothes provided by Kevin, his hair was tousled, his face dirty, and the few who noticed him at all saw no difference between him and the other two in the cart, except that the son was much paler than the father or daughter. And at one stop Kevin saw fit to remark to a countryman who paused to pass the time of day: "My son's ill. I'm taking him to a doctor in Dublin."

"Ay," said the countryman, "I thought he looked somewhat peaked."

"Yerra, yerra; I'm ill," muttered Michael with a broad country accent—and then he remembered Doherty and smiled sadly to himself. "They will take the dress for the man," Doherty had said, and it was proving out.

Here and there they saw small parties of dragoons as they neared

Dublin, but they were not menaced once. Towards the last, Michael grew very weak, and Maureen held him upright with a long arm about his waist.

They deposited him in the courtyard at Nine Steps at two o'clock of a misty, rainy morning, and at last Maureen had the courage to kiss him on the mouth and call: "Good luck, Captain. Good luck. I'll pray for you." And Michael returned the kiss and gave her a long hug, and Kevin said with a sigh: "The poor girl will remember that to her dying day."

But Kevin almost fell off the cart when Michael gave him twenty guineas, and at once Kevin became very eager to get out of Dublin, "where a man with money is not safe."

Kevin turned the cart around and started off; and Maureen stood up to wave, crying at the same time, and then hostlers appeared from the stables, and there was a shout somewhere in the midst of the tavern itself, and Michael heard the clatter of feet rushing downstairs. And there was Big Tom, also some others, mere dark shapes—and then, at last, Trim—and Michael turned and slipped sideways down to the cobbles of the courtyard in a faint before the men could reach him.

BIG TOM sent for a doctor at once, and then, with the help of Trim and two of the hostlers, he carried Michael to the "Fort" and made him comfortable.

The Fort was Big Tom's best hide-out, exclusively for important, badly wanted men. It was entered through an innocent-looking disused smoke-house, off the courtyard. In the back of the smoke-house wall was a small hidden wooden door; this opened into a large, low-ceiled, comfortable room with two beds, a double and a single, a big table, and many chairs. There was even a small fire-place, for the room was very damp, and several high-up portholes for air. Best of all, there was a secret exit which led down through the cellars of Nine Steps, where there was a warren of basement rooms and wine-cellars and storerooms, a bewildering labyrinth for the uninitiated.

The doctor, a small, hawk-nosed, whisky-faced, wizened little man, came at once, and when he saw the wound in Michael's leg, he demanded: "And who cut the ball away, a blacksmith with a hammer and chisel? Good God!"

"It was gnawing at me like an uneasy conscience," said Michael.

"You should have let it gnaw. You may have trouble now with this leg, my boy. But on the other hand you may not." Then he chuckled to himself. "I've been surgeon in His Majesty's Navy, and yet I've never seen anything like this. You're a damned rough and ready fellow, I must say."

And Michael looked up proudly at the solemn, respectful faces of Big Tom and Trim.

Later, after some soup and grog, he felt better, and Trim sat down with him for a conference.

"The black?" asked Michael.

"Safe in the stable, sir." Trim smiled wanly. "I had no trouble at all, and the black walked out of his lameness, and we made good time. He's lame again from the journey, but the hostlers say he'll be right again in a day or two."

"So they've taken Regis Donnell?"

Trim nodded slowly. "We walked right into it, sir. 'Twas bad luck."

"Oh, no," cried Michael. "We did not walk right into it. We brought it on, Trim. I led them right to him, and it was all the damnedest black-hearted accident, just because I wanted to see . . . but never mind that. What else?"

"The apartment is being watched night and day. Miss Aga has been warned to do nothing. But she's frantic, Captain."

"Warned how?"

"I had a note slipped to the butcher, who gave it to Mary when she was marketing. It was risky, but I had to do it, Captain. No telling what Miss Aga might do. Some wild thing, like Doherty. I hope she will remain calm."

"That she will not," said Michael, smiling sadly. "But maybe in a little while I can talk to her."

"No, no," cried Trim. "Impossible. You're safe here, Captain; but one move outside and you'd be gone."

"I can't stay here for ever," shouted Michael impatiently, rising from the bed.

"No, not for ever. Things do not last for ever in Ireland." Trim studied Michael's face shrewdly, then he lowered his eyes and went on: "Doherty was a great one for lying low at the right time. That's how he went on to forty. Twenty years of such a life without a moment in prison is somewhat in the nature of a record. It was all from lying low at the right time."

Michael lay back and stared thoughtfully at the ceiling. After a while he fell into a deep sleep, and Trim tiptoed out.

THE NEXT AFTERNOON Michael, lying more or less at ease and reading a novel Trim had brought him, was surprised to hear a tapping at the smoke-house door. He slipped a pistol from under his pillow and lay waiting; but finally he heard Big Tom's voice, very low: "Are you asleep, Captain? Are you asleep?"

Michael called impatiently: "Come in. Come in, man."

The door opened, and Big Tom looked in. "Captain, do you feel up to hearing great news and speaking a word to Mahony and his lads?"

"Yes," cried Michael, perking up at once.

And then Big Tom entered, followed by Mahony, Tuer O'Brien, and Willie the Goat. They had all been drinking, and their eyes were blazing with triumph.

"We heard the sad word," said Mahony, "that young Donnell has been taken. But he's avenged already, and so is Doherty—and you yourself, Captain. Clagett has been directing the narks, and they say that he alone is responsible for the taking of Donnell. Well . . . Clagett is no more."

Tuer O'Brien and Willie the Goat cheered savagely, and Willie did a few wild dance-steps like a primitive man celebrating a great triumph over his enemies.

"What!" cried Michael, sitting up and staring at them.

"He died of fright, the little rat," said Mahony, "while Tuer was putting the finishing touches to Villona, who fought like a devil from hell."

"The cutlass did it," cried Tuer O'Brien. "None of your thrust and parry for me. I like the slash and the slice."

"We found them at last," said Mahony, "with the help of poor doddering Jimmie Wren, who is sick with the excitement and keeps drinking and may not last the night."

"Ay," cried Willie in savage wonder, "he died of fright like a rabbit. He collapsed like a punctured sack. I have never seen a man so white. I thought it was a feint to put us off. It was not." Willie took a small object from his pocket and tossed it on the table in front of Michael. It was a human ear with a gold ring in it. "A receipt, by the gods!" yelled Willie, then he laughed loudly.

Michael repressed with difficulty a sharp recoil; then he looked steadily at the ear for a moment and said: "Very well. So much for Clagett. Take it away."

Willie put the ear back in his pocket. "Why, thank you, Captain. I was hoping I could keep it for a memento." Now he drew his cutlass and made it whistle. "Death to all Castle narks!" he bellowed, and Tuer O'Brien followed suit with the bellowing and the whistling cutlass.

"Easy, easy, boys," said Mahony, looking at them with distaste.

Michael got his purse from under the mattress and distributed the guineas, and finally the bellowing and chortling Willie and Tuer were ushered out by Mahony. Big Tom remained.

"I'll put the two of them in a room, take their weapons away, give them plenty of whisky, and lock the door," said Big Tom. "We don't want them wandering the town in this state."

"Ay," said Michael, feeling more than a little sick and hoping he hadn't turned green.

Michael was a bold and ruthless fighter when his anger was roused, but such unmitigated callous savagery appalled him.

Big Tom laughed wryly. "And I think the old one is going back to his harp in the street, now that Clagett's had his *quietus est.*" Big Tom shook his head in wonder. "He's near eighty. What a man he must have been fifty years ago!"

"Ay," said Michael, pouring himself a drink.

REGIS DONNELL'S TRIAL was "short and sweet," as all the proponents of Dublin Castle boasted proudly. As a matter of fact, it was to all intents and purposes drum-head, and Regis was sentenced to hang in two weeks' time. The back-country people of Ireland were stunned by his sudden taking and by the summary nature of his trial. They were now rudderless; what leaders they had were little bickering men who could not hold their own local groups together, let alone speak for all; and the famous Captain Martin was hardly more than a legendary figure in far-off Dublin, or maybe already taken or dead by now. He had certainly disappeared.

And at the Castle itself, Crewe, the hard-bitten old political veteran, had been proved right, and several other more moderate advisers wrong. No insurrection developed. Not even a sign of one. The Lobsters now galloped the country roads safe from brick-bats, and the gentry in far-off counties began to unbar their windows, and there was sadness and gloom and inertia all over Ireland.

"We broke their backs," said Crewe over his port to the great Lord Castlewood, Lord-Lieutenant of Ireland, with young Lord Glen hovering in the shadows, fawning a bit and also strutting a bit, owing to the huge success of his master's policies. Oh, Crewe was the man of the hour!

"God, what they did to your man, Crewe!" said Lord Castlewood with a delicate shudder as he took a pinch of snuff. "What was his name?"

"Clagett," said Crewe. "They hacked off his ear in death. What savages! But there are always plenty of Clagetts in this world. God, how the port's deteriorating," he went on, without a change of tone. "When I was a young man in London, it was the drink above all. Now it's bilge, and the sack's not much better. I think I'll turn lady and drink claret."

And now Lord Castlewood and Lord Crewe, both elderly men, held a long nostalgic discussion about the good old days when port was port, and sack sack, and the best Continental wines were being imported and not just your rubbishy "bubbly," which all the young blades were drinking at present. And young Lord Glen listened politely, and in his secret heart he had contempt for these two old men who would not relinquish the reins of government to younger and abler men, but must fight on in their dotage—for what?

Yes, Regis Donnell's fate had been settled so swiftly that Michael was still in the Fort, hobbling about on a blackthorn stick, cursing his fate, drinking too much, reading too many damned books, and shouting irritably at Mahony, Trim, and Big Tom. He was like a caged beast, and one night he got very drunk indeed and smashed all the bottles he could find against the wall.

He wanted to be free. He wanted to sit in front of the little grate at the apartment with Aga on his knee and Princey frisking happily about and the Dublin rain falling soft as an angel's touch against the windows. Above all, he wanted to tell Aga what an ass he was; what a reckless, headlong fool. He wanted to ask her pardon for all the trouble he had caused her.

Meanwhile, the Lord-Lieutenant's men combed Dublin—in fact, all of Ireland—for one Captain Martin, and emboldened by the lethargy of the population, they were rough in their methods and very thorough, which had not been the case before when it was two to one they'd get a brick-bat in the face at an inopportune moment.

And late one night, to everybody's horrified surprise, old Mahony began to bawl the "Highwayman's Song" at the top of his voice on the pavement in front of Nine Steps, and Big Tom could not believe his ears. What—the Lord-Lieutenant's men at last after all these years? The old one must be mistaken.

But the words were loud, sharp, and clear as Mahony sang:

> "As I was riding over Hunslow Moor
> There I saw a lawyer riding before,
> And I asked him if he was not afraid
> To meet bold Turpin, that Mischievous Blade."

And now as Big Tom beat on the Chinese gong in the hall, there was a scurrying through the place like rats in a barn, and a banging of doors and a clatter of bootheels, and when the Lord-Lieutenant's men appeared, pale and nervous, with pistols cocked and sabres bared, taking no chances in this macabre hell of the deepest stews, there were only a few ragged men at the bars, and a few playing cards quietly, sucking on old pipes, and a few rolling dice, sailors from the quays mostly—and no real prey at all: not even a low pimp or pickpocket wanted for breaking gaol.

No one spoke a word to the Lord-Lieutenant's men. Big Tom followed them about calmly, smoking a short clay pipe and spitting contemptuously from time to time. And the Lord-Lieutenant's men were not quite so thorough here as elsewhere, though they searched the place from room to room and from top to bottom—but sketchily. And finally when Big Tom led them to the basement and they saw its gloom and its shadows and the many passageways leading off from the wine-cellar, they looked at each other in trepidation and decided they'd had enough. What a wonderful place for a murderous ambush!

Clagett's end had not gone unremarked. Not one of the Lord-Lieutenant's men had the least desire to face his Maker, particularly mutilated. They left with a clatter of warlike sabres, and at the door the leader warned Big Tom about harbouring wanted men, and Big Tom spat contemptuously at his feet.

"All the same," said Big Tom afterward, "it was humiliating and must be discouraged." Mahony was of the same opinion.

AND THEN one night there was a faint tapping at the secret door in Michael's room, and Michael leaped from bed, where he'd been reading, fully dressed, blew out the candles, and stood waiting with a pistol in each hand and a crazy hope in his heart that it was somebody looking for trouble. He'd had a bellyful of inaction.

But it was Big Tom, and he was calling: "Open, Captain. Open. Very important."

So Michael put down the pistols, relighted the candles, and unbarred the door—and then he started back in amazement as a slender girl, her identity veiled by a shawl, rushed past him into the room and flung herself face down on the bed, sobbing wildly. There was a pale, apologetic-looking little man with her. Brady!

Big Tom closed the door. Michael turned slowly away from Brady, stunned, and looked at the slender form on the bed. Catherine!

"I had to bring her," wailed Brady, very much upset. "She devilled the life out of me. I says to her: 'But, darling, what can Mick do? He's a wanted man himself.' But she wouldn't listen. I've had one hell of a time with the girl."

Michael was speechless. Now Catherine rose slowly, turned, and sat on the edge of the bed, facing him. Her cheeks were tear-stained and she was very pale, but she was lovely, lovely!

"You've got to save him, Mick, love," she pleaded. "You've got to."

"Ay," said Michael quietly. "I've been thinking along those lines myself. I brought the whole thing down on him by my silliness. I wouldn't listen to anybody."

Hope showed so nakedly in Catherine's face that Michael felt a pang of remorse at his heedless words. Heedless, always heedless! "You will do something foolish and rash," Regis had said to him ages back, and Regis had known him since childhood.

"But what in God's name can I do?" cried Michael. "Storm the Castle? Would take three regiments—and then who knows? It's a puzzle, Cath; a puzzle."

"Ay," said Brady, "an impossible puzzle, I keep telling her. Of course, there are all of those petitions with thousands of names!"

"Petitions!" cried Catherine, jumping up. "And what are they petitioning for? Banishment! And that means to Botany Bay. A fine thing, those damned petitions. Oh, God—the Irish! I hate them. I hate them all. Give me the English any day!"

Michael stepped back as if he'd been struck in the face with a whip. "What the devil do you mean, girl?"

Quickly Brady intervened: "She's distracted, Mick. Can't you see it? The poor girl's distracted."

"Distracted and be damned! What kind of a way is that to talk? What are the O'Herlihys, then—Italians?"

"And you're one of the worst!" screamed Catherine, raising her fist as if to hit him. "Talk, talk, talk. Drink your whisky, race your horses, lie in the bushes with your trollops. I know you—the lot of you! You no-good, drunken, gambling, whoring loud-mouths! And he's going to die for you—all of you! And what is he? Why, he's a gentleman. Does he get drunk? He does not. Does he gamble? He does not, but saves his money for the family he hoped to rear. Does he run after trollops? I'm the first girl he ever had. Is he a loud-mouth? He is not. He speaks nothing but sense. What kind of way is that to talk, you say? There is no other way to talk about the likes of you, Mick Martin— and all your friends and kind. And to hell with you, Mick Martin!"

Brady turned away with a groan and hung his head, as Michael shouted: "So it's a hell-cat you are behind your pretty face, and me dreaming of a swan-boat and all that silly nonsense! I'll get Regis Donnell out of that damned Castle if it kills me—and to hell with you double, Catherine O'Herlihy."

"You'll do nothing," screamed Catherine. "Nothing! You'll talk, talk, and drink—and then you'll feel sorry for yourself. I want to go now, Aloysius."

She hurried over to the door.

"Well, that was a pleasant visit," said Michael as she disappeared into the darkness of the cellar.

Poor Brady shrugged, and as Michael said nothing, he turned and went out. Michael saw the reddish flickering of Big Tom's torch in the cellar, then he slowly closed the door, threw himself on the bed, and lay staring up at the ceiling.

"Where's the difference?" he demanded. "Aga or Cath—it's all one."

And finally, exhausted by his anger and his frustration, he fell asleep.

IT ALL came to him in a dream, and waking, he leaped violently out of bed, in spite of his game leg, and danced about, shouting: "God, Doherty, you're watching over me in my sleep. I've got it. I've got it!"

And then, although it was just dawn, he began to yell and beat on the doors with a chair, and he raised such a commotion that Big Tom thought that he'd gone mad through confinement and came in to see him at last, pale and sweating.

"Good God, what is it, Captain?"

"Tom," cried Michael, all but dancing, "get Trim, Mahony—right away. Ah, Doherty—the parson! God, man—I've got the most wonderful idea in the world."

You WOULD THINK that a man of Clonmel's delicate nurturing would be appalled by Nine Steps, but this was not the fact. "Sir Andrew" looked at everything with deep interest, and he seemed to be especially taken with Big Tom, the ex-heavyweight champion of Ireland, James Mahony, the ex-pirate, and particularly with Michael's place of hiding, the Fort. He wanted to look at everything, examine everything, test everything. Michael showed him through the labyrinthine cellars, the big torch he held high flaring in the draughts that blew from unseen doors and windows.

And at last when they were back once more in the Fort and sitting at table, drinking, Clonmel said: "I find, Captain, that you lead a very interesting life. No dullness here."

"That's an outside view," said Michael. "I've been damned dull in this room. What's going on in the sporting world?"

"Nothing," said Clonmel. "The 'trouble' frightened a lot of people, of course, especially when your name was dragged into it. Bracken has left for the Continent. Poor Clayton is writing his daughter in London pathetic letters. He wants the money to go to her. But she's married to a Scottish prig who reprobates Clayton, and wants nothing to do with him. Very sad. Our friend Glen, I understand, is being promoted at the Castle, and Crewe, a vindictive old man, is in the saddle. Castlewood himself is a gentleman and a very good friend of my father's, the Earl. Though the Earl is far from a moderate, as you know. He's for hanging the disaffected and be damned to them. He has bored me from childhood with such talk—because, you see, the Earl is a tender-hearted man, at bottom, and wouldn't harm a fly. So why does he talk in that manner?"

"It's in the air," said Michael. "And how are you getting along with your father?"

"Not at all, as usual. Why?"

And then, after a long pause, Michael broached his project to Clonmel, who sat listening in stunned silence, taking a minute pinch of snuff from time to time; and then when Michael was all through, he carefully brushed the front of his coat with a handkerchief and inquired: "And you yourself, Captain? Are you so anxious to hang, then?"

"Oh, I'll not hang," shouted Michael. "Don't give that a second thought."

Now "Sir Andrew" rose and began to mince about the room, flicking his handkerchief here and there, and finally, to Michael's surprise, he threw back his head and laughed as raucously as a parrot. "I'll do it," he cried. "Oh, God, what a lark! If I'm apprehended, the Earl might lock me up for life—he's threatened to for less; but, oh, the look on his face! I'd love to see it. 'Twould be worth ten thousand guineas."

"Good," said Michael. "Tonight."

Clonmel recoiled slightly. "So soon?"

"The sooner the better."

Now Clonmel turned and studied Michael's face for a long time. "There is no way I could refuse, Captain. You are risking your neck—I'm risking hardly more than discomfort and disapproval; for, as you know, the Earl is one of the most powerful men in the British Isles—powerful through wealth, let me modestly add, not ability. No. There's no way I can refuse. I'll tell you, Captain. The duel with Hood endeared you to me for ever. 'Reload his pistol.' And you meant it. Such a thing has never been heard of before. Very well. I'm at your service." Then he brightened and began to laugh. "Oh, God above, what a thing this will be if we pull it off! Why, Patrick may be in the history books yet—his one and only chance."

And finally Clonmel left, and then the arguments began. First, Trim, then Big Tom, then Mahony, who was so upset that his voice began to quaver like a very old man's, an unusual thing for Mahony, though he was nearly eighty. But they might as well have been talking to a brick house, and when finally they began to realize that all argument was useless, they relaxed and shook Michael's hand and looked at him with the deep admiration such men as these have for courage, even when it borders on the rash and the idiotic.

And when at last Trim and Michael were alone, Trim asked: "And Miss Aga, Captain?"

"She's to know nothing till it's an accomplished fact; then she's to be taken in with it. She has all the money in the strong-box, near ten thousand guineas, and we may need every penny of it."

"Let me say one thing, Captain," said Trim, "then I'll be quiet. Crewe is an ill man to cross. He will see that you suffer, one way or another."

"Ah, well," cried Michael impatiently, "that's a chance I'll have to take."

"Yes, sir," said Trim.

AT EIGHT O'CLOCK that evening a sumptuous, crested six-horse coach, with liveried postilion, driver, and boot, was admitted at the big gate of Dublin Castle, but halted inside by red-coated guards.

Clonmel leaned out and screamed at them: "Stand aside, boobies! What—stop Clonmel?"

The guards paled and glanced into the coach. In the far corner sat a Trappist monk in a dirty habit and cowl. Clonmel slapped the captain of the guard across the face with a document. "Here," he shouted; "if you must make a nuisance of yourself. Permission for this monk to visit the prisoner Regis Donnell."

Shaking, the captain glanced at the document quickly by the light of a lantern, then handed it back.

"What's your name, my man?" bawled Clonmel belligerently.

But the captain stammered and then cried: "It's perfectly all right, my Lord. A mere formality. Pass on." Then he turned and shouted into the darkness: "Pass them—ho!"

They were admitted to the wing for political prisoners by an obsequious warder, who cringed and almost abased himself as Clonmel strutted and damned Dublin Castle and all the thick-witted boobies in it and shouted that they'd all see what it was like to treat the Earl of Aire's son as if he were a common ordinary man of no influence whatsoever.

"I'm sure, my Lord," said the warder, "that no one—"

But Clonmel cut him off and went on raving as the warder led them down a dark corridor, with the monk following silently, his arms crossed in his sleeves, his face hidden by a huge, dirty, greasy cowl. At last they stopped at a great wooden door with a rather large grille in it, and Regis Donnell could be seen sitting on a cot in his shirtsleeves, reading a book by candlelight. He looked up quickly.

"Mr. Donnell, sir," said the warder, his voice full of respect now, "here is Lord Clonmel, Aire's son, bringing a reverend father for your comfort, sir."

Regis started and stared for a moment, but as he was far from a fool, he realized at once that something was up, so he rose and said: "Why, excellent. Most happy. Thank you, warder."

And then Clonmel and the monk were admitted, the door was locked, and the warder walked heavily back down the corridor. Regis stood staring at Lord Clonmel as Michael had once looked at Clayton, as if he were a tiger, and he demanded:

"Well, my Lord, and what the devil is this?"

And then Michael lowered the cowl, and Regis was so amazed that he staggered back and reached for the wall.

"Good God, man," he gasped, "what are you doing here, Mick? You'll hang if they catch you."

And Michael said abruptly: "In a little while you will put on this habit and walk out of here with Lord Clonmel."

Regis paled slightly and a wild hope showed in his eyes, and then his face stiffened, and he set his jaw. "No. I'll be damned if I will. I'll not see you hanged for me, you rash fool!"

"Catherine's waiting," said Michael patiently, deeply pleased by Regis's reaction, though he'd been expecting it. "Everything is arranged. Clonmel will see you to the Continent personally."

"In fact," said Clonmel, giggling a little out of nervousness, "I'm in as much of a hurry to get away now as you yourself, Donnell."

"No," said Regis quietly. "I will not."

"You will," cried Michael, "if I have to beat the living hell out of you—and then tell the warder the monk has fainted dead away and must be carried out."

"Quiet," cautioned Clonmel suddenly, and they all stood listening, and there was the sound of heavy footsteps in the corridor, and Michael pushed Regis to his knees beside the cot and then knelt down with him as if in prayer, and the heavy footsteps drew nearer and nearer—but at last passed on harmlessly and died away around a corner.

Regis and Michael rose. "Get out, Mick," cried Regis. "Get out while you can. Tempt me no longer. What do you suppose I've been thinking of all this time but Catherine? She's waiting, you say?"

"Yes," said Michael. "Do you want to break her heart?"

"Oh, my God, man," cried Regis, "it was all her idea, this marrying, and now look. She's just twenty and has lived enough already for a woman of fifty. I hate to see her suffering. She would never have so much as a headache if I could prevent it, but—"

"Oh, stop making speeches, God damn it," cried Michael violently, "and get out of here."

Regis shook his head stubbornly and emphatically. "No, Mick. I could never live so, thinking I was responsible for your hanging."

"And then I'd be responsible for yours!" cried Michael. "And besides, my boy, they will never hang me."

Regis looked at him blankly. "What's this?"

"I'll do 'em," laughed Michael. "I'll be got out—don't worry about that. The arrangements have already started."

Regis turned to Clonmel. "Is this true?"

"Yes," said Clonmel, "it's true. It's a damned chancy business. But it's true."

Regis still hesitated, deeply troubled.

"If you will just stop thinking about yourself for a moment," said Michael bluntly, "and start thinking about Ireland and all the people depending on you, Regis Donnell."

"Ay," said Regis, with a deep sigh.

"And think about how this victory over the Castle will give people heart again!"

Regis looked at Michael in wonder. "Such sentiments from you, Mick!"

"And now will you stop holding one of your bloody meetings and go before you get us all caught—and that would be a pretty thing, wouldn't it?" shouted Michael so vehemently that Clonmel put a hand on his arm to quiet him.

Regis, shaking, reached for the habit, and Clonmel helped him put it on. "Mick, you've surprised me, man. You've surprised me. God bless you, Mick—and the first boy we have will be called Michael Martin Donnell."

Now Michael rapped loudly for the warder, and when they heard him coming down the corridor, Michael blew out the candle and lay down on the cot in his shirt-sleeves.

The key grated, the door swung open. "He has fallen into a deep sleep, owing to the ministrations," said Clonmel, "and here, my man, are ten guineas for your understanding services."

And the warder almost bowed to the ground—ten guineas, what munificence!—and bowing and cringing, he ushered Lord Clonmel and the reverend father to the door, and even went outside with them for a moment, still bowing, overcome!

He saw a huge coach, its side-lights flashing, drive off, and he heard the guards cry: "Pass. Pass on," and then he went back inside, dreaming what he would do with his ten guineas. Hide them from his wife—that was the first thing!

Michael lay with his arms under his head, staring up at the ceiling. "Ah, well," he told himself, "it's no worse than the Fort, at that."

BUT IN THE MORNING there was hell to pay. Whistling blithely, a day warder unlocked the door of Regis's cell and entered, carrying a tray of food.

"Morning, sir," he chirped.

"Morning," said Michael, smiling.

And the warder stared like a man in a nightmare, and then he ran out into the corridor, leaving the cell door ajar, and looked at the other cells, then he rushed back and stared blankly at Michael, who stood grinning at him; and finally he locked Michael in the cell and went screaming down the corridor as if all the devils in hell were after him.

AND NOW the venerable Castle had a great problem on its hands. Crewe's first idea was to cover up the escape entirely, say nothing; ignore it; but the Castle was rife with gossip, the warders were sure to talk volubly at home, especially as many of them were true-born Irishmen and only pretending to be subservient in order to draw their pay. What a blow for Crewe and the Castle! He'd broken their backs, had he? Crewe was apoplectic, and was avoided by all who could reasonably avoid him; and there was a session with the stiff-necked and bewildered Earl of Aire that ended in loud, vulgar yelling, and the gossip was that a duel between these two august gentlemen was prevented only by quick thinking and adroit manœuvring on the part of Lord Glen, the coming power, as all agreed.

So . . . the Castle was forced to release the news that the Great Rebel and Traitor, Regis Donnell, had escaped, but the bulletin went on to state that his reapprehension was expected in a matter of hours. Then the next day a new bulletin was issued: the Great Highwayman and Thief, Captain Michael Martin, referred to vulgarly as Captain Lightfoot, had been captured after a wild chase by men of the Lord-Lieutenant's personal forces, and was now incarcerated in Dublin Castle and would shortly be tried and hanged.

But the bulletins did not achieve their object. Gossip spreads in Ireland like fire in straw. The truth of the matter was soon known even in the Aran Islands, and a roaring defiant laugh went up over the whole country.

Oh, that Lightfoot! He was the boy for you!

CREWE, exhausted by age, dissipation, excitement, and frustration, took to his bed at last; and Castlewood, appalled by the scandal of Lord Clonmel and Aire's disaffection from the Castle, took it upon himself to travel to Aire's country seat and try to reason with the powerful and wealthy Earl, who was not accustomed to insults, even from a man of the stature of Crewe.

So Glen was in charge. He had Michael brought to him in an elegant, panelled little room with fine engravings on the walls and beautiful English furniture. Michael sat opposite him.

"You are a damned rash fellow, Captain," said Glen.

"Ay," said Michael.

"You will hang for this, you know."

"Perhaps."

"I think you need a lesson first, however."

"When a man is to hang, lessons are a little late."

Glen burst out laughing, and dismissed him.

BUT GLEN'S LAUGHTER was not kindly, as Michael found out soon enough. Michael was arraigned before an old, deaf, hard-eyed magistrate who used an ear-trumpet but was not comical for all of that.

Angus Desmond, urged on by Lord Devereaux, whose old friend Crewe was in such a pickle at the Castle, identified Michael and gave evidence against him. Nothing more was needed, and at last the magistrate said:

"This prisoner, Michael Martin, vulgarly known as Captain Lightfoot, is to be branded 'Thief' on the right hand, and held for trial on the capital offence of armed robbery on the highway. Dismissed."

Michael was stunned. What—branded? He couldn't believe it. He heard a sympathetic murmur, and turned. An ugly little warder he hadn't seen before was looking at him with anguished eyes. As Michael passed him on his way out, the warder slipped him a note.

Once in his cell, Michael looked eagerly at it.

It read:

A. *disappeared with the strong-box. Mystery. T.*

From Trim! Good God, what did it mean? They needed that money for the bribing of guards.

Michael fell down on his cot and took his head in his hands. Things were not working out as his optimistic nature had led him to expect.

But the branding! God above!

AFTER HIS MORNING MEAL next day, Michael was moved from the political prisoners' wing into the section reserved for the common criminals. Regis's cell had been a nice one, more like a country-hotel bedroom than anything else, except for the grilled door and the barred windows, but there was certainly nothing like it to be found in the old, dungeon-like part of the Castle down whose dank, sweating stone corridor Michael was now walking, manacled, between two powerful warders.

One of the warders opened a small iron door while the other one unlocked the manacles. Michael recoiled slightly at the look of his cell. There was a narrow, slitted window high up in the far wall, and for the rest, nothing but masonry, top, sides, and bottom, and straw on the floor—not even a stool. As he looked, a large rat scuttled through the straw with an impudent rustling and disappeared into a drain-pipe.

"Ah," said Michael, "an Englishman just went past."

And both of the warders laughed loudly; then one of them hurried away down the corridor, but the other one pushed Michael into the cell and whispered: "You've got friends, me lad. Don't lose heart."

Then he slammed the door quickly and locked it.

Michael stood in the miserable twilight of the narrow cell, looking about him with distaste. Not fit for animals even, the place! It stank to high heaven, and a clammy cold seemed to ooze from the walls.

"Ah, well," said Michael, "it won't be long, one way or another," and he moved over below the slitted window and looked up at the feeble ray of sunshine cutting diagonally across the gloom. Bad news and good news all at once. First, the branding. Michael shuddered and quickly put it out of his mind. Second, Aga. Where had the crazy girl got to with the guineas? Was she the kind who ran off when there was trouble? Michael doubted it very much, and yet you could never be quite sure of a woman; of a man, yes, in spite of the opinion of Doherty. Two counts of very bad news. But the warder's words had heartened him. He had friends. Just let him get out of here once, and to hell with the rest. He'd worry about that later.

LATE THAT AFTERNOON Michael was taken to a room in the cellars. Outside, the sky had clouded over, and in spite of many low, grilled windows the room would have been pitch-dark if it hadn't been for the lanterns hanging here and there.

He saw the red-hot glow of a small forge, and a huge man in a leather apron heating a long-handled iron. Near by stood a hard-faced officer of dragoons in a red coat.

Michael felt a sudden wave of panic and struggled violently for self-control. The manacles had been taken off earlier, his hands were entirely free, and he had a wild desire to strew men about the floor as he'd once strewn them about the floor of Doherty's Castle. But then what? He'd be branded all the same, and forcibly, as there were at least twenty men in the big room. Little by little he composed himself, and then of a sudden he thought of Mahony and what he'd said of the branding—"like pork sizzling in a pan"—and Michael's mind winced violently away from the image, and his hard-won composure was gone in an instant. But now he noticed that all eyes were on his face, and by a great effort of the will he pulled himself together, indicated with a jerk of his thumb the huge man in the leather apron, and demanded: "What is he going to do, shoe me for the Darby?"

A loud laugh rang through the room. The red-coated officer shifted uneasily and said: "Prisoner Michael Martin, we are about to carry out the sentence imposed by Mr. Bradley of Magistrates' Court, Dublin Castle. Have you anything to say?"

"Yes," said Michael. "Rare will suit me fine."

A warder rushed out suddenly and could be heard laughing uncontrollably and hysterically in the outer corridor.

"Your levity is misplaced here, my man," said the officer stiffly.

"I hope your iron will not be," Michael replied.

And now half a dozen men were laughing helplessly, impatient to rush out and repeat Captain Lightfoot's words all over the prison, where they would be spread ultimately all over Dublin and Leinster and Connacht until the far-western fishermen on the Atlantic coast would be roaring over them in the taverns at night.

Oh, Michael was killing them with his wit, but all the same his flesh was creeping and wincing as two warders put him in a chair, ready for the iron, and one of the warders fussed over him so much that

Michael grew irritated and was about to shove him away, when the man whispered very low: "It will be as light as Hughes can make it with the Lobster looking on."

And the other warder called loudly to mask the whispering: "He's ready, sir. The prisoner's ready."

And so Michael was branded "Thief"—a crude capital T on the back of his right hand. And there was definitely a sizzling as of pork in the pan, and tongues of cold-hot pain leaped up his arm, and the world went all black and vague; and then his head cleared, and he felt such a violent hatred of all men and everything for one blind moment that it took a half-dozen of the warders to prevent him from attacking the red-coated officer, who did not move once during the struggle, but stood looking on with a calm, pale face and an air of weary indifference.

And when finally Michael had been subdued and the manacles put back on and soothing oil poured on his right hand, the red-coated officer said in a low voice: "Why do you jump at me, Martin? I make the laws no more than you do. Nor do I impose any sentences. I merely see that they are carried out."

"I lost my head," said Michael sullenly.

"I hate and detest the branding," said the English officer with such force that they all looked at him in wonder. "It is barbarous. The blacks of Africa could think of no worse. What would you have me do, Martin? Throw up my commission?"

Michael looked at the pale Englishman and wondered. Could it be possible that he felt a certain sympathy with him? Good God, not with an Englishman! Preposterous!

"I do not give a hoot in hell what you do," said Michael, then he turned and was led off by the warders.

As he was passing into his cell, one of the warders handed him a note.

It read:

A. *had ideas of her own. All's well.* T.

And in spite of the terrible pain of his hand, Michael danced a step or two, and as the rat rustled through the straw into the drain-pipe, he called after him: "I doubt you're an Englishman after all."

MICHAEL WAS TRIED before Mr. Justice Banks, and his trial was as summary as Regis's—cynically so. Legally it was a very simple matter: Michael's word against the word of Lord Devereaux's steward. The fact that all the money had been returned was considered irrelevant by the judge, as he stated in his summing up. It was all over in the space of an afternoon, and Michael was sentenced at once: to hang within two weeks' time.

AND MICHAEL soon found that all was *not* well—far from it. At the conclusion of the sentencing a head warder was assigned to the job of watching Michael until he was hanged. Apparently the Castle was taking no chances.

The head warder was a huge, brutal-looking man, well over six feet and very wide in the beam, with a shock of coarse, curly blonde hair and a pale, square face of outsized ruggedness. He had fists as big as hams, and he seemed to take an instant dislike to Michael and handled him roughly in front of the other warders, cursed him for a damned Irish peasant, and even tried to kick him once, though he was restrained from it by two horrified under-warders.

He was a man of uncertain origins by the name of Grimshaw; what he was—English, Scotch, Welch—nobody knew. He was well hated in the prison, and also feared. He watched Michael's cell all day long from a chair halfway down the corridor, and at night he slept at the same spot on a cot put out for him; he even had his meals in the corridor.

The other warders, friendly to Michael, began to shake their heads gloomily and avoid Michael's eyes as the day of his hanging neared.

There were no more notes.

AND NOW Grimshaw had taken complete charge. Half a dozen warders, all more or less friendly to Michael, had been moved to other sections of the prison, and Grimshaw had assembled his own crew, a hard-bitten, silent, surly lot who scarcely so much as looked at Michael, let alone spoke to him.

His three meagre meals a day were brought to him, and the tray later taken away, in complete silence, while Grimshaw looked on at the door. From time to time Michael, violently irritable and surly himself through confinement and inaction, would bait the warders, in spite of the glowering presence of Grimshaw, but they kept their eyes on the ground and ignored him; and during one of these attempts at baiting, Grimshaw laughed ferociously and cried: "Ah, the rat's squeaking. What a way to die—trapped!" And then later, to the warders in Michael's hearing: "Well, boys, you won't have to put up with this Irish impudence much longer. A matter of a few days."

Each morning Michael, the quenchless optimist, woke early, hoping for a note, some word, a sign. But the day would pass, night would fall, and once more he'd be in his corner, lying on the straw, listening to the activities of his friend, the rat, grubbing about the floor, looking for the bits of food spilled from the plates. And he could hear the big prison pulsating about him, and the clink of the keys, and the heavy footfalls of the warders on the stone floors, and Grimshaw laughing ferociously in the corridor or bickering irritably with a murmuring warder. At times there would drift in from the outside the faint clinking of accoutrements and the hollering of orders and the stamp of foot troops or the hoofbeats of the dragoons, and even, once in a while, faint cries from beyond the walls, voices in the night from Dublin—a Dublin lost to him now, the old grey eternal city he had taken so lightly when he had been a free man: the city that had irritated and bored him in so many ways: the city he had wanted to escape from. And now, as he lay in his cell, it seemed to him like a city of fabulous wonder, a fairy-tale place, beautiful and desirable; and at last he understood Doherty's words: "Lad, there is only one Paradise. Paradise lost."

And one night he woke from an uneasy doze, sweating, and such a feeling of apprehension was nagging at him that he could just barely restrain himself from rising and beating on the door and begging for mercy, for help of some kind, at least for a word of comfort. Was this a way for a man to die—like a rat in a trap? And then he heard Grimshaw laughing unpleasantly in the corridor and some little obsequious warder was murmuring respectfully to him, and at once all of Michael's apprehensions left him and he was filled with a wild rage and he prayed profanely for one moment of freedom, just one moment, so that he could change Grimshaw's tune before the cart was driven from under him at the gallows and he was left standing on air.

Now as the time shortened, Grimshaw grew more and more abusive. He'd come to the door and shout and jeer at Michael and tell him how few hours he had left, and how the cart was being newly painted in the carpenter shop just for his benefit, and how his execution was going to be witnessed by Lord Glen himself, and how it was rumoured that several ladies of quality were to be allowed to watch from a hidden place high up in the Castle—and then he would laugh wildly, kick the door, and pass on.

And Michael noticed that even the surly, obsequious warders were getting a bellyful of Grimshaw, whose actions began to seem to be those of a lunatic. Why torture a man locked helplessly in a cell? It was stupid, useless, completely without reason. And one night at supper a warder even went so far as to grunt a greeting to Michael and give him a quick look of compassion.

. . . And now the big clock at the Castle ticked off the minutes inexorably, like a dispassionate second tolling the count for duellists. "No turning back now," the clock seemed to be saying. "The die is cast. There is no stopping the remorseless march of time." And Michael tried not to listen to the gloomy bing-bong of the clock as it struck the hours, one by one.

. . . Two days, two nights left, and Michael was restlessly pacing his cell like a big cat in the zoo. He heard the Castle clock strike eleven, then twelve; and finally his friend, the rat, appeared from the drain-pipe and began to rummage fearlessly in the straw almost at Michael's feet, and Michael looked down at the rat in the gloom of his cell and said: "At least you are under no sentence of death—such as you are!"

Suddenly there was a banging at his cell door, and Michael saw a face looking in at him through the small grille. "How goes the night, rebel?" the face asked, then there was a jeering laugh. Grimshaw!

Michael made no reply.

"I think I caught you weeping," jeered Grimshaw. "The great Captain Lightfoot blubbering in his cell. Ah, God! What a joke! What a thing to tell later."

Now Michael walked over to the door. "If you would step inside, Mr. Grimshaw, we'd soon see who would do the crying."

Grimshaw laughed. "Oh, I've handled three like you at a time, rebel. I could hug you and break your neck."

"Would you like to try?"

"Yes, my handsome lad, I would. But it wouldn't be legal, you understand? Your neck will be broken soon enough—and legally, and in public."

And now Michael lost his head completely and began to rage about his cell and kick his door like a demented man and scream insults at Grimshaw that flashed and corruscated and were like the blows from a whip.

Turning, Grimshaw called down the corridor: "Mullins, bring me the butt. The Captain's gone mad, and needs taming."

Michael pressed his face to the grille, a terrible joy in his heart. "Only open this door," he wanted to shout. "Just for one second—then to hell with the hanging!"

Dimly through the small grille he saw a warder hand Grimshaw a short, ugly black whip with a heavy leaded butt, and the warder said: "Have you lost your senses, Mr. Grimshaw? Let him rage. I'd do the same in his case."

"Hold your tongue, Mullins—you chicken-hearted fool! Get down to the solitaries in the cellars—open one cell for this beast. Then if he rages, it's all one. Our rest will not be disturbed."

"Mr. Grimshaw . . ." Mullins still persisted.

But Grimshaw turned towards him menacingly and shook the whip. Mullins wheeled and disappeared rapidly down the corridor.

And now Grimshaw unlocked Michael's cell door, then jumped back quickly as Michael came raging out into the corridor. Grimshaw, five or six inches taller than Michael and much wider, stood with his legs apart and the whip ready for a blow as Michael crouched before him, eying him, feinting, ready for the do-or-die rush . . . and then . . . Grimshaw's left eyelid was lowered briefly, and Michael stared and there was a passing inner shock and he wondered for a moment which of them was mad . . . and then it happened again, and there was a wild joy in Michael's heart. "All's well!" Trim's note had stated. "All's well."

Now Grimshaw grabbed him by the collar and hustled him down the corridor past the other cells, and awed faces were pressed to the grilles, and screams of reprobation were sent after Grimshaw, who cracked his whip viciously and kept shouting: "Ah, you will, will you? We'll see about that, my man!"

Michael struggled and writhed and made an ungodly uproar in the stone corridor, where all noises echoed and reverberated until it began to sound as if huge beasts were fighting to the death.

And finally they were at the head of the spiral stairway with the iron hand-rail which led down to the deep dungeons, and Michael heard a violent metallic rattling that puzzled him, and then Grimshaw released him and said: "The landing. Hit me! Hit me!"

And Michael swung from the waist, and his right fist landed with a terrible impact on Grimshaw's unprotected chin, and a look of wild surprise showed in the big man's eyes for a moment, and then slowly he sank to the floor, sat down, stared foolishly, and lay back with a sigh, unconscious.

Michael rushed down the spiral stairway, stumbling and almost falling in his haste. The small metal door on the first-floor landing was being taken off its hinges from the outside. Sweat poured from Michael as he waited, looking about him warily from time to time. And finally the door gave, with a violent wrenching sound that sent long, sinister echoes through the corridors, and then the blunt end of a big oaken four-by-six made its appearance, and at last the door was bent back far enough for Michael to slip through.

He found himself in a narrow stone gallery. Mahony was holding a torch at the far end of it, and Tuer O'Brien and Willie the Goat, who had just demolished the door, were hurrying down the corridor towards the torch. Near the door, Trim was standing with a pistol in his hand; and just beyond him was a slim boy with cropped black hair, also holding a pistol. Now the torch was put out.

"Down the gallery, Captain," cried Trim, giving Michael a gentle push. "I'll cover you."

In a few hurried paces Michael encountered the mysterious boy. A small, slim hand reached out and took one of his, and a light, familiar voice whispered eagerly: "Mick."

"Good God! Aga!" cried Michael, staggered. "And what in God's name have you done to your beautiful hair, girl?"

But Aga pushed him ahead of her down the gallery.

In a moment Michael encountered another demolished door, and then he slipped through into a space so large that, owing to his long confinement, he was startled and momentarily frightened by it. But he noticed a faint winking overhead—stars, for the love of God! He was clear, free, out in the open air once more. He saw dark shapes moving up ahead of him, and followed them. Aga was hurrying on his left, taking three steps to his one. And Trim behind with a cocked pistol, covering the escape.

And now they came to a dark courtyard, and Michael saw the towers of Dublin Castle looming back to his right, with a few lighted windows here and there, and he wanted to shout and leap in his wild delight, but at that moment he noted a great wall rising directly in front of him, but as he hesitated and stared up, a hand reached out of the darkness and he was hustled through a breach in the wall and found himself in a pitch-dark roadway, and off to his right he heard a concourse of horses and men, and before him he could see a few dim lights and the shapes of houses and trees.

Aga came through the breach, then Trim; and at once there was a great bustle and grunting and scraping as the breach was plugged with a piece of planking that loomed like an upturned raft in the darkness, and the planking was braced with oaken four-by-sixes anchored in the mud.

Michael made for the horses, hoping to find his black thoroughbred —once astride that wonderful animal, no one could overhaul him: but Aga pulled him back and whispered: "No! No!"

And now an alarm bell began to ring in the Castle, and they could hear a scurrying of men and loud shouts of: "This way! Out this way!"

And Michael cried impatiently: "And why the blazing hell are we standing here?"

Many running feet, hitting the earth out of time, could be heard clattering across the back courtyard now, and one man, swifter than the rest, reached the wall and began to work at and kick against the breach-plug.

At this moment there was great activity among the horses and men down the wall, and Michael heard Tuer O'Brien shouting in a loud, raucous voice: "South, Captain. South does it. The rendevous in Wicklow. South!"

And now the cavalcade started off along the wall southward with an uproar of shouting and hoofbeats, and covered by the great clattering, Trim and Aga drew Michael across the road and into the shadows.

"In God's name—" Michael began.

But Trim hissed: "The decoys, Captain. The decoys."

And now, as if they could see perfectly in the dark, they led him down an alley and in at a gate and through a courtyard and out at another gate, then down another alley and through another gate and across another courtyard until Michael was completely bewildered, like a man in a maze, and allowed himself to be led along like a child —and finally they came out into a wide alley beyond which loomed some tall dark houses, and they were admitted into the servant's entrance of a big mansion, and a silent flunkey led them through a vast cellar, lit only by a few dim lamps, and up a front stairway to an immense entrance hall where one tall candle was burning on a table.

Two flunkeys were standing at attention on the opposite sides of a big doorway, and Lord Clayton was pacing up and down nervously between them in a greatcoat, mopping his brow with a big white silk handkerchief, and as they all emerged, he turned and shouted: "Thank God!"

No one wasted any time talking. A flunkey brought Michael a magnificent cavalry greatcoat and helped him into it, then handed him a steel officer's helmet with a red crest and a sword-belt and sabre. Aga was also getting into a greatcoat, as was Trim. Through the glass of the huge front door Michael could see a big coach waiting with postilion, driver, and boot.

"Aga! Your hair!" cried Michael, and Lord Clayton glanced at him in irritation. A young man just saved from hanging worrying about his wife's hair! Wouldn't it grow?

"Don't you think I make a wonderful boy?" Aga demanded. "There is only one thing; or rather, two. That's why I wear the loose jacket."

Lord Clayton gave a delighted whinny, and Michael stared about him with compressed lips. Oh, there'd soon be a stop put to this sort of thing!

Now they hurried down the big front steps, where Michael found the black waiting for him. He mounted. Trim mounted the roan. Aga rode inside the coach with Lord Clayton. The postilion gave a shout; the driver cracked his whip, and they made off northward through the sleeping streets of Dublin.

Michael rode knee to knee with Trim, who was wearing a non-com's rig. "Why did you let Aga take such chances?" he demanded.

With a sigh Trim replied: "How could I prevent it, Captain?"

Michael fell silent. True, all too true.

"Besides," said Trim after a moment, "she recruited Lord Clayton, and that was the crux of the matter."

"I see," said Michael, compressing his lips again. He thought he had detected an air of undue familiarity between Clayton and Aga.

AND SOON they had left Dublin far behind and were driving through the open country, and after a while Michael turned his horse over to Trim and got into the coach with Lord Clayton and Aga. The old Lord was asleep in the corner, worn out by days of anxiety, and Aga was in another corner, as wide awake as if it were broad morning, humming to herself and looking out at the dark rolling countryside lit only by the stars. Michael took off his helmet and his sword, and sat for some time with his arm around Aga and her head on his shoulder.

"Weren't you proud of me, Mick?" she asked.

"No," said Michael. "My impulse was to give you a good spanking. You might have been killed."

"I liked it," said Aga bluntly. "I wanted to prove to myself that I was truly Doherty's daughter."

"Oh," said Michael. "I thought it was to get me out of prison."

Aga laughed and pinched his ear and kissed him, then she said casually: "That, too, Mick."

And the well-hung coach swayed gently, and there was the monotonous, unending clatter of hoofs, soothing as a lullaby, and after a while they both fell into a doze, clinging to each other, while the exhausted old Lord snored dolefully in his corner.

TRIM, on horseback at the coach window, woke them all. It was still black night.

Trim waved a long arm. "There's bivouac fires spread for a mile up there along the road, and though it's three o'clock, the market-town up ahead has got lights all over it. I don't understand it. Shall I ride on ahead?"

"We could turn back and take a side-road," suggested Clayton wearily, coughing in the morning chill, then yawning.

"No," said Michael. "A coach such as this on a side-road is a very suspicious thing. Let's chance it, whatever it is."

He kissed Aga quickly, then buckled on his sword, picked up his helmet, got down, and mounted the black Trim was holding for him.

They moved slowly into the market-town, where there was a jam of soldiers, gigs, carts, coaches, and an unholy ho-lo-boloo as of a fair, with torches flaring and men shouting, and women talking in loud voices, and dragoons dashing in and out among the terrible jam of vehicular traffic on the King's Highway. Michael noticed that the side-streets were patrolled by dragoons but completely empty otherwise. With a wave of his arm, he led the coach from the main road, and shouting: "Make way for Lord Clayton's coach! Make way!" He tried to force a passage down a side-street so the highway could be detoured, but half a dozen dragoons quickly blocked his way and stopped the coach. Michael screamed at them: "This is Lord Clayton's coach, boobies!"

But a dragoon said: "Sorry, sir. Orders. All traffic is to be cleared through the main highway. No exceptions. Sorry, sir."

Lord Clayton yelled from the coach: "How would you like to find yourself in military prison, young man?"

The non-com, followed by several others, rode up beside the coach, and the non-com dismounted, turned his horse over to the man nearest him, and walked to the window of the coach.

"I'm awfully sorry, sir, but you will have to move this coach back onto the highway, sir."

"I'll be damned if I will," cried Lord Clayton. "Who's in command here?"

"Why, Lieutenant Cooley, sir."

"Damn it, fellow, I'm not speaking of subalterns. I see an encampment. A regiment, likely. Who's in command?"

"Colonel Bascomb, sir."

Clayton gave a loud laugh. "What—Whisky Billy?"

The non-com recoiled slightly and cleared his throat nervously. "Sir William it is, sir."

"Where is he?"

"He's at the tavern, sir, right down the street."

Lord Clayton pulled out his card-case, extracted a card, and handed it to the non-com. "Take this to him, and you'll hurry, my man, if you know what's good for you. Sir William is an old friend of mine."

"Yes, sir," said the non-com, saluting.

"Meanwhile, we'll stay where we are."

"Yes, sir."

They waited in silence while the noise and the confusion continued behind them. But finally Michael grew impatient and rode up knee to knee with one of the privates of dragoons. The private was a youngster, not over nineteen. At the sight of Michael's crested helmet he stiffened in his saddle and sat staring straight ahead.

"What's all this?"

"They've blocked the road, sir. Some great criminal has escaped from Dublin. I don't rightly know who, sir. I'm told there are couriers all over the place."

"Does it take a regiment to catch one man?"

"Oh, it's not that, sir. We were in encampment here. Manœuvres, sir."

"Thank you, private."

"Yes, sir."

Michael rode back to the coach, and then in a moment there was a clattering and hollering, and a small group of horsemen turned the corner with a little turkey-cock of a man leading. All the dragoons stiffened and stared at the stars, rigid as ramrods. A bustling aide got unsteadily from his horse, almost falling into the dust and bringing a loud guffaw from someone; then he helped the little turkey-cock of a man to dismount: Colonel Sir William Bascomb. He was drunk and strutting.

"Ah, good God! Binny, is it you?" he cried, looking into the coach.

"Yes, yes," said Lord Clayton impatiently, "and they've stopped me, and I'm in a great hurry to get to Belfast."

"My orders. Iron orders. Sorry, old man. In a hurry, you say? When I was handed your card, I was hoping you could stay for a while and drink with me till this silly business is over. One gets tired of sycophantic underlings. I say, can't you stay?"

"Impossible. I'm behindhand now, Billy. What the devil is going on?"

"Oh, those idiots at the Castle have let their number-one man get away from them. First Donnell. Now Martin. Utterly ridiculous. If I was governor of the prison, I guarantee there'd be no escapes. But Colonel Blunt's an amateur. He'll see India for this. However, that's no worse than Ireland. It's a silly thing up here. The man escaped south. The courier they sent me says it's all over Dublin already that he escaped south. Oh, hell, Binny—the Army's the Army. Fine soldiers at the bottom and woodenheads at the top. Ah, God, Binny, can't you stay?"

"Sorry, Billy. Will you pass us on?"

The Colonel turned abruptly and spoke to the non-com. "Escort them through town by the back road—my orders." Then he returned to Lord Clayton as if reluctant to see the last of him. "Is that your grandson with you there?"

Lord Clayton recoiled slightly. "Grandson! Of course not. Would I have a grandson that size? No, it's the son of a friend."

"What—Binny! Have you taken to boys now?" And the Colonel roared, then wheezed asthmatically and choked. "Oh, God—what an unlikely thing, if I remember rightly."

"You remember rightly," said Lord Clayton, laughing. "I'll be in London soon. Will you look me up?"

"Yes, of course, Binny," cried the Colonel. "I'll look in at your daughter's. Well . . . I suppose I'd better let you pass on. Not even one drink—a stirrup-cup, Binny?"

"Sorry, old man. Sorry."

And so they passed on, escorted by the non-com, and Whisky Billy stood in the dust of the roadway, regretfully looking after the big coach. Ah, God, when would he be removed from this desert of sullen peasants and bungling politicians! Oh, to be in London with Binny! Binny was the boy for you, all right—always had the prettiest girls!

Now beyond him one of his escorts fell from his horse with a clank and clatter, and there were roars of laughter.

"Who was it—Meigs?" shouted the Colonel, above the uproar.

"Yes, Colonel."

"It had to be Meigs," said the Colonel. "He was looking a little green in the tavern."

There was a roar of loud guffaws, but all the common soldiers ignored the merriment and sat their horses stiffly, staring at the stars.

AND so Lord Clayton and party passed on unremarked to Belfast. It was dawn when they arrived, and the still water of the Lough was dark greenish, with faint glazes of pink and gold from the rising sun. A mild west wind was blowing.

When the coach drew up at Cavendish's, there was Brady nervously pacing. He was almost incoherent with relief, but he finally managed to tell Michael that the *Northern Star* of Belfast was ready to clear from Cavendish's number-three wharf as soon as they could get aboard.

And now in a way it was as it had been once before. The two thoroughbreds were loaded aboard, the loading supervised by Trim this time, and the ship was ready to sail, and there was only space for a brief good-bye. Lord Clayton, more than a little upset, shook hands with Michael and said: "Good-bye, lad, and good luck. And for me it's good-bye to Ireland for ever. I'm taking the Liverpool boat at ten." And then he kissed Aga on the cheek and patted her somewhat unnecessarily, Michael thought, compressing his lips; and at last Michael and Aga were aboard, and the *Northern Star* drew away slowly, and

Belfast seemed to be moving rather than themselves, and Lord Clayton waved and waved and finally turned away with a despairing shrug.

And now Michael and Aga hurried below to their cabin, and no one saw them for a good two hours and more, and then at last they reappeared on the gently swaying deck and walked forward to the bow, where the salt wind was blowing strongly and freshly from the Channel. Ahead of them at the horizon was a huge white fog-bank, and Michael remarked about it to a sailor who was working forward.

"Ay," said the sailor. "We're for it, though she may shift."

And now Michael and Aga stood alone, holding hands.

"I am glad to see the last of Clayton," said Michael finally.

Aga glanced at him, then laughed lightly. "Oh, we needed him, Mick. Mick, do you know we haven't but a little over two hundred guineas to our name?"

"So?" said Michael indifferently. "Where did it all go?"

"Roughly," said Aga, "thirty-three hundred guineas to Lady Anne, who has promised to look after Princey. Oh, Princey! I miss him so."

"Yes, the poor little fellow," said Michael, sighing.

"That was Anne's share—one third. And six thousand to Binny for the bribery and for himself—didn't have a guinea to his name, poor old man! Even so, he didn't want to be mixed up in it, but I persuaded him."

"I thought as much," said Michael coldly.

Aga laughed. "Would you rather hang, then?"

"I could tell you better if I knew the truth."

"Oh, God, Mick—it was no more than a little cuddling. I could twist him round my finger. Princey is more trouble."

Michael was silent for a long time. Finally he said: "Aga—you're a wicked girl."

"Yes," said Aga, "it's true. And as for you, Mick—you are not a wicked man at all. You are just a creature of circumstance."

And now, little by little, they sailed into the fog-bank, and as the *Northern Star* of Belfast was slowly swallowed up by the dense white fog of the North Channel, Michael Martin, sometimes called Captain Lightfoot, silently disappeared from history's stage and was heard of no more. And the years passed, and there was much gossip about Michael Martin around the peat fires at night, and finally he was added to the pantheon of Irish hero-villains, the Rapparees—Paddy O'Bryan, Patrick

Flemming, and John Doherty himself—until all memory of the flesh-and-blood Michael Martin had been lost and nothing remained but the flashing, gallant, comet-like figure of legend, Captain Lightfoot.

AND NOW our long story's told, and if it is a good story it will show a moral at the end, but for the life of me I can't make out what the moral can possibly be except the obvious and usual one: Man is born to trouble as the sparks fly upward.